THE CHRISTMAS GENIE'S WISH

Michaela Trueman

CONTENTS

For Steph.

CHAPTER ONE

As Victoria walked along the dark Lanes and alleyways of Colchester, she clutched her handbag tightly and kept a close eye on the people who slept in the doorways along the Lanes when she passed them.

'Hi, Auntie!' a voice called out from an alleyway behind Victoria.

Automatically, Victoria span round to see a woman of around half her age with pale hair standing before her.

'Jesus Christ, Eugenie! I nearly had a heart attack!' Victoria cried.

Eugenie frowned. 'I was just saying a friendly hello. There's no need to take the Lord's name in vain,' she replied.

As Victoria did not believe in God, she didn't care that she'd taken His name in vain. She cared that Eugenie had scared her, that the wind was blowing down the Lanes, and that the roads and their pavements were uneven, but she didn't care about blaspheming. She also cared about being late for the meeting she was on her way to.

'Well, that's enough about that. Come along, Eugenie, as quick as you can in those shoes. We don't want to be late now,' Victoria said.

With that, Victoria stormed off down the lane. Her niece followed her, the tip-tapping of her high heels pounding the pavement echoing off the windows of the closed shops and cafes lining the lane.

-

The moment she walked into the stockroom of Bygones, Victoria felt smug. She felt smug because she believed herself to be the most well-dressed person in the room. In addition to seven business owners, who Victoria considered herself to be better dressed than, there were nine chairs. Victoria and Eugenie sat in the unoccupied chairs, because, like many humans and some pets, neither of them wanted to sit on someone's lap.

'You're Toothill's, aren't you?' asked the woman in the most comfortable-looking of the nine chairs.

In order to confirm she was the owner of Toothill's without moving her pursed lips, Victoria nodded.

To show how proud she was to work in her aunt's shop, Eugenie announced: 'Yes! I get to dress women up all day in contemporary clothes and see them leave with huge smiles on their faces and lighter purses.'

'This is my niece, Eugenie. She is tasked with merchandising for Toothill's, which is why I brought her along,' Victoria explained.

The person Victoria was referring to wasn't listening. She'd realised she'd said something wrong, so was considering correcting herself. She decided that she would.

'Customers purses are lighter *metaphorically* speaking when they leave us, but as most people pay by card, they're not *literally* lighter,' Eugenie explained to her aunt and the assembled crowd of business owners they were meeting with.

'I understood that,' the woman in the comfy-looking chair said.

Before anyone could interrupt her and steer her meeting off course, the woman in the comfy chair cleared her throat to signal she was about to say something important.

'I'm Helen, and this is my little antiques and vintage clothing shop. Thank you all for coming. I've brought you together to discuss united plans for Christmas,' the woman in the comfy chair said.

The only man in the room looked around at the eight women he was sat with. 'United plans? We've got a couple of fancy clothes places, a couple of cafes, her with her arty bits, and my hardware store. What do we have in common, and what are you thinking getting us to work together? We're like chalk and cheese here,' he questioned.

As a woman who'd sent enigmatic handwritten letters to thirteen business owners requesting their presence at short notice, Helen knew she'd be questioned. This meant she had already answered the hardware store owners question in her head laying in bed one night, so it was easy to answer out loud in the backroom of her shop.

'That's a good question, Clive. The answer is that we are all mothers, fathers, daughters, sons, aunties, uncles, etcetera, trying to make a living in this tough world. Our businesses *are* like chalk and cheese, but might I point out that you can buy both of those things in the same place? The same shop sells chalk and cheese, shoes and sandwiches, perfume and picture frames, oranges and ornaments, and they'll happily take your money for them and give it to their bosses in big cities to spend on extravagant holidays and high-performance cars. What I'm suggesting is, we make people buy those things from *us,* thus keeping their money in Colchester to spend on putting food on our family's' tables,' Helen replied.

Clive folded his arms. 'Yeah, that'd be great, but I don't see any magic wands around here. I don't wanna spend my hard earned cash on some Instagram campaign to get millennials to buy drills and nails from me. We all want more people through our doors. This just isn't the way to go about it,' he said.

At this point, it occurred to Helen, and everyone else sitting in her backroom, that she hadn't outlined her plan. As yet, the only person who knew the details of her vision for Colchester at Christmas was her husband. She hadn't told Clive, or anyone for that matter, that she was planning an Instagram campaign targeting millennials.

'Clive, *what* isn't the way to go about getting customers? What aspect of my plan are you rejecting?' Helen questioned.

'The bit about... I mean when you said...' Clive stammered. After several seconds thought about why he couldn't get his words out, he concluded: 'I don't know. I don't get what you want to do yet.'

Unnoticed by most of the room, Helen shared a smile with the proprietor of Trinity, her favourite coffee shop. The subtle smile communicated that they felt the same about Clive.

'I don't remember you telling us about your plan. Did I miss it?' Eugenie asked.

The smile on Helen's face grew wider. 'No, I haven't explained what I want to do yet. That's why I was confused by Clive's comments. Instagram and millennials have not been mentioned by *me* once,' she replied.

'Yeah, but it's always about that sort of thing, so I know I'm right,' Clive retorted.

'It's interesting that you *know* you're right, for you are not. If I'm allowed to speak, then I can explain that, while Instagram is *part* of it and hopefully some of our customers *will* be millennials, my plan doesn't focus on either. It focuses on the thing that makes small businesses like ours better than anywhere else; customer service,' Helen revealed.

Just as she'd hoped they would, Helen's words silenced Clive. They silenced everyone else too, which allowed Helen to unveil her grand idea for saving Colchester's independent businesses over Christmastime.

'We need shopping to be an *experience*, and we need to introduce customers to a variety of stock from various suppliers. When I think of a good shopping experience and a wide range of products, I think of department stores. When I think of department stores, I think of personal shoppers. To customers, personal shoppers are the best shopping friend imaginable. They have the killer combination of product knowledge and people skills. With a good personal shopper by your side, you're virtually guaranteed to blow your budget and not care because you've had such a good time. To businesses, they're invaluable, because they introduce customers to brands they may never have tried before and they encourage them to spend more than they'd planned to. They do all this while making the experience so good that customers want to come back for more,' Helen told the people in her backroom.

Instead of the impressed gasps Helen had hoped for, there was silence.

The silence was broken when the proprietor of Trinity asked: 'Are you planning on hiring a personal shopper for us? To take people from shop to shop, or something of that ilk?'

Only then did Helen realise that she hadn't actually revealed what she wanted to do. She'd explained *why* what she wanted to do was good, but not *said* what it was that she wanted to do.

'Yes, Lynne, that's the gist of my plan. I want to offer a service where customers make a list of presents they need to buy or people they need to buy for, and then, using their knowledge of what we have to offer, a personal-shopper-type person takes them around the local shops to buy things off their list. We'll set up a membership scheme, and the personal-shopper-type will only take customers to businesses that are members of the scheme. If I can get enough of the shops along the Lanes to sign up, there'll be no present that customers can't buy. I've contacted a few eateries too because, on a long shopping trip, you need to pause for coffee and cake. The personal-shopper-type could recommend places to customers, and use them as drop-off or pick-up locations,' Helen explained.

A loud squeal came from someone in the room. Eight heads turned to stare at Eugenie, who, as well as squealing, was clapping her hands and beaming. Eugenie's glee was so overwhelming that she didn't notice she was the only one reacting in the way she was.

'I *love* it! It's an amazing idea! An idea I really, truly, very much, desperately want to be a part of!' Eugenie enthused.

'Control yourself, Eugenie! This is a business meeting. You must behave like an adult. Besides, of course you'll be a part of this. You work in one of the shops that will take part,' Victoria scolded.

'Oh, so Toothill's will do it. That's good. The idea does work then,' Helen thought to herself.

The part of Helen's plan that bothered her the most was hiring the personal shopper. The whole thing hinged on them being just right. She defined "just right" as: "friendly and dedicated, with a creative mind and a good knowledge of the participating businesses and their stock and services". It was a challenging role. A role Helen suddenly knew how to fill perfectly.

'If Victoria can cover you in the run up to Christmas, would you like to be the personal-shopper-type, Eugenie?' Helen asked.

Dreams of helping people find the perfect presents flashed through Eugenie's head. She visualised herself dancing through streets packed full of shoppers, with a merry customer at her heels as they made their way to a tiny boutique that sold the *perfect* dress for their mum.

When Eugenie considered the alternative, she imagined herself confined to Toothill's with her aunt. She pictured the occasional customer popping in and brightening up her day while she found them the right skirt for their party and then them taking the aforementioned skirt home, leaving Eugenie alone in the shop, or with only Victoria for company.

'Please, please, please! I'd love to do that!' Eugenie cried.

Victoria sighed. 'I need her for merchandising and dealing with stock deliveries, but I suppose I could spare her at times. I could cope with doing extra hours to cover her,' she agreed.

'That's sorted then. Eugenie can be our personal-shopper-type person,' Helen said.

Inside, though not out loud, Helen breathed a sigh of relief. For the first time since she'd thought of it, she had confidence her plan would come to fruition.

-

For the next hour, Helen sought agreement from her fellow business owners to join her personal shopper scheme, and she fleshed out the details.

By the time everyone went home, they had a clear idea of how everything would work. This included Eugenie, who believed she was on course for the best Christmastime she'd had as an adult.

While walking home that night under the stars, Eugenie wondered what people would put on their Christmas shopping lists. She knew what *she'd* put on her shopping list, but it wasn't something she could buy at any of the participating businesses. Even without the thing she wished for, Eugenie was sure she was going to have a happy Christmas.

CHAPTER TWO

'I've got a new job for Christmas!' Eugenie told Holly, her flatmate, the morning after finding out about the new job.

Like most people who knew Eugenie, Holly was aware of her feelings towards her job at Toothill's. This meant she was surprised that Eugenie had a new job.

'Really? Did your aunt get too much for you? She is *such* a grumpy cow,' Holly questioned.

Eugenie frowned. 'I'm not leaving auntie Victoria. If I did, she would probably be even more miserable. I've just got another job for Christmastime as well as Toothill's,' she replied.

Just as Holly was wondering what to say to break the awkward silence that had fallen, the toaster popped.

'Ooh, I meant to say, can I try that new spread you've got?' Eugenie asked.

The spread Eugenie was referring to was supposed to taste like biscuits. Holly had bought it on her last shop, and was quite happy to share it with Eugenie, especially if it eased the tension she felt she'd created.

'No problem. I'll pop some on this,' Holly said, putting Eugenie's toast on a sandwich plate.

Silence then fell again, but as it was caused by eating toast, Holly felt comfortable with it.

-

When she'd finished eating her breakfast, Holly went to her room to put her make-up on and do her hair for work. While blending her eyeshadow, she wondered what Eugenie's new job was. Only then did she realise she hadn't asked her what it was. She'd asked her what she thought of the biscuit spread on her toast, but not what she was going to be doing for a living.

Upon realising her mistake, Holly burst out of her room to find Eugenie dashing out of the bathroom, hastily doing her belt up.

'I never asked what your Christmas job is! Sorry,' Holly said.

Eugenie shook her head. 'Don't worry about it. We live together. We have plenty of time to catch up. I'd tell you now, but I need to get to work. I'd forgotten that the window display needs changing before we open,' she replied, brushing crumbs off her trousers.

Being Eugenie's housemate didn't just mean Holly had plenty of time to catch up with her. It also meant that she cared about her, and wanted to know any news she had as soon as possible. This meant she was happy to pay coffee shop prices for an Americano and panini in order to discover what Eugenie's job was a few hours earlier than she would otherwise.

'You can tell me over lunch. I'll pick you up and take you somewhere nice. My treat,' Holly told Eugenie.

Being told she was being taken out for lunch inspired Eugenie to kiss the person taking her out for lunch.

Having kissed Holly, Eugenie headed for the door, calling: 'Thanks, Holly. I'll see you later.'

CHAPTER THREE

Like she was on a lot of Wednesday's, Eugenie was bored. She was in charge of the window display and layout of Toothill's, but those responsibilities didn't interest her. Dressing a mannequin left her cold. Considering how customers would travel around various potential shop layouts failed to engage her full attention.

'Eugenie! What are you doing?' Victoria asked her niece when she noticed she'd been staring out the window for two minutes.

'Nothing. There's nothing to do,' Eugenie replied, gesturing at the customerless shop.

Victoria shook her head. 'This is retail. There's always something to do,' she argued.

The sound of the bell on the front door ringing stopped Eugenie complaining that jobs that didn't directly involve customers were dull.

Whenever she had a new customer to serve, Eugenie tried to guess what they needed. Based on one look at the woman who'd just entered Toothill's, she decided they had to dress up for an event that they'd been given very little notice for.

'Hi! I've got to meet my brother's new partner *tonight*! I

don't want to show him up, but I don't do dressing up. The last time I wore heels, it nearly killed me, and I hate showing my arms. What does someone like me wear to impress their brother's partner?' the customer asked.

The customer was in luck. Eugenie knew exactly what a woman like her newest customer wore to meet her brother's partner.

'I'll answer that question as soon as you tell me your dress size, shoe size, and name,' Eugenie told the customer.

'Marian, six, Fourteen,' the customer replied.

Armed with the information she needed, Eugenie started rifling through a rail of long dresses. She pulled out a white one and checked the label. She glanced at it, and then the customer.

'Well, Fourteen, I've never heard of dress size Marian,' Eugenie said.

Despite being stressed, the customer giggled. 'My *name* is Marian. I ordered the questions in the wrong answer,' she explained. A second later she added: 'And I just said that in the wrong order. What is going on today?'

Eugenie laughed. 'Whatever it is, I hope it continues. You're hilarious,' she said.

Without looking up from the paperwork she was checking at the counter, Victoria commented: 'Well, I don't know about *hilarious*, but you're certainly *stressed*. I hope that *doesn't* keep up. There's no need to worry about meeting your brother's new girlfriend. She's dating him, not you.'

Marian frowned. 'I *am* stressed. Yes, my brother's partner is dating my brother, not me, but they might think less of him for having a scruffy sister like me,' she replied.

'If she does, she's not worth having,' Victoria pointed out.

'But that's not my decision to make. What if I mess everything all up?' Marian questioned.

Picturing them on Marion, Eugenie snatched a pair of ankle boots off the shelf and whipped a smart black jacket off the sale rail. Along with the white dress she'd picked up before, she whisked the ensemble off to the fitting room.

'You won't mess anything up, so it's not worth worrying about,' Victoria replied.

Once she'd hung up the clothes she wanted Marian to wear and put the boots to go with them on the floor in the fitting room, Eugenie tottered back out to the shop floor.

'If the heels you wore were anything like these, no wonder they nearly killed you. I've paired your dress and jacket with boots, which will still look good but should be safer. It's all in the fitting room,' Eugenie told Marian, looking down at her stilettos.

Getting off the shop floor, away from Victoria, seemed like a good idea to Marian. She thanked Eugenie and ran off to the fitting room.

-

When Marian returned to the shop floor, dressed up in the clothes that had been left for her in the fitting room, she found someone was talking to Eugenie.

'I'm really excited about this. This should be perfect,' Eugenie was telling the person she was talking to.

The sound of Marian's boots echoed on the plywood floor, alerting Eugenie to her presence. She span round to see exactly what she hoped to see.

'Does it work?' Marian asked.

Eugenie looked to the person she'd been speaking to. 'Holly?' she asked.

The sight of Marian rendered Holly speechless, so she just nodded.

'See for yourself,' Eugenie suggested, gesturing at a mirror that existed for customers to look at themselves in.

As requested, Marian looked at herself in the mirror. What she saw made her smile.

'What's your name?' Marian asked Eugenie.

'I'm Eugenie,' Eugenie replied.

'Genie? Well, that's apt, because you *are* a genie. This is perfect,' Marian said.

Being told she was a genie made Eugenie so happy that she twirled around on the spot, sending her pastel pink hair flying into Holly's face.

'Watch it! You're whipping your poor friend with that hair of yours,' Victoria cried.

To show she wasn't at all bothered about Eugenie's hair flying into her, Holly smiled.

Seeing the smile, and knowing Holly wouldn't be bothered, Eugenie ignored Victoria's comment.

'Please tell me you're taking this lot home,' Eugenie said to Marian.

Before committing to spending over £200, Marian took one last look in the mirror. She pictured herself in a few hours time, shaking the hand of her boyfriend's partner.

'I feel better about tonight already, so yes, I'm buying this. Thank you so much, Genie,' Marian confirmed.

Eugenie beamed. 'It's *Eugenie*, and it's my pleasure,' she replied.

-

After Marion left Toothill's with a paper bag of clothes and £209.97 less in her bank account than she'd entered with, Eugenie and Holly left with no paper bags and the same amount of money that they'd entered with.

Together, Eugenie and Holly traversed the varied lanes of Colchester, passing an arguing couple, a busker "singing" *A Team* to a crowd of people who were ignoring him while they ate their respective lunches, and a colourful display in the window of Red Lion Books. The pair only paused when Holly spotted someone she knew.

'Darren! Hi! How are you?' Holly asked the person she knew.

Before Holly had called his name, Darren had been striding up the road, head looking down at the reddish-brown bricks of the road. When he heard his name, he looked up, his blue eyes momentarily looking straight into Holly's.

'Holly? From Bridge House?' Darren questioned.

'*He barely knows who I am. That makes sense though. I don't know why I thought he'd remember me,*' Holly thought to herself.

It was obvious to Eugenie that Holly knew Darren from work. She guessed he was a colleague of Holly's, for he didn't look like Bridge House's usual clientele.

'Ah, you work with Holly. Are you a fellow receptionist, or behind the scenes?' Eugenie asked.

Darren shook his head. 'I don't work with Holly. I'm not that lucky. I *am* lucky enough to stay at Bridge House sometimes, so I see Holly then. I'm amazed that she recognised me considering I must have only seen her four or five times at most,' he explained.

Knowing Holly, Eugenie *wasn't* amazed that she'd recognised Darren. One of the things they had in common was affection for their customers and a good memory for them. If asked, Holly could probably tell Eugenie whether Darren liked down, memory foam, or polyester pillows, and if he was an early bird or a night owl. If asked in private, Holly could tell her if Darren was rude or polite.

Based on the fact that Holly was silent, Eugenie guessed Darren was rude. If that was the case though, she wondered why she'd called out to him.

'I forgot to answer your question, didn't I? I'm not feeling too bright today. Overall, I'm not too bad, all things considered. I'm with a mate at the minute, so that's all good,' Darren told Holly.

It didn't escape Eugenie's attention that Holly's face lit up when Darren said he was with a mate. She took it as a sign that Darren was a troublesome guest, so Holly was pleased not to have him at the hotel. Suddenly, she understood why Holly had called out to Darren when she didn't like him. Eugenie realised it was so she could find out if he was staying at Bridge House, so if he was, she'd have warning and could walk into her next shift mentally prepared to deal with him.

'I'm so, *so*, pleased for you!' Holly enthused.

The delight Holly expressed that a rude customer of hers was "not too bad" confused Eugenie. She understood that, as a professional, Holly would hide any dislike she felt for her customers, but it seemed like, in her efforts to cover up, she'd gone too far the other way.

'Are you doing alright?' Darren asked Holly.

'Me?' Holly questioned, as if there was someone behind her who Darren might have been talking to. As Eugenie was to the side of Holly and unknown to Darren, and the street was otherwise empty, there wasn't anyone other than her who he could have been talking to.

'Yes, you, Holly,' Darren confirmed.

'Thank you for asking. That's so lovely of you. You don't need to ask about me, a receptionist. It's kind that you did though. I'm fine, thank you. I'm really well,' Holly replied.

Having established that they were "fine" and "not too bad", Holly and Darren fell silent.

As far as Eugenie knew, silence made people uncomfortable. She didn't like people to be uncomfortable, so she thought of a subject she considered to be universally loved and brought it up.

'I can't believe it's Christmas in a couple of months! It's the best time of the year, isn't it?' Eugenie said.

Darren frowned and started paying close attention to the ants wandering around on the bricks at his feet.

Turning to Darren, Holly said: 'It was nice to see you, Darren. I hope we bump into each other again sometime.'

'Yeah, thanks. Bye now,' Darren replied before running off up the street.

'Ah, there was no need for me to bring up Christmas. Holly managed to get rid of him,' Eugenie thought to herself.

'Shall we?' Holly suggested, gesturing down the street in the direction of the café they were having lunch in.

As there was no reason for her to disagree, Eugenie replied: 'We shall.'

CHAPTER FOUR

The first thing Eugenie noticed when she entered the cafe Holly had taken her to were the citrus colours of the paint on the walls. In stark contrast to the walls, the tables, including the one Eugenie and Holly sat at, were white.

'It feels so cheerful in here! I wish our flat had walls like these,' Eugenie commented.

'We could always paint them. We are allowed to,' Holly suggested.

'Yes, please. That would be so fun,' Eugenie replied.

As much as she liked the idea of redecorating their flat, Holly didn't want to talk about it at that moment. She had taken Eugenie out for lunch to ask her about her new job, so she wanted to do just that.

When a waitress came to the table to take the drinks order, it formed a natural break in conversation. Holly took this as her opportunity. As soon as the waitress had walked off with a notepad with "1 X Mocha frappe, 1 X Americano" written on it, Holly asked: 'So what is your new job?'

Before Eugenie even told her what the job was, Holly knew she liked it, for a beaming smile appeared on her face.

'I'm going to help people buy Christmas presents in the Lanes. Basically, customers will call me and tell me what they want to buy or what sort of thing the people they're buying for like, and we'll arrange a time to meet up. Then, when I see them, I'll take them to little shops in the Lanes that sell the things they want, and hopefully, they'll buy stuff there. Whatever present they want, with a few exceptions, I'll find it for them in a little local shop. It's inspired by department shop personal shoppers, and it's the perfect Christmas job for me. I get to help people get lovely presents and get them to support family-run places that need their money,' Eugenie revealed.

'You really *are* a genie then, because you'll be making Christmas wishes come true. It sounds great, Eugenie. Very you,' Holly replied.

When Holly called her a genie, Eugenie clicked her fingers. 'That's it! I'm a Christmas genie!' she cried.

The volume of Eugenie's voice turned the heads of a few of her fellow diners, but she didn't notice. Holly did, but she saw no reason to acknowledge it. It didn't matter to her what people thought of her friend.

'Helen didn't know what to call my role. I'm a personal shopper really, but that description sounded too dull to her. This is a new and exciting idea, and she wanted it to sound like one. Christmas Genie would be *perfect*! It would make people curious, so if they saw it on social media at the top of a post, they'd read on and find out what we're up to. I *love* it. Thank you, Holly. You're a genius,' Eugenie said.

Holly didn't know who Helen was, but she decided it didn't matter, so she didn't ask.

Holly didn't think she was a genius, and being called one

made her uncomfortable, so it mattered to her. The easiest way to deal with it, she thought, was to pretend Eugenie hadn't said it.

'When do you start this Christmas Genie slash personal shopper thing?' Holly asked.

'Next week, and it will run all the way up to the day before Christmas Eve. Hopefully, I will help people grant lots of present wishes over that time,' Eugenie replied.

Realising how close Christmas Eve was, Holly wondered what she'd be doing on it. She also wondered what Eugenie would be unwrapping the day after, because she hadn't bought her present yet.

'What's *your* Christmas wish?' Holly asked.

'To introduce a lovely new boyfriend to Mother over turkey at our place,' Eugenie told Holly.

Before Holly could work out what to say about the fact that Eugenie would probably be single on Christmas day, hundreds of miles from her mum, a waitress came with their drinks and asked what food they wanted.

-

As they hadn't looked at the menus they'd been given, it took Eugenie and Holly a minute or two to work out what they wanted. The length of time wasn't long enough to forget what they were talking about though.

When the waitress left with their order, Eugenie and Holly picked up where they'd left off.

'I know you were asking about presents, but I don't care what you get me. For Christmas, I want to be with Mother, and I want a boyfriend. You can't buy me either of those things,' Eugenie said.

The sadness in Eugenie's voice made Holly want to hug her. Instead, she grasped her hand across the table. 'I'm so sorry, Eugenie,' she murmured.

Eugenie laughed and shook off Holly's hand. 'Holly, it's fine. I didn't mean to sound negative and miserable. I don't *need* a boyfriend, and though she isn't down here with me, at least I have a mother who loves me, who is alive. I was just talking about an *ideal* world, that's all,' she replied.

The swift change in Eugenie's mood seemed unnatural to Holly. 'It's okay to admit you're lonely, Eugenie. Christmas is the loneliest time of the year,' Holly told her.

The idea of Christmas being the loneliest time of year made Eugenie scoff. 'I work in a shop. I speak to dozens of people a day. I'm not lonely. Christmas isn't lonely either. It's all about togetherness,' she argued.

Before Holly could point out that talking to dozens of people doesn't necessarily stop you being lonely, Eugenie asked: 'Do you think the Christmas lights will be good this year?'

When Holly didn't answer immediately, Eugenie answered her own question by saying: 'I think they'll be bigger and better than last year.

-

Until their food came, Eugenie talked rapidly and endlessly to Holly about various aspects of Colchester's Christmas decorations, making it impossible for them to discuss anything else. Food prevented Eugenie and Holly from speaking about *anything*, and when they'd cleared their plates, it was time to go back to their respective workplaces.

CHAPTER FIVE

The moment Eugenie stepped through the big wooden doors, a wave of calm settled on her. The light streaming through the many tall windows seemed to make its way into her heart.

As she walked along the tired tiled floor, Eugenie waved hello to people she knew. Most of them had content smiles on their faces, and waved back to her. A few frowned at her and exchanged whispered words with each other, just as they did most weeks. It didn't upset Eugenie, for she knew it wasn't personal. Anyone who didn't fit their idea of who a person should be, and there were a lot of people who didn't fit their idea of who a person should be, got the same response as her.

When she sat down, Eugenie noticed that the smooth wooden surface of her pew was very cold. So cold it made her shiver.

'Hello, darlin-. Cold, ain't it? Heating's still broke,' said a man who sat next to her.

'Steve, hello! I hope it's fixed for Christmas,' Eugenie replied.

'Yeah, so do I an- all,' Steve agreed.

-

It wasn't long before Eugenie, Steve, and most of the people around them, stood up again. They all rose to sing.

'I love this one!' Eugenie commented to no-one in particular when she heard what they were all about to sing.

The people who'd frowned at Eugenie when she'd entered looked up from the orange books they were reading to frown at her again. They then realised that they didn't need the orange books, so they put them down again, but continued to frown at Eugenie. Eugenie, who hadn't picked up her orange book, was too caught up in her excitement to notice the frowning people.

As a soprano, Eugenie's voice rose above many of the other singers as they praised the creator of nature in all its varieties.

While listening to herself and dozens of other people singing together, Eugenie felt that they were all sending a collective message that they meant and believed the words they were singing. It made her feel like part of something much bigger than herself.

-

After the song had ended, Eugenie and those around her sat down. The room was silent, except for one voice, which told a story. Eugenie recited the words of the tale in her head and contemplated what they meant to her, the life she lead, and the world she found herself in.

Usually, Eugenie was a person who struggled to concentrate, but something about her surroundings helped her to focus. In that room, she could think about what mattered most, and what direction her life should take. Just sitting there, in the presence of like-minded people coming together to celebrate the most important thing in their lives, made Eugenie feel blissful.

CHAPTER SIX

In the flat Holly shared with Eugenie, the television was in the kitchen-diner, for the kitchen-diner was the main room. This meant that every Sunday, the sound of Holly chopping veg merged with hymns from the program that Eugenie was watching.

Listening to the hymns on Eugenie's favourite show made Holly smile. She couldn't imagine herself going to church every Sunday and learning the Bible by heart though, which, as far as she understood it, was what being Christian was about.

Listening to the hymns on her favourite show made Eugenie feel like part of a diverse and inclusive community. To her, the shots of the congregations showed people from every walk of life. As far as she understood it, the faith they all shared was about belief in God and a will to make the world a better place in His name.

'That smells *divine*, Holly. I can't wait for it to be on the table. Thank you for cooking,' Eugenie said after sniffing the air.

'I don't cook during the week, so I'm happy to do this, especially as you like it so much. Eating it is a good excuse to spend quality time together,' Holly replied. As she was modest and liked Eugenie, Holly didn't add that she wanted Sunday roast but, as she preferred it not burnt, she had to do it herself.

The mention of quality time and people singing on the television gave Eugenie an idea.

'We spend a lot of time together here, but we rarely go out. We should though. Let's go out for karaoke one night. I've always wanted to, and you'd be the perfect person to do it with,' Eugenie suggested.

As a shy woman with little confidence in her singing voice, Holly did *not* think she was the perfect person to do karaoke with.

While trying to work out how to politely reject Eugenie, Holly checked how cooked the joint of beef in the oven was. It was perfect, so she took it out.

'It's almost done here, so I'll be plating up soon,' Holly announced.

'Great! Katherine's just singing us out on here, so that's perfect timing,' Eugenie replied.

-

Just as it usually did, Holly's Sunday roast kept herself and Eugenie quiet.

When she'd mostly cleared her plate, Holly asked: 'Are you looking forward to tomorrow?'

'Very much so. I've got a regular customer from Toothill's in the morning to kick things off, and then a young man with quite a large family in the afternoon. Both seemed just as excited as me. I can't wait,' Eugenie replied.

Happy with this news, Holly gulped down the last of her carrot slices.

'Lot's to look forward to then,' Holly commented.

'Yes. I've got bookings throughout December, and, when we can fit it in, we've got karaoke! Life's good,' Eugenie enthused.

In her head, Holly said: *'Oh, so you didn't forget. Looks like I'll be making a fool of myself some time soon then.'*

CHAPTER SEVEN

On account of her mood, Eugenie threw open the heavy glass door of Trinity Café with such gusto, it slammed into the wall.

'Oops. Sorry, Lynne!' Eugenie called to the owner of the door she'd thrown open, who'd seen her do it.

'Don't worry about it. It happens twenty times a day,' Lynne replied.

Nodding at a table in the window, Lynne told Eugenie: 'He's over there. Been waiting for ten minutes.'

When Eugenie laid eyes on the man Lynne was referring to, she couldn't help thinking he looked familiar. They'd chatted on the phone for nearly an hour to arrange this meeting, and he hadn't *sounded* familiar then, but he *looked* familiar sat in the café.

'Are you Hamish?' Eugenie asked.

The familiar man nodded and stood up, his hand extended for Eugenie to shake. When she took it, the man confirmed: 'Yes. That's me.'

Having greeted the man, Eugenie laid her hand on a chair to pull it out so she could sit on it.

'Wait! Allow me,' Hamish cried.

Before Eugenie could work out what it was Hamish

wanted to be allowed to do, he glided over to the chair she'd earmarked as hers and pulled it back with both hands. Somewhat bemused by this, Eugenie sat on the chair, which Hamish then pushed up to the table.

'Can I get you anything? Coffee, tea, cake?' Hamish offered.

For a moment, Eugenie wondered if *she* was the customer and *Hamish* was the personal shopper.

'No, it's fine. I had lunch before I met you. Besides, isn't it my job to ask *you* those questions?' Eugenie questioned.

Hamish blushed. 'Ah, yes. Sorry. I got confused. For a moment there, I thought we were friends, when in fact I'm your customer. I think it's because you're so warm and gregarious. It makes me feel like I've known you forever,' he replied.

While trying not to meet Eugenie's eye, Hamish shuffled back to his own seat and sat down.

It was clear to Eugenie that Hamish felt awkward. She wanted to put him at ease, and she decided complimenting him would be the best way to do that.

'You've nothing to apologise for. You're charming,' Eugenie told Hamish.

Much to her dismay, Eugenie's comment made Hamish blush harder. He was now so uncomfortable that he couldn't speak.

Having failed miserably on her first attempt to put Hamish at ease, Eugenie changed tack.

'On the phone, we talked about your mother. You were unsure what to get her. Is that right?' Eugenie asked.

Just as Eugenie had hoped, Hamish's cheeks paled. He

even smiled a little bit.

'Yes, that's correct. She has a great dislike for objects in general, unless they have a purpose or, as she puts it: "Someone has poured a lot of love into them." That makes it quite a challenge to know what to buy her. To make things harder for you, I absolutely adore her, so I want her present to be perfect,' Hamish confirmed.

'I could tell you love her. You talked about her with such affection,' Eugenie revealed.

Once again, Hamish's cheeks reddened. 'Oh, you could? I am a proper Mummy's boy, so I suppose that would come across,' he replied.

Eugenie smiled. 'I love a boy who loves his mum. You really are charming,' she said.

Silence fell, as Eugenie realised that, in a way, she'd just told Hamish she loved him. The words slipping so easily out of her mouth made her wonder if she actually *did* love him. As her relationship with Hamish was a professional one, she decided it was best not to dwell on those thoughts.

'I think I know *exactly* what you should buy her. Would you like to see what I have in mind?' Eugenie asked.

Before answering, Hamish gulped down the last of his coffee. 'Yes, let's,' he agreed.

The lunchtime rush at Trinity had died down. This meant that, on his way to the door, Hamish could walk up to Lynne behind the counter and say: 'Thanks for the coffee. I'll be back.'

'I look forward to it, Arnie,' Lynne replied.

As he wasn't called Arnie, this confused Hamish. It confused him even more because he hadn't introduced himself to Lynne. She had no reason to think his name was Arnie, or any other name in particular.

'My name is *Hamish*,' corrected Hamish.

Lynne laughed. 'You said "I'll be back", an Arnie catchphrase. I didn't think *your* name was Arnie. I've never met anyone whose name *was* Arnie,' she explained.

As he had never watched any Arnold Schwarzenegger films, Hamish was unaware that "I'll be back" was one of his catchphrases. Now he knew, he felt silly, for he suspected most people would have known Lynne was making an Arnie reference.

'Sorry. Goodbye now,' Hamish mumbled.

'Hasta la vista, baby!' Lynne called.

In order to get out of Trinity Café and away from its Arnie-reference-making owner, Hamish opened the door. He held it open for Eugenie to walk through.

It had been a long time since Eugenie had had a door held for her, and Hamish doing it made her feel like a grand lady.

On the street outside Trinity, Eugenie gazed up at the church that loomed before her. There were stark black metal railings between her and the building, but she still felt a connection to it.

'Breathtaking, isn't it? It's the oldest standing building in Colchester. Older than the castle, even. It has reused Roman bricks in it, so it has serious age to it,' Hamish commented when he saw what had grabbed Eugenie's attention.

'I love it,' Eugenie replied. She was so in awe of the ancient church before her that she could only manage a whisper.

Hamish cleared his throat. 'Sorry, I didn't need to tell you about it, did I? We're on a shopping trip, not a history tour,' he said.

'You didn't *need* to, but I'm glad you did. Now, every time I eat my lunch gazing up at it, I'll hear your voice in my head telling me about it,' Eugenie told Hamish.

'Is that a good thing?' Hamish questioned.

Eugenie nodded energetically. 'Yes, it is. You have a kind and calm voice,' she replied.

Suddenly, Hamish found he couldn't use his kind and calm voice. Eugenie's words had rendered him speechless.

Seeing that Hamish was having difficulty speaking, Eugenie decided to fill the silence. 'The shop is this way,' she said, gesturing to the right.

-

The "shop" Eugenie thought sold a good present for his mother looked more like an art gallery to Hamish. Busy acrylic seascapes adorned the walls. Below them were tables with shell necklaces laid out on them. Nothing he saw interested Hamish, and nothing looked like something his mum would want.

At the back of the shop was a stepladder. When he first saw it, Hamish wondered if it was an art installation. He then noticed that there was a woman at the top of it, so he decided it wasn't.

'Good afternoon, Suzi!' Eugenie called to the woman up the stepladder.

When she realised she had customers, Suzi made her way down the stepladder to greet them.

'Yes, it is actually. What can I do for you?' Suzi replied.

'Do you have any of your painted pebbles, from Sheringham?' Eugenie asked.

That one question told Hamish why Eugenie had brought him to that shop.

As she *did* have painted pebbles from Sheringham, Suzi nodded. 'I put the basket away because I didn't think anyone would want them. Give me a minute and I'll go get it for you,' she told Eugenie.

To get the basket of requested painted pebbles, Suzi scuttled across her shop to a door that, because it was behind the counter, Hamish hadn't noticed. He watched her go through the door and pick up a large wicker basket. After looking inside the basket at its contents, Suzi shook her head and returned it to its shelf. A moment later, she pulled out an identical basket and, just like the last one, put it back again.

'I'll just be a minute,' Suzi called, going deeper into her stockroom.

As the moment when she got to show Hamish what she'd found for his mum's Christmas present drew closer, Eugenie's excitement reached a fever pitch.

'You remembered that Mum lives in Sheringham? How? I only mentioned it once or twice,' Hamish questioned.

'My job is to listen to you and make present suggestions based on what you tell me, so that's what I've done. You told me your mum is in Sheringham and doesn't like clutter, but loves things that people have poured love into. You also told me that, despite being less than a hundred, Sheringham feels like a million miles away. From that, I worked out what you should buy her. It's simple,' Eugenie replied.

At last, Suzi found the basket she was looking for. She brought it up to the counter, where Eugenie and Hamish were waiting for her.

The basket was full of pebbles, each one with a colourful painting on. Most of the scenes depicted were familiar to Hamish. He picked one up with a reddish-orange rectangular building on it.

'I remember saying to Mum once that this church looks like a power station, and her telling me that the man who designed it also did Battersea. We spent the rest of the day wondering how on Earth the same man ended up doing both things, before I had to come home,' Hamish told Eugenie.

Unnoticed by Hamish, who was captivated by the pebbles full of memories, Suzi and Eugenie shared a smile.

Once he'd put the pebble with the unusual church on to one side, Hamish picked up a flat grey stone that Suzi had painted a beach on. He stroked a thumb along the representation of familiar great expanses of sand, broken up by the brown lines of groynes.

'She walks the dogs along this, out of season. They love it. It's heaven to them,' Hamish murmured.

'The beach is *my* favourite thing about Sheringham. My partner lives there, and every time I go to see her, we catch up while walking on the beach. I take my art things and, if I see something nice, I take a stone from the beach, which I know you're not supposed to do but I don't do it that often, and I paint it. That's how I've ended up with all these pebbles on with scenes from Sheringham. Until Eugenie text me last night, I didn't expect to sell them. Why would anyone in Colchester want pebble paintings of Sheringham? Happily, it seems like you do,' Suzi said.

For some reason, knowing he wasn't the only person in Colchester with a connection to it made Sheringham feel closer to Hamish. Giving pebbles adorned with scenes from the town she lived in painted by an artist from the town he lived in would make Hamish feel closer to his mum.

'My mum moved to Sheringham when Dad left her, so that's why *I* want them. Paintings by someone from where I *still* live of where Mum *now* lives seem like the perfect Christmas present,' Hamish explained.

It was Suzi's main ambition for her art to move people. Knowing how much her pebbles meant to Hamish made her want to jump up and down with happiness because she'd been successful and cry because she knew how painful it was for loved ones to be far away, all at the same time. She ended up doing neither.

'How many do you want? They're four pounds each, but I'll do you a deal if you buy a few,' Suzi asked. Asking a question she had to ask for her job distracted her from the ache caused by the distance between her and her partner.

The formal question also stopped Eugenie and Hamish ruminating on how much they missed their distant loved ones.

'I want every one that means something to me, even if you charge me a *fiver* each,' Hamish told Suzi.

-

It turned out that seven of Suzi's pebbles meant something to Hamish, and, because she could see how much they meant to him, she asked for twenty pounds for the little lot of memories.

With his seven pebbles wrapped up and stowed away in a tote bag, Hamish left the shop with Eugenie. As soon as he was exposed to the air outside the heated shop, he grimaced.

'Winter is coming,' Hamish commented.

'I don't know what that means,' Eugenie replied.

What Eugenie said made so little sense to Hamish that he replayed her words in his head. How could she possibly not know what he meant? Surely everyone knew what "winter is coming" meant.

'It means the season is changing. It won't be autumn much longer, if you can even call it autumn *now*. You can feel the onset of winter in the wind,' Hamish explained.

'Oh, you meant it literally! I thought you were making a *Game of Thrones* reference. I know "winter is coming" is a phrase from the show, but I don't watch it, so I have no idea what it means! Sorry,' Eugenie cried as she realised her mistake.

Like Eugenie, Hamish hadn't watched *Game of Thrones*. Unlike her, he didn't know "winter is coming" was a phrase from it. It reminded him of something.

'You don't need to be sorry. It's not as bad as when the lady in the café made a joke about Aaron someone, and I didn't get it,' Hamish said.

Eugenie shrugged. 'It doesn't matter. I only know about Arnie because Holly loves him. She says he's her celebrity crush. I guess he *is* handsome, but I find it hard to fancy someone who always seems to have blood on him and be killing people. My ideal man doesn't have any bodily fluids on him and wouldn't hurt a fly,' she replied.

Thinking about the sort of films Arnie starred in made Hamish shiver. He hadn't watched any films with Arnold Schwarzenegger in, but he'd seen *Die Hard* and *Robocop,* and they'd told him that action films weren't for him, regardless of who starred in them.

It occurred to Hamish that *Game of Thrones* and action films were popular. It also occurred to him that, because he didn't watch them, many people would think him strange.

'I'm an odd creature. Many popular things are of no interest to me. Some disgust me. I seem incapable of being trendy. I cannot fit in,' Hamish mused aloud.

'If *you're* odd then so am *I*, because I don't fit in *anywhere*. I want to let the world know how happy I am and share my joy, but, and I don't know why, not everyone likes that. I get the funniest looks sometimes,' Eugenie revealed.

The idea that some people didn't like Eugenie was inconceivable to Hamish. He gazed into her grey eyes, a window into her soul, and saw nothing to dislike.

'I think you're wonderful. You've made my day with those pebbles for Mum, and for not being the only one to get muddled up over references,' Hamish told Eugenie.

The word "wonderful" made Eugenie's heart flutter. She found she could no longer hold Hamish's gaze, so she looked down at her excitable heart.

'I'm glad the pebbles worked out well. Shall we look for something for your uncle now?' Eugenie suggested.

'Yes, let's,' he agreed.

Looking straight ahead, Eugenie lead Hamish around the lanes to continue their shopping trip.

CHAPTER EIGHT

Laying on the sofa with a book was Holly's favourite thing to do when she got back from work. The tale of a grieving wannabe author working all hours as a waitress just to survive made Holly forget about the hours she'd spent correcting her favourite colleague's work. As Holly had told her workmate, it was worth doing to avoid their boss being in a bad mood, but it was still hard work.

When Eugenie got home from her first day as a Christmas Genie, Holly was *physically* at their flat, but *mentally* she was in Boston, Massachusetts.

'Hi! I'm back from one of the best days of my life!' Eugenie cried as she danced into the kitchen-diner.

The sound of Eugenie's lilting tones brought Holly fully back to Colchester, Essex. Knowing she would no longer be able to concentrate, she placed her book to one side.

'Good evening, Eugenie. What made the day so good?' Holly asked.

As she took her long white coat off, Eugenie twirled around the room. Once removed, the coat was thrown at the coat hook on the wall, which it lopsidedly hung from.

'I had the *best* day! This job is going to make my Christmas, I'm sure. My first client can't *wait* to give her sister the vase that's exactly like the one their nan had when they were little, and my second was *charming,* and nearly cried when I showed him what I'd picked for his mum. It couldn't have gone any better. Happy customers makes a happy me,' Eugenie told Holly.

It was unnecessary for Eugenie to tell Holly that her customers being happy made her happy. Anyone who knew Eugenie knew that.

Just like customers (and anyone she met) being happy made Eugenie happy, Eugenie being happy more often than not made Holly happy.

'Sounds great, Eugenie,' Holly said.

Eugenie sighed and flopped down on the sofa, next to Holly. 'It was,' she replied.

Only when she sat on her sofa did Eugenie realise how tired she was. When guiding Hamish around the Lanes, she'd felt as if she'd drunk litres of energy drinks. Every step had had a spring in it, her senses had been at their sharpest, especially touch and smell, and her heart had pounded along eagerly like a drum. Hours later, she felt like she hadn't got a sap of energy left.

When she thought about the fact that she had to cook dinner, Eugenie felt a little less happy. To show this, she groaned.

'What's wrong?' Holly questioned.

'I still have to cook dinner, but I'm exhausted. Don't worry, though. I'll do it,' Eugenie told Holly.

The knowledge that Eugenie didn't want to cook gave Holly an idea.

'If you don't want to, *don't* cook. Let's go out. We can celebrate your first day in your new job,' Holly suggested.

The idea of not having to cook made Eugenie's spirits soar.

'Can we? Can we go out? Isn't that giving in and being lazy?' Eugenie questioned.

'I don't see why we can't. Neither of us will be taking our families out for dinner over the Christmas period, but we still deserve to go out. Better to do it now than closer to Christmas itself, because it will get busier and busier as the day gets closer,' Holly replied.

No more justification was needed for Eugenie. She had no reason to object to Holly's plan, and lots of reasons to agree.

'Yes, let's. Let's go out,' Eugenie agreed.

After her words had left her mouth, Eugenie realised they were familiar. 'I sounded like Hamish just then,' she told Holly, who had never met Hamish.

Holly smiled and said: 'To me, you never sound or act like anyone other than yourself.'

CHAPTER NINE

The first thing Eugenie noticed about the restaurant Holly took her to was that it was warm and bright inside. As it was cold and dark outside, this pleased her.

There was a lectern just inside the door with a sign that read: "Welcome! Hang on here a minute and we'll be right with you." Eugenie and Holly obeyed the sign.

"We" turned out to be someone whose uniform wasn't at all creased or stained, and "a minute" was actually thirty-four seconds. The person was wearing a badge that informed readers that the wearer's name was Sam, and they were a waitress.

'Have you booked?' Sam asked Eugenie and Holly.

The idea of her booking a table made Eugenie giggle. 'No, I'm never that organised. Besides church and work, I don't know what I'm doing one day to the next. I only decided to come here an hour ago,' she told Sam.

Sam frowned. 'We have availability tonight, so you'll be pleased to know that's not an issue,' she replied.

As they'd never thought not booking would be an issue, Eugenie and Holly didn't know what to say to Sam.

'Follow me,' Sam ordered, striding off across the restaurant.

On the way through the restaurant, Sam snatched two menus from a holder on the wall.

Once Sam reached their destination, a booth with striped red and white banquettes, they slapped the menus down on the table.

'Is this for us?' Holly asked, looking at the table she and Eugenie had been shown to.

'Yes. It should be suitable. Sit here and have a read of the menu. I will be along to take your order shortly,' Sam replied.

Having said that, Sam embarked on a return journey to the lectern, but not before Eugenie said: 'Thank you for all your help, Sam.'

Just as they'd been told to do, Eugenie and Holly read the menu. Something on the bottom right caught Eugenie's eye.

'They do cinnamon apple pie!' Eugenie cried.

Holly smiled. 'Trust you to look at desserts first,' she said.

'I can't help it! My eye is drawn to anything sweet,' Eugenie replied.

Chuckling softly to herself, Holly continued to read the main meals section of her menu. When she'd decided what she wanted, she turned her attention to the drinks. One in particular appealed to her, so she committed its name to her memory and shut the menu.

'It all sounds so yummy! I don't know what to choose,' Eugenie said, her menu still open.

'There is a lot of choice. I'm having pizza, because I fancy it,' Holly told Eugenie.

When Eugenie perused her menu once again, she made

her mind up.

'I want the burger that has everything, as long as you don't mind. It's one of the most expensive things on the menu,' Eugenie declared.

'Eugenie, it's okay. It's not like this is fine dining. There's nothing on this menu I can't afford. It's partly why I came here,' Holly reassured her.

A few seconds after Eugenie closed her menu, she heard the purposeful footsteps of a member of staff approaching. It was the same woman who had greeted her.

'Do I see you've decided what you want?' Sam asked.

'Yes. Yes we have,' Eugenie replied.

Looking at Holly, Eugenie asked: 'Shall I go first?'

When Holly nodded, Eugenie proceeded to say: 'I would like a Jumbo Burger and a cosmopolitan, please.'

With a miniature pencil from a catalogue shop, Sam committed Eugenie's order to the paper of a plain brown notepad.

'And you?' Sam asked Holly.

'Hawaiian and rum and Coke for me, thanks,' Holly told Sam.

'Individual, for the pizza, or a sharing one?' Sam questioned.

'*There are two of us, and she's having a huge burger. What do you think?*'' Holly thought.

Out loud, Holly said: 'Individual, thanks.'

'Very good. I'll get this off to the kitchen. As you can see, we're quite full here, so I'm afraid it might be a wait of more than forty minutes for food,' Sam told Eugenie and

Holly.

Having taken their order, and warned them there would be a wait, Sam left Eugenie and Holly to it.

Having ordered, and been warned there was a wait, Holly reclined in comfort on her bench. She looked around at her fellow diners. Most of them looked as if they, like Holly, had made a last minute decision to have dinner out and had wandered in in the clothes they'd been in all day. There was a group of four, all in plain black and grey clothes with smart hairstyles and minimal make-up, behind Holly, and a couple with two children who were still wearing their school uniforms in front of her. No-one stood out.

Like Holly, Eugenie took in her surroundings. She noticed that people seemed to be there for all sorts of occasions. There was a couple hunched over their table, whispering and holding hands, who she was sure were on a date, and across from them were five smiling people, one of whom was wearing a big round pin badge, and she guessed they were celebrating a birthday. There were some tables of people where their reason for being in the restaurant wasn't obvious. Eugenie wondered if, like her and Holly, they were simply there because they were hungry and didn't want to cook.

Most of the people Eugenie and Holly had observed were engaged in conversation. Laughs and gasps of shock rose above the multi-tonal murmurs of steady chatter. Eugenie decided to add to the noise.

'Holly, I haven't asked about your day yet. How was it?' Eugenie asked.

'My day was dull. I had to fix some errors Sally made yesterday on some paperwork. It was *so* boring. You know how mind-numbing I find that side of my job. Poor Sally was really apologetic, but she didn't need to be. She didn't do it deliberately,' Holly told Eugenie.

'Oh, what a shame for Sally. She's a lovely girl. I hope she wasn't too upset about her mistakes. Good for her that you fixed them. I know you'll have been kind about it,' Eugenie replied.

'I couldn't hide how bored I was, but I did try to make it clear that it wasn't a big deal. As you say, Sally is lovely,' Holly said.

Discussing Holly's work made Eugenie recall when Holly had met one of her customers in the street. One who Eugenie thought must be rude.

'At least that man didn't come in. The one we bumped into one day on our way to have lunch. Then your day may not have been boring, but it wouldn't have been interesting in a good way,' Eugenie pointed out.

Holly frowned. 'Why? Why would Darren staying be a *bad* thing?' she questioned.

'That day when we saw him, you hardly spoke to him, so I thought he was a rude or awkward customer,' Eugenie explained.

'No, I... Well, the reason I can't speak to Darren is... I must have been tired that day. Darren isn't rude or awkward. He's a good man, nowadays at least. His heart's in the right place,' Holly rambled awkwardly.

'Oh, I misread it then. Never mind. Silly me. I do that sometimes. I'm glad he's not rude or awkward,' Eugenie replied.

Just as Holly was thinking it would be nice to have something to sip, Sam appeared with two glasses.

'This is the rum and Coke, and this is the cosmopolitan,' Sam announced as she placed the aforementioned drinks on the table.

'Thank you, Sam. These'll warm us up on this cold night,' Eugenie said.

'I hope they do. It's freezing out there,' Sam replied, already walking off to the next table.

The moment her drink was in front of her, Holly took a gulp from it. Eugenie took a moment to admire the bright pink colour of her cocktail before she tasted it. When she did take a sip, she emitted a little squeak.

'Wow! I forgot how sharp a cosmopolitan is! I love it though,' Eugenie told Holly.

Raising her glass of warming rum and cola, Holly declared: 'Cheers.'

-

An hour and a half later, Eugenie and Holly trundled along the lanes between the restaurant and their flat.

'I loved showing Hamish around here. It was such a pleasure to share this with him. He really seemed to appreciate the magic of pretty, family-run, independent little shops,' Eugenie commented, referring to the locked-up shops she was passing with Holly.

'Yes, it's the perfect job for you. This is utopia to you, and I know you'll love showing it off to people,' Holly replied.

'Heaven, more like, and the perfect place to spend this month,' Eugenie murmured.

Having admired the shops beside her, Eugenie turned her attention skyward. Above her, she saw twinkling dots of white against a deep navy background.

'Look! Aren't they the perfect Christmas lights?' Eugenie asked, pointing at the stars.

When she looked up herself, Holly found that she agreed. The stars were far prettier than any artificial lights could be.

Eugenie giggled. 'For a moment, I thought it already was December. I think the cinnamon in my dessert confused my brain. To me, that is the taste and smell of Christmas. That and oranges,' she replied.

Under the Christmas lights/stars, daydreaming of kitchens where the air was heavy with oranges and cinnamon, Eugenie and Holly made their way home.

CHAPTER TEN

'It's the switch-on tonight, Eugenie. I imagine you're excited about it,' Victoria said to Eugenie at Toothill's one Tuesday morning in late November.

Eugenie shook her head. 'Not really,' she replied.

This confused Victoria, and Victoria didn't like being confused. It unsettled her. She folded her arms.

'I thought you loved Christmas, but you don't care about the lights switch-on? That makes no sense. Do you like Christmas, with the lights, the trees, presents, terrible music and all that, or not?' Victoria questioned.

A dress amongst the trousers, falling off its hanger, caught Eugenie's eye. As soon as she spotted it, she was compelled to take it off the rail, rehang it, and put it in its proper place with the other dresses.

As she hadn't yet been answered, Victoria said: 'Well? Which is it? Make your mind up.'

'None of the things you listed are what Christmas is really about,' Eugenie replied.

Victoria shook her head and busied herself with some paperwork.

While Eugenie was pondering redressing the mannequins in the window, a man walked in off the street.

Customers walking in excited Eugenie. It meant that dress-up time was imminent. She was slightly disappointed when she saw her latest customer, because she assumed he wasn't shopping for himself, so wouldn't try any of the clothes on.

'Welcome to Toothill's. I'm Eugenie. How can I help you?' Eugenie asked.

The customer extended his hand to shake and said: 'Cool. Ronnie's my name, and you can help me by picking out some outfits for my stunner of a girl.'

Because she felt it would be rude not to, Eugenie shook Ronnie's hand.

From her vantage point at the counter, Victoria observed Ronnie and Eugenie. She drummed her real nails on the counter in an attempt to shift the uneasy feeling the sight gave her.

'I'll be out the back, Eugenie, but I'll still be able to keep an eye on you. I'll certainly be able to *hear* you,' Victoria told her niece.

Waving a hand dismissively, Eugenie replied: 'Yes, of course. I'll be fine here with Ronnie.'

Not entirely convinced that Eugenie *would* be fine, Victoria snuck away to her stockroom.

'Are you buying your girlfriend outfits for an occasion?' Eugenie asked Ronnie.

'Yeah, some parties we've got coming up. This is all a sort of challenge. I asked Ems what she was wearing for one of the parties and she laughed at me. Apparently, it's pointless telling me what she's going to wear. I know nothing about clothes. She said if I had to dress her for the party, then she'd turn up in jumper and jeans, which apparently is unacceptable. Right then, I knew I had to prove her wrong, so I argued. I said I'd pick her out something as stunning as she is. She laughed some more and said if I was so confident, then I should go shopping for her. The one thing I one hundred percent am is confident, so now I'm here, in her favourite shop, to buy her some nice bits,' Ronnie revealed.

The idea of a challenge made Eugenie rub her hands together with glee. Already, she was creating potential outfits in her head.

'Let's get to it then! What do you want?' Eugenie asked.

Ronnie blushed and twiddled his thumbs. 'See, here's the thing, Eugenie. All my confidence, it's just bravado. I don't have the first idea what to buy for her. This was such a stupid idea. I'm gonna go home looking like an idiot,' he replied.

The sudden shyness that had overcome Ronnie made Eugenie warm to him. Now, more than ever, she was determined to choose something good for his absent girlfriend.

Before Eugenie could finalise an outfit in her head, she needed to know a little bit more about Ronnie's stunner of a girl.

'I can sort this, if you answer a couple of questions. What colour are your girlfriend's eyes? Also her hair. I'd like to know its colour too, and style,' Eugenie asked.

'Oh, thanks so much! You're a lifesaver! She's a natural brunette, but she dyes her hair honey blonde because she thinks it looks better. Her eyes are just a dull grey,' Ronnie told Eugenie.

'Perfect! I'll get to work then, if you can tell me her size,'

Eugenie declared.

'She's a twelve now, almost a fourteen. Probably because it's Christmastime,' Ronnie informed Eugenie.

As she had no comment to make on Ronnie's girlfriend's dress size, Eugenie glided through the shop in silence, whisking clothes off the rails. The clothes she removed, she draped over the counter.

Once she had everything she wanted, Eugenie plucked a black suit jacket and a purple blouse back off the counter she'd placed them on a moment ago, and held them up together for Ronnie to see.

'Nice. I can see her in that,' Ronnie said.

'The black should go well with her grey eyes, and I love putting purple or orange with black. The contrast is so fun!' Eugenie explained.

Having studied the clothes, Ronnie's gaze drifted to the eyes of the person holding them. He blinked, as if he couldn't believe what he was seeing.

'Speaking of eyes, yours are really pretty. They're like a window into your sparkling soul. I bet they get you a lot of attention from men... along with some of your other attributes,' Ronnie told Eugenie.

Any warmth Eugenie had felt for Ronnie left. Her feelings for him turned so cold, she almost shivered. She did *not* shiver, but she *did* put her hands on her hips.

'Yes, I do have pretty eyes. I also have a slender figure, eye-catching hair, I wear nice-smelling perfume, and I am the perfect height in heels,' Eugenie replied.

In the stockroom, Victoria was listening to the exchange between her niece and Toothill's latest customer. Hearing

Eugenie praise herself brought a rare smile to Victoria's lips.

On the shop floor, hearing Eugenie praise herself made Ronnie frown. 'Erm, yeah. That's right,' he mumbled, unsure of what to say.

'Shall I show you the rest of this lot so you can pick out what you'd like for your *girlfriend*?' Eugenie suggested.

As he had no alternative ideas, Ronnie agreed: 'Yeah, sounds alright.'

-

Twenty minutes after he'd walked in, Ronnie left Toothill's with two bags of clothes and a lighter purse.

Eugenie was only alone on the shop floor for a few moments, for her aunt joined her.

'I like what you said earlier,' Victoria told Eugenie.

'What? Do you mean about how, as lovely as our clothes are, it's the thought that counts when giving gifts?' Eugenie questioned.

As that was not what she meant, Victoria shook her head. 'I meant about you having a slender figure and being the perfect height in heels,' she explained.

Eugenie didn't understand why Victoria would like that she'd praised herself. It was quite unlike her. She believed in the adage "Self-praise is no praise". There was a reason why she'd spoken about herself in that way, but she didn't think Victoria knew that reason.

'I only said those things so *he* couldn't say them. I could see where things were going, and I knew if I didn't nip it in the bud then he'd keep paying me little compliments, and the thought of that made my skin crawl. I do desperately want a man, but I'm not *that* desperate,' Eugenie explained.

It hadn't occurred to Victoria that Eugenie had said what she'd said for a reason. She'd just thought Eugenie was making a statement about how body-confident she was. It pleased her that Eugenie was comfortable with herself, or at least her appearance. Often, Victoria had wondered if Eugenie's upbeat demeanour was a front for insecurity. Victoria found it inconceivable that anyone could truly be as bright and sunny as her niece appeared to be.

'That's clever, to say it so he didn't. I didn't know you could think like that, but I'm impressed that you can,' Victoria said.

Behind her back, Eugenie pinched herself. It hurt, a lot, which confirmed that she wasn't dreaming. Her aunt really had just paid her a compliment.

All Eugenie could think of to say after being unexpectedly praised was: 'Thank you.'

A woman pushed her way through the door, into Toothill's. Eugenie got excited, because she thought she had another customer to dress. When the woman dragged a trolley with two boxes on through the door, she realised that they were a delivery driver, not a customer. This didn't disappoint her though, for it meant she had new clothes to look at, which was almost as good as having a new customer to dress.

'This Toothill's?' the driver asked Victoria.

'Yes,' Victoria confirmed.

The delivery driver pulled a phone with a blank white screen out of her fleece pocket and held it in front of Victoria.

'Sign here,' the delivery driver ordered.

Using her index finger, Victoria wrote her name on the delivery driver's phone. She took great care doing it, so it looked exactly like the signature on her driving license. As she had many drop-offs to do, and no-one ever checked the signatures she collected, the few extra seconds it took Victoria to sign her name properly irritated the delivery driver.

'Good day,' the delivery driver said.

It was unclear to Victoria whether the delivery driver was saying it *was* a good day or was telling her to *have* a good day. Whichever it was, Victoria didn't care, for she knew the delivery driver didn't mean what she'd said.

While Victoria was busy writing her signature with a finger, Eugenie had removed the boxes from the delivery driver's trolley. This meant that the driver could easily haul the empty trolley out of the shop and down the lane to where she'd dumped her van.

Looking at the two boxes in the middle of her shop, Victoria said: 'I think you know what to do, Eugenie.'

Looking at the two boxes full of new clothes that she could dress the people of Colchester in, Eugenie replied: 'Oh, I *do*.'

Knowing what she was supposed to do, Eugenie lugged the boxes, one at a time, to the stockroom.

-

To allow Eugenie to sort through Toothill's new stock, Victoria stayed at the counter. While she did so, someone teetered through the door.

'Good afternoon. I am looking for a handful of new outfits

for some functions I'm attending this season,' the new-comer said.

Recognising her latest customer, Victoria replied: 'I would be delighted to assist with that, Hermione, if you don't mind.'

As the very reason she'd come to Toothill's was for Victoria to assist her with buying new clothes, Hermione didn't mind. She showed this by nodding.

While Victoria sauntered around her shop, perusing her rails, she noticed there was noise coming from the backroom. She could hear the clicks of a tagging gun and the rustle of tissue paper being removed from clothes and folded neatly for future use. This didn't bother her, for the noises were quiet, and ones she expected. She knew Eugenie was unpacking new stock and preparing it for display.

Just as Victoria was wondering if Hermione would look good in a peach dress that had been on the rail for two months, Eugenie cried: 'Oh, so soft! Soft and beautiful!'

The sound of Eugenie crying out about something soft and beautiful startled Hermione. She looked up from the magazine she'd been engrossed in with a frown on her face.

Seeing the expression on Hermione's face, Victoria told her: 'I'm terribly sorry about this. I'll just be a moment.'

Leaving a slightly perplexed Hermione on the shop floor, Victoria marched through to the stockroom. There, she found a rail half-full of new dresses, and Eugenie hugging a white faux fur coat.

'Stroke this! It's so soft!' Eugenie told Victoria.

Victoria shook her head and snatched the coat from Eugenie's hands. 'What do you think you're doing? We've got a very important customer out there and you're yelling away in here,' she hissed.

'It was so soft, I couldn't help myself,' Eugenie replied.

'Well, you *must* help yourself! I can't have you making silly noises about furry coats, understood?' Victoria snapped.

Unable to speak for fear of saying something cheeky, Eugenie nodded.

Having dealt with Eugenie, Victoria stormed back onto the shop floor. Hermione was still there, reading the label on a jacket while she waited for her.

'Is everything okay?' Hermione asked Victoria.

'Oh yes, my niece was just overwhelmed by the softness of a coat, which is typical of her. Sorry about that,' Victoria replied.

'I'm just glad she's okay. That's quite cute, that she exclaimed about a soft coat. I think I like this niece of yours,' Hermione said.

'Well, someone has to, I suppose,' Victoria murmured.

Despite it not making noise, Hermione got her phone out and looked at the screen. She frowned at whatever she saw, and returned it to her shoulder bag.

'I have an important business meeting to attend at which decisions will be made involving big sums of money, of which I will take a cut. Big sums, huge. I must dash. Good day,' Hermione announced.

'Well, that's unfortunate. I hope to see you again about those new outfits,' Victoria said.

Pretending not to hear Victoria, Hermione headed out

onto the street.

Some of the shoppers on the street outside Toothill's were confused. They were confused because a woman was walking down the street giggling to herself. They may not have been confused if they'd have known that the woman was giggling because she'd made a *Pretty Woman* reference to a shop owner who she didn't like very much and pretended to have a text about a meeting so she could leave the woman's shop. Then again, they may have still been confused, for the woman didn't look like the type of person who did such things.

It frustrated Victoria that Hermione had walked out without buying anything. She suspected that Hermione had many hundreds of pounds to spend, which could have gone into Toothill's till. She also suspected that Hermione didn't actually have a meeting, and had left because she was unhappy with the behaviour of the staff. Both of Victoria's suspicions were correct.

'Now look what you've done! That rich woman left, and it's because of you!' Victoria yelled through to Eugenie, who was still in the stockroom.

While silently admiring a navy shirt with sparkling silver snowflake buttons, Eugenie thought: '*Oh, so now Auntie's back to snapping at me. Normal service is resumed. Oh well. I've got lots of pretty clothes to look at, and my lunch break is less than an hour away.*'

CHAPTER ELEVEN

The bench with a view of Holy Trinity Church was Eugenie's favourite place to eat her lunch. As she sat on the bench with her cheese sandwiches, gazing at the captivating ancient church, she thought about Hamish. In her head, she heard him say: *'Breathtaking, isn't it?'*

Because she was daydreaming about Hamish and replaying his voice in her head, Eugenie didn't realise her phone was ringing until it was halfway through its ringtone. She whipped it out of her pocket and answered it without looking at the caller ID.

'Hi, sorry to interrupt whatever you're doing. Are you free to talk?' the caller asked in the same voice Eugenie had been listening to in her head.

Overwhelmed by the excitement of being called by the very man she'd been thinking about, Eugenie cried: 'Hamish!'

'Yes, that's me. I was wondering if I could use your services again,' Hamish replied.

'Yes! Yes, of course you can! I'd love that!' Eugenie told Hamish.

A couple walking past Holy Trinity Church wondered what the pink-haired woman on the phone would love.

The pink-haired woman on the phone wondered if she was the luckiest girl in the world.

'The team I work alongside have gone above and beyond this year, and I'd like to recognise that with decent Christmas presents. You know where to buy decent presents, so I thought I'd call you,' Hamish said.

A pigeon started pecking some crumbs from Eugenie's sandwich that had fallen at her feet, but she didn't notice. She was distracted by hoping that Hamish had hundreds of colleagues.

'I was just thinking of you,' Eugenie revealed to Hamish.

'*You* were thinking of *me*?' Hamish questioned.

Looking up at Holy Trinity Church, Eugenie explained: 'I'm by the church you told me about. The very old one with Roman bricks.'

What Eugenie didn't tell Hamish was that she'd thought of him in many other places.

'That's where you go to eat lunch, isn't it? Am I stopping you eating?' Hamish asked.

As she never talked with a mouthful, and Hamish didn't talk long enough for Eugenie to scoff bites of her sandwich while listening to him, he *was* stopping her eating.

'I *did* come here to eat my lunch, but I've finished it. Please feel free to talk to me,' Eugenie lied.

'Would it be possible to see you Friday?' Hamish asked.

Because her calendar was on her phone, which she was using to talk to Hamish, Eugenie wasn't sure if she could do Friday.

'I think I can. I'll check for sure later and text you,' Eugenie replied.

'Great, you're a lifesaver. Thank you ever so much!' Hamish cried.

Despite the fridge-like temperatures in Colchester that day, Eugenie felt warm when she heard the delight in Hamish's voice that he could see her Friday. It was the second time a man had called her a lifesaver that day. Her feelings about the first man were very different to her feelings about the second man.

'Morning, or afternoon?' Eugenie asked.

'Morning, please. Nine o'clock, if possible,' Hamish replied.

'If nine o'clock on Friday is possible, then nine o'clock on Friday we shall meet,' Eugenie confirmed.

In the background on Hamish's end of the line, Eugenie heard someone call his name.

'I'm sorry, Eugenie. I have to go. Thanks for taking my call. See you on Friday, if possible,' Hamish said.

'Yes, see you then. It was lovely to speak to you,' Eugenie replied.

As soon as Hamish hung up, Eugenie opened her phone's calendar app. When she swiped across to Friday, she saw only one event. The event was a Christmas Genie appointment with a single dad who worked as a teaching assistant. The man had to finish work and then pick his daughter up from school to take her to his parents house before he could meet with Eugenie, so their appointment wasn't until 4pm. That left plenty of time for her to see Hamish.

Having looked at her calendar, Eugenie tapped and swiped to switch from that app to her texts. She told her phone to start an SMS conversation with Hamish.

In the box her phone brought up, Eugenie typed: "Have checked and can do Friday 9am see you then x x".

Once she'd sent the text to Hamish, Eugenie navigated to WhatsApp, on which she brought up her conversation with a contact called "Housemate Hotel Holly".

To Housemate Hotel Holly, Eugenie wrote: "I just got a call from Hamish. He needs presents for his colleagues, so I get to see him again!!! I was eating lunch when he called. The bread you made is scrummy!!! It makes a perfect cheese sandwich. If I get you the ingredients, will you please make some more on Sunday? Love, Eugenie x x".

When she saw that her message to Holly had sent, Eugenie slipped her phone in her pocket and turned her attention back to her cheese sandwich.

The pigeon that had been pecking at Eugenie's feet when she'd been on the phone to Hamish was still there, and cooing. 'No, this is far too good for you,' Eugenie told him.

The pigeon wandered off to harass someone else, leaving Eugenie to enjoy her perfect cheese sandwich in peace.

CHAPTER TWELVE

When trying to arrange a meeting point by text, neither Eugenie nor Hamish could decide where to find each other. It didn't matter to either of them where they met up, just that they did meet up somewhere.

On account of not caring where their meeting place was, Hamish suggested somewhere where there was a big sign with "meeting place" on it. Eugenie had no idea where it was, so Hamish had to tell her that it was in Culver Square. Once they'd agreed to meet there, they exchanged texts about how you can not notice little things, like a pillar with "meeting place" painted on it, despite walking past it every day.

As she didn't want to be late, Eugenie strolled into a square full of stalls and food vans at 08:50. When she did so, she spotted Hamish standing by the "meeting place" pillar.

Feeling bad that she was the second one to arrive, Eugenie tried to dash across the square, to reduce the amount of time Hamish had to wait for her by a few seconds. Due to her knees suddenly weakening, and her high heels, dashing proved to be impossible. Instead, Eugenie had to walk at a sensible pace towards Hamish while he smiled at her.

'Sorry! I meant to get here before you! I hope you haven't

been waiting long!' Eugenie cried.

'I've not been waiting long. I was so eager to see you that I left home far too early. That's hardly your fault though,' Hamish replied.

'You were eager to see me?' Eugenie questioned with a smile on her face.

Hamish cleared his throat and shuffled on the spot. 'Yes, well, I have been looking forward to seeing you. You are...' he started to say, running out of words mid-sentence.

For a few seconds there was silence while Eugenie wondered what she was, and Hamish wondered if it was appropriate to tell Eugenie what he thought she was.

While waiting for Hamish to finish his sentence, Eugenie asked herself what *she* thought *Hamish* was. '*Charming,*' Eugenie thought in answer to her question. '*Also handsome, and a true gentleman,*' she added.

Eventually, Hamish decided what to tell Eugenie. 'You are a very talented personal shopper. I was eager to see what you suggested for my hard-working colleagues,' he told her.

The end of Hamish's sentence disappointed Eugenie. Disappointment wasn't something she wanted to feel, so she told herself to put a smile on her face and move on. It was her job. Hamish was just a client.

'Then let's get going so I can do the job you're eager for me to do,' Eugenie said.

-

To distract herself from Hamish as she walked with him to a shop that sold sugar-free sweets, Eugenie paid attention to her surroundings. She noticed old-fashioned-looking lanterns mounted on some of the shop fronts she walked past. They reminded her that many of the buildings she walked past were old. She didn't know how old, specifically. If she had to guess, she'd say they were Victorian. For all she knew though, they were Georgian. As the life she lead meant it wasn't necessary for Eugenie to know much about architecture and history, she knew very little about them.

One of the old buildings Eugenie passed was Toothill's. She waved through the window at her aunt. Despite noticing that someone was waving at her, Victoria didn't wave back, or smile, or nod, or acknowledge Eugenie in any way.

'Do you know that shopkeeper?' Hamish asked.

Eugenie nodded. 'That's my aunt. I work there, with her, dressing up the ladies of Colchester,' she replied.

'That must be nice, working with your aunt,' Hamish commented.

'I *love* my job, and my customers. Auntie Victoria and I have our differences though. Because my mum helped her set up the shop, Auntie is honour-bound to employ me. If she wasn't, she'd probably have fired me by now,' Eugenie told Hamish.

It shocked Hamish that, if not for a family debt, then Eugenie would have been fired. He couldn't think of any reason why someone would want to fire Eugenie, especially her own aunt.

Although he wanted to ask why Eugenie's aunt would fire her, Hamish didn't. He considered that it would be impolite to ask that. Instead, he asked: 'Does your mum help out, at your aunt's shop?'

A haze of sadness descended on Eugenie and clouded her thoughts, like a mental mist. Much to her surprise, she found that she wanted to burst into tears when she thought about the idea of her mum working with her. Bursting into tears was the last thing Eugenie wanted to do at any time, let alone on a crowded shopping street with a client next to her. In an attempt to steady herself, she took in a lungful of the crisp December air.

'It would be too much of a commute for my mum. She lives up in Manchester,' Eugenie revealed in an approximation of her lightest, happiest tone.

'*That's* how you understood about my mum! It's personal. You know how it feels for a loved one to be miles away at this special time of the year,' Hamish realised aloud.

What Hamish said reminded Eugenie of the sadness in his voice when he'd talked about the fact that his mum lived in Sheringham, so wouldn't be with him for Christmas. Those memories didn't help with Eugenie's wish not to cry about the fact that her mum lived in Manchester, so wouldn't be with her for Christmas.

'Yes, I do. It's okay though. Mum's in Manchester to help the poor, hungry people up there, and they need her more than me. Manchester makes her happy, so I'm happy she's in Manchester,' Eugenie explained.

Hamish sighed, his breath visible before him when he did so. 'That's a very sensible view to take. I wish I could think like that, but I'm afraid I'm more selfish than you. My mum is happy in Sheringham because there are no memories of my father there, but all I seem to think about is how much happier I'd be if she'd stayed down here,' he said.

It was difficult for Eugenie to know what to say to that.

Part of her was screaming at her to admit that she'd lied and, actually, she felt the same way Hamish did. Another voice in her head pointed out that admitting that she missed her mum just as much as Hamish missed his would bring the mood down, and shopping was supposed to be light and fun.

Thankfully for Eugenie, she didn't have to make any further comments about distant loved ones, for she and Hamish had reached their destination, a sweet shop.

'This is the place. They do delicious sweets, including sugar free ones, vegetarian ones, and dairy-free ones,' Eugenie told Hamish.

'You remembered the dietary requirements I told you about! I'm impressed!' Hamish said.

'It's my job,' Eugenie replied with a smile.

Before Eugenie could, Hamish got to the door of the sweet shop. He held it open and nodded for Eugenie to go in in front of him.

Once inside the shop himself, Hamish gazed around him at the hundreds of jars of sweets on the walls.

'Wow! This is perfect. A bag of traditional sweets is the perfect Christmas present for colleagues,' Hamish cried.

In front of a wall of sweets, behind a dark oak counter, was a man in an apron. 'I wish more people thought like you. Might get a bit more money in the till if they did,' he said.

'Now you've signed up to Christmas Genie, you will. I'm sure Hamish won't be the only person who needs to buy a small present for someone with a sweet tooth,' Eugenie replied.

The man behind the counter nodded. 'Yeah, clever Helen for coming up with something. It'll help a bit, I guess,' he agreed.

The many jars of sweets had captured Hamish's attention, but he caught the shopkeeper's words. Something about them irritated him.

'Clever *Eugenie*, really. She's the one doing all this,' Hamish pointed out.

Being called "Clever Eugenie" made Eugenie's cheeks burn, and put a smile on her face.

'It's my job,' Eugenie murmured.

'A job you excel at,' Hamish pointed out.

Being complimented twice in quick succession by Hamish rendered Eugenie speechless. She watched in silence as Hamish ordered sweets for his workmates.

-

Once Hamish had got all the sweets he needed, he left the shop with Eugenie. Out in the cold, about to say goodbye to Eugenie, he shivered.

'Thanks for helping me get all these wonderful things. My friends and family will be so happy on Christmas day,' Hamish said.

'You're in their lives. That should be enough for anyone to be happy,' Eugenie replied.

'You think so? I didn't realise you knew me so well,' Hamish questioned.

Only when Hamish questioned it did Eugenie realise how personal what she'd said was. When she'd said it, she'd forgotten that Hamish was just her client.

'From what I've seen, you're a nice person. I'm sorry if

I overstepped the mark or crossed any boundaries,' Eugenie said.

A smile spread across Hamish's face. 'No, Eugenie, it's fine. You're just naturally friendly. I think you're a nice person too. I've enjoyed shopping with you. I wish my social circle was wider, so I had more present wishes for you to grant,' Hamish told Eugenie.

It wasn't just Hamish who wished his social circle was wider.

With it firmly in her head that Hamish was a client, who she wouldn't be seeing again, Eugenie decided to be formal and professional until she'd said goodbye.

'Thanks for using the Christmas Genie service,' Eugenie said.

'My pleasure. As I say, I've enjoyed it,' Hamish replied.

As neither Eugenie nor Hamish went on to say goodbye, silence fell. They both knew it had to be said, but neither one wanted to say it.

After almost twenty seconds, Hamish accepted that he had to drag himself away from Eugenie.

'Goodbye, Eugenie. Good luck with Christmas Genie and Toothill's, and I hope you have a merry Christmas,' Hamish said.

'Goodbye. Merry Christmas to you too. I hope your friends and family like what we've bought together,' Eugenie replied.

There was nothing more Eugenie or Hamish could say, so they walked in opposite directions through Colchester with similar thoughts in their heads.

CHAPTER THIRTEEN

As someone who rarely read print books, Eugenie hardly ever went to the library. She wasn't a member, because she had no reason to be.

When, one Saturday in December, Holly asked Eugenie to come with her to the library, she did, because then she had a reason to go.

When Eugenie arrived at the library, she found Holly admiring a display of sweetly-titled books with robins and snow on their covers.

'They all look good!' Holly moaned.

To Eugenie, all the books looked the same.

'How many can you take out at one time?' Eugenie asked.

'Fourteen, but I only get to keep them for three weeks if someone else wants them. I can't read fourteen books in three weeks,' Holly replied.

Judging by the pensive look on her face, deciding which books to take was one of the biggest challenges Holly had ever faced. Eugenie couldn't understand what was so difficult about choosing a few books. They were all free, so money wasn't an issue.

'How many *can* you read in three weeks?' Eugenie asked.

'*Be sensible. Restrain yourself, Holly,*' Holly told herself in her head.

After a lengthy sigh, Holly answered: 'Four. With work, stuff around the flat, and present buying, that's all I can fit in. It's so hard though! There are a few by people I love, and some really interesting ones by authors I haven't yet had a chance to read!'

It was clear to Eugenie that the decision was too much for Holly. She felt that if she left Holly to her own devices, the question of what to read and what to leave would make her explode. Not wanting her friend to explode, Eugenie decided to make the decision for her.

'What if you choose two by authors you know and like, and I pick two at random by other people? Does that work?' Eugenie suggested.

Holly beamed. 'Yes! That's perfect. That way, I don't have to agonise about what new authors to take a chance on. It's not my fault if I miss out on something. Thank you, Eugenie,' she agreed.

With the weight of responsibility lifted, Holly picked a couple of books bearing familiar names off the shelf.

While Holly took two books to the counter, Eugenie picked up another two that had titles that made her smile.

At the counter was someone whose badge told readers that they were a library assistant called Blair.

'Has the festive season officially begun now?' Blair asked Holly.

Holly nodded. 'Oh yes! To me, there's nothing better in this weather than curling up in front of the fire with a book. I don't have a fire, but at least now I have books,' she replied.

With a knowing smile on their face, Blair scanned the barcodes inside the books that would be keeping Holly company in the run up to Christmas. When they reached the fourth one, they paused.

'Oh, I *love* this one! They all get together to save their town market. It's one of those where you know the two of them should get together, but neither of them will admit it. Such a good read! You even fall in love with the side characters too, like the heroine's friend, who's already in a relationship and desperate for her boyfriend to propose,' Blair enthused.

Standing at Holly's side, listening to her chatting to the library assistant, Eugenie wondered if *she* should read the book Holly and Blair were discussing. She decided not to, because she already had half a dozen books on her Kindle that were waiting to be read. One had been waiting for over a year.

While Holly and Blair chatted in soft voices about their favourite books, Eugenie's mind wandered. It ended up fixating on something, or rather, *someone*, who had nothing to do with books.

-

When Blair noticed a disgruntled-looking woman waiting, they let Holly go. She and Eugenie wandered out of the library together, one of them paying very little attention to her companion or her surroundings.

Noticing that Eugenie was distant, Holly asked: 'What's up?'

'I was thinking about Hamish, my charming Christmas Genie client. I liked him a great deal, and I was just thinking about the fact that it's a shame it would be unprofessional to call him and ask to be friends,' Eugenie replied.

Thinking about the fact that Eugenie wanted a man for Christmas, Holly wondered if she wanted to call Hamish and ask to be *more* than friends.

'I understand. There's a regular guest at work who I wish I could see outside of the hotel. He's made some terrible mistakes in his life, but I can see he's got a heart of gold, and I'd love to know him better,' Holly told Eugenie, hoping to make her feel better.

Nodding solemnly, Eugenie said: 'Yes, it's sad. I wish I could bump into Hamish on the street one day, like when we saw one of your guests. The one I thought was rude. If only I could see him outside of work, perhaps I could ask to see him again properly.'

-

As they walked home along the Lanes of Colchester, both Eugenie and Holly kept an eye out for men they'd met at work. Neither of them saw who they were looking for.

CHAPTER FOURTEEN

The scent of oranges hung heavy in the air when Eugenie entered the building. It reminded her that it was Christingle service.

By the time she'd sat down on a pew, Eugenie was no longer thinking about the fact that it was Christingle service. She was thinking about Hamish.

-

When Eugenie was handed a Christingle, she thanked the person who gave it to her but didn't pay them much attention.

'I remember that the orange is the world, the ribbon is Jesus's love and blood, the candle is Jesus's light in the world, and the sweets are God's creations, but I have no idea what the tin foil is. Does it represent how our kindness to others is reflected in them being kind to us, or something like that?' a man next to Eugenie asked.

'Probably,' Eugenie answered, having not really listened to or considered the question.

The man next to her wasn't the only thing Eugenie couldn't focus on. When a hymn started, she made roughly the same noises as those around her, but didn't give it much thought. Had Eugenie have realised she was absent-minded, she would have been mortified. The subject occupying her mind was so pleasant that she felt no mortification or any bad feelings of any kind. All she felt was love for a man she'd only seen for a few hours.

-

It was only when the people around her rose to leave that Eugenie realised she'd been thinking about one thing for the entire service, and that one thing had nothing to do with God.

'I can't believe I did that! That's like going round a friend's house and completely blanking them. In fact, it's exactly that. You are my friend, and I haven't thought of you once since getting to your house. I'm so sorry,' Eugenie told God in her head.

There was no tangible response to Eugenie's apology.

For once, when Eugenie noticed people frowning at her, she felt their disapproval was justified. She kept her gaze fixed firmly on the toes of her stilettoes as she made her way out of the building.

The gravel of the path outside crunched under Eugenie's feet, but she didn't notice the noise. All she could hear was her own voice in her mind telling her what an awful person she was for thinking about a human man when she should have been thinking about God, and how stupid it was considering that she'd probably never see the man again.

A male voice called Eugenie's name. That, she *did* notice, and she stopped in her tracks. The voice belonged to the man who'd been the sole focus of her thoughts for over an hour.

'Eugenie! Good morning, it's me, Hamish. I wanted to talk to you,' Hamish said, appearing in front of Eugenie as if by magic.

When Eugenie had first met Hamish, she'd thought he looked familiar. Now she knew why; he was a fellow churchgoer. They hadn't spoken until he'd called her to use the Christmas Genie service, but she'd seen him every week.

The idea that there was something Hamish wanted to talk to her about excited Eugenie. Her deep feeling of shame at not paying attention during the service was forgotten.

'You want to speak to me? That's *great*! What about?' Eugenie asked.

'A chapel that is around an hour's drive away. It is one of England's oldest churches. Because you admire Holy Trinity, like I do, I think you'll like this place,' Hamish replied.

How long it would take to drive to the chapel was irrelevant to Eugenie. What *was* relevant was that Hamish had remembered that she loved Holy Trinity Church, and had thought to tell her about another place she would like.

'It sounds lovely, but I don't drive. Thank you ever so much for thinking of me though,' Eugenie told Hamish.

Hamish blushed. 'Ah, I didn't make myself clear. Sorry,' he murmured.

Recalling what Hamish had said, Eugenie couldn't see anything ambiguous about it. There was no cause for confusion that she could think of.

'What do you mean?' Eugenie questioned.

'I mean that I wasn't just suggesting you visit the chapel. I was asking, or at least *meant* to ask, if you wanted to go there *with* me,' Hamish explained.

Before she'd fully considered Hamish's offer, Eugenie cried: 'You're asking me out!'

To confirm that he was indeed asking Eugenie out, Hamish nodded. 'This chapel is a special place, and I think you'll appreciate it,' he told Eugenie.

'I hope so, and I appreciate you taking me. I look forward to it,' Eugenie replied.

Hamish looked up the path. It lead to the road, where a woman was leaning on a maroon Volkswagen Sharan, looking at him. He nodded at the woman, who smiled and jumped into the car.

'The children are waiting for me, so I have to go now. I'm ecstatic that you want to come with me to the chapel. Is Wednesday acceptable to you? It's a half day for me this week,' Hamish said.

'Yes! I've got no Christmas Genie clients on Wednesday, and it's the quietest day of the week, so Auntie can spare me. I'd love that!' Eugenie agreed.

As he set off down the path, Hamish called over his shoulder: 'I'll text you about time and pick-up. It'll be afternoon, and I'll come to your house if you want.'

Emotion froze Eugenie. She stood stock-still on the gravel, from which she watched Hamish jump into the Sharan and kiss the woman behind the wheel on the cheek. The woman wiped her cheek and laughed before turning her head to say something to her four passengers in the back of the car. She then turned her attention back to the road and drove off.

As she watched the car drive off, Eugenie thought: '*I get to spend time with Hamish, and it's not for work.*'

When the Volkswagen Sharan Hamish had got into disappeared from view, Eugenie thought: '*It looks like he's got a wife and kids, and an ugly car to put them in. What a shame.*'

CHAPTER FIFTEEN

The hotel Holly worked at sometimes demanded she worked Sundays. It was part of her contract. The same contract that stated she'd be paid 25% more an hour on Sundays and bank holidays.

On the Sundays Holly worked, Eugenie didn't miss her much. Sunday was her day of rest, and she could rest just as easily without Holly as she could with her. The Sunday Hamish asked Eugenie out was an exception to this. On *that* Sunday, Eugenie didn't feel restful at all. She was in the mood to chat, and she couldn't chat without Holly.

Knowing that Holly had an early lunch on Sundays, Eugenie made her way straight from church to Bridge House Hotel.

-

It didn't take Eugenie as long as she expected to get from her church to Holly's work. She strolled into the reception of Bridge House a few minutes before Holly's break was due. This meant that Holly was still behind the desk, talking to a guest.

'Yeah, so the bad news is that they kicked me out, but the good news is that they did it because I'm moving on. I've got keys. Keys of my own,' the guest was telling Holly.

When she heard the guest speak, Eugenie realised it was

Darren, the man she'd once thought was rude.

The smile on Holly's face was wider than any Eugenie had ever seen before.

'Yes! I'm delighted for you!' Holly cried.

'Me too, but it means I don't get the pleasure of staying here anymore. Not that I could stay here that often, but I loved it when I did,' Darren replied.

The smile on Holly's face vanished. 'That's true,' she mumbled.

Darren glanced at the clock on the wall behind Holly and said: 'Look, I'm gonna go now so you can get on. I just wanted to tell you my news and say goodbye. You've always been so nice that it just seemed right.'

'Thanks. I appreciate that you thought of me,' Holly replied.

Having said his piece, Darren walked out of the hotel with a spring in his step. Holly watched his every step, and didn't turn her gaze to Eugenie until Darren was out of sight.

'Nice to see him again,' Eugenie said.

'Yes, for the last time,' Holly murmured.

To Eugenie, there seemed to be a mist of sadness emanating from Holly. She hoped the good news she'd come to tell her would blow those clouds away.

'I've had an interesting morning, and I want to share it with you. Would you join me in a cafe somewhere?' Eugenie asked.

'Oh, we probably can't afford it. We did eat out the other night,' Holly replied.

Eugenie shook her head. 'We can, or at least *I* can.

I'm earning lots of commission for my Christmas Genie work, but my salary from Toothill's is more than enough for me. Besides, I want your company, and that's priceless. Let me treat you with money I've earned helping people treat others. It seems appropriate,' Eugenie begged.

When Eugenie really wanted something, Holly, and most people, found it impossible to refuse. As hard as she tried, Holly couldn't bring herself to say no.

'How can I say no? Of course I'll let you treat me,' Holly agreed.

-

Once they'd sat down inside Trinity café and ordered, she told Holly about her morning.

'In church this morning, I couldn't concentrate. All I could think about was Hamish. I walked out feeling so ashamed of myself for not paying attention to the service, and guess who calls my name?' Eugenie started.

As Eugenie had been leaving church, where she hadn't paid attention, Holly wondered if it was something or someone religious who'd called her. Growing up, Holly's parents hadn't taught her anything about any religions, and she hadn't paid attention in R.E., so she didn't know what religious thing or person could have called Eugenie.

Hazarding a guess, Holly asked: 'God himself? Was he having a go at you for thinking of a mortal while in his presence?'

It was clear that Holly was way off the mark, for Eugenie started laughing. 'No! Firstly, I'm always in His presence. He is everywhere. The church is His house. To me, going there is like visiting a friend. He's always with me though, in other people's houses as well as His own. Secondly,

He's never called my name. I don't think that's something He does. He's more subtle than that. His ways wouldn't be mysterious if He told you in words what He wanted, would they? Thirdly, I don't imagine He's that cross with me for thinking about Hamish. For all I know, He wants me to think of Hamish and for us to be a couple,' she pointed out.

As she was clueless about religion, there was nothing Holly could think of to say to Eugenie. That meant she fell silent. The silence felt awkward to Holly. Eugenie had asked her out to chat, and she wasn't chatting.

When it dawned on Holly who had *actually* called Eugenie's name, she was relieved, for it meant she had something to talk about. 'It was Hamish, wasn't it? He goes to the same church as you, he saw and recognised you, and he called out to you to say hello,' Holly said.

'Yes, but it's even better than that. He didn't *just* want to say hello. He wants me to come with him to an ancient chapel. He asked me out!' Eugenie revealed with a vast smile on her face.

'Asked you out? Is this trip to the chapel a date then?' Holly asked.

The corners of Eugenie's mouth drooped and her gaze dropped to the table. 'No. His *wife* and children were waiting for him outside the church,' she murmured.

Ever since Eugenie had mentioned Hamish, Holly had wondered if she had romantic feelings for him. The way Eugenie said "wife" confirmed Holly's suspicions. Holly knew all too well what it felt like to love someone you hardly knew and for them to not return your feelings or even be aware of them. This meant she knew just how much pain Eugenie was in, and she was pleased she'd come to see her.

'Oh, Eugenie. I'm so sorry,' Holly whispered, reaching out to take her friend's hand.

When offered it, Eugenie took Holly's hand and stroked the palm of it with her thumb. No words came out of Eugenie's mouth, but the light grip she had on her hand told Holly a lot.

'Why are you sorry? This is *great*! I've got a potential new friend, a kind and caring family man, and he's taking me to what sounds like an amazing place. What reason have I to be unhappy?' Eugenie questioned, still stroking Holly's hand.

Watching Eugenie's thumb, Holly said: 'I'm sorry because you *love* him, and now you know he's unavailable. Not having your feelings returned is *agony*, Eugenie. I know this. It's okay to cry if you need to.'

Eugenie laughed loudly, turning every head in the cafe. '*Love* him? I just met him, and it was a work thing. I'm not in *agony*. I'm at a cafe with my best friend, and I'm going to a new place with a new person on Wednesday. I couldn't be *happier*,' she argued.

'If that's so, why don't you sound it? Why are you stroking my hand if not for comfort?' Holly questioned.

As soon as Holly mentioned her hand, Eugenie released it.

'I was stroking your hand because your skin is soft, and I sound sad because I'm still upset about being distracted in church. It's not like me. Church is usually the one place I can concentrate. It's just a temporary blip though, I'm sure,' Eugenie explained.

While wondering how to make Eugenie admit her feelings, Holly saw a waitress bringing food over to their table. Food had a way of ending conversation, especially the food served by Trinity Café. Holly had no choice but to give up on her mission to get Eugenie to speak the truth. For now, at least.

CHAPTER SIXTEEN

The rooftops outside Holly's window sparkled, as if they had been sprinkled with white glitter. It was frost though, not glitter, that coated the road and the cars to the side of it. Unlike glitter, frost was slippery and could cause serious accidents. This was especially true if you wore inappropriate footwear.

With inappropriate footwear in mind, Holly dashed through to the kitchen-diner, where Eugenie was perusing the shoe rack.

'Don't wear heels today! It's a death trap out there,' Holly warned Eugenie.

Sliding a black pair of trainers off the shoe rack, Eugenie replied: 'Yes, I'll have to wear running shoes today. I don't mind though. It's so pretty!'

A smile spread across Holly's face as she thought about how predictable Eugenie was.

That smile remained as she watched Eugenie, full of energy at before seven on a Monday morning, shove her trainers on, and jog out the door.

-

When Eugenie unlocked and stepped through the door of Toothill's, she, and her chattering teeth, were met by the heavy warmth created by the heating system, which was on full blast. This was a surprise, because it suggested Victoria was around, but the reason Eugenie had come in early was so her aunt didn't have to.

'Good morning! It's freezing, but fabulous outside!' Eugenie called to Victoria, who she knew had to be somewhere in the building.

'I'm cold to the bone, and the heating just isn't shifting it,' Victoria replied from the fitting room.

Already, Eugenie could feel herself warming up. So much so that, before she'd even got to the coatrack in the shop's staff kitchen, she took her parka off.

'It was nice of you to come. I'm quite happy to supervise the electrician myself, but it's reassuring to have you around,' Eugenie told Victoria as she returned to the dark shop floor.

'I *had* to come. The company sending the electrician demand that a member of staff with the authority to make decisions is present. Apparently, it's because if they have to do extra work, they need to know we'll pay them for it. Of course, they didn't tell me until yesterday evening, by which time I'd downed a whole bottle of red in the hope it would make Paul more interesting. It didn't, it's not a magic potion, but it *has* given me a banging headache,' Victoria explained.

Eugenie laughed. 'Oh dear! Bless uncle Paul. He gets so passionate about things, and he doesn't realise that we're not as interested as he is, or that he's told us that story before,' she said.

'Try being married to him. After thirty years, you've heard *every* story, he *knows* you're not interested, but *still* he witters on, and all the passion you *and* he had has been sapped out of you to be replaced with bitterness,' Victoria moaned.

The way Victoria talked about her husband left Eugenie speechless. She thought of marriage as the pinnacle of happiness. Victoria was married to her childhood sweetheart, and had been for three decades. That sounded like a dream to Eugenie, but Victoria made it sound like a nightmare.

It wasn't just the artificial heat that made the atmosphere in Toothill's seem heavy. The sadness emanating from the owner was like a dense fog.

Wanting to lighten the mood, Eugenie said: 'I'll make tea, and then we can take this opportunity to spruce up the window while we chatter away.'

-

After spending two minutes undressing the mannequins in silence with Victoria, Eugenie was bored. She decided to talk about the first thing that came into her head.

'One of my Christmas Genie clients goes to the same church as me. When we went shopping together, we both admired the church up the road. The one behind the black railings. He came up to me after church yesterday and offered to take me to a chapel that's one of the oldest churches in England,' Eugenie announced.

'Creepy. He's talking about St Cedd's, which is in the middle of nowhere. He could do anything to you out there. Did he get angry when you refused him?' Victoria asked.

'Refused? Why would I do that? He's charming, not creepy. We arranged to go on Wednesday, as I'm not working here and have no Christmas Genie appointments that day,' Eugenie replied.

It hadn't entered Victoria's head that Eugenie would agree to go somewhere she'd never been with someone she didn't know. She couldn't understand why anyone would do that.

'Why? You don't know the guy,' Victoria pointed out.

It had occurred to Eugenie that Hamish was a virtual stranger (not that he felt like that to her) and they'd be alone together. Over coffee, she and Holly had discussed the safety concerns of this.

'Holly will know who I'm with and where I am, and I'll warn Hamish of that. Not that he needs warning. He's a nice man. A father too, married to a beautiful and happy-looking woman. All he wants is to share with me a place he loves that he thinks I'll appreciate,' Eugenie explained.

This allayed Victoria's safety concerns about her niece. She was satisfied that Holly knowing Eugenie's plans was good enough.

No longer concerned, Victoria was curious about Hamish's relationship.

'How do you know he and his wife are happy? What's he told you? Does he do thoughtful things like cook her dinner when he knows she's had a hard day, or entertain her with witty tales to distract her from the misery that is everyday life? How can you tell what a happy marriage looks like? What's the secret?' Victoria questioned.

Most questions, Eugenie answered immediately, but something about the wistful look in Victoria's eyes made her pause.

'He hasn't talked about her at all. He didn't even mention

her when I asked who he needed help buying for. I was surprised to see that he *had* a wife. As I'm single, I don't know what makes a happy marriage,' Eugenie replied.

'If you find out what makes a happy marriage, tell me,' Victoria ordered.

Eugenie giggled. 'Surely, as you and Paul have been together for so long, you should be able to tell me,' she pointed out.

A knock at the door made both Eugenie and Victoria jump. They turned their heads to see a man with a name badge staring into the shop.

'That's the electrician. I'll let him in. Of course, to work on the lighting system, he'll have to turn the power off, so we'll lose the heating. Prepare for this place to become like the Arctic,' Victoria said, striding to the door.

-

The physically demanding work of lugging shop fittings around, and thoughts of Hamish, kept Eugenie perfectly warm while the heating was off.

When the heating and lighting was restored, Victoria opened the shop to the public, and Eugenie spent the rest of her morning dressing up the few women who found their way to the shop.

CHAPTER SEVENTEEN

From half an hour before Hamish was due to arrive, Eugenie gazed out of her window, hoping to see his car. He hadn't told her what car he drove, so every time someone pulled up on her street, she thought it was him.

While staring out of the window, Eugenie considered what to buy for someone. One of her Christmas Genie clients had a grandmother who disliked clutter. They had very few things, but what they had, they loved. Apparently, they got very upset when their beloved things broke, and, one of the last times they'd spoken to Eugenie's client, the main subject had been a vase that had smashed. The client's grandmother was so attached to the vase that she couldn't bring herself to throw away the pieces. She'd picked them all up and put them in a shoebox.

On the street below Eugenie's window, a red Jaguar pulled up. Out of it got Hamish, the very man Eugenie was waiting for.

With a squeal, Eugenie launched herself off the bed she'd been sitting on and dashed out of the flat.

'Good afternoon! I'm really excited about this!' Eugenie

told Hamish when she reached him.

'You look it! You look incredible!' Hamish replied.

Due to the inclement weather of December in Essex, Eugenie was wearing her green parka coat with clumpy black boots. This outfit was practical, but she didn't consider it to be incredible.

Before Eugenie could reach it, Hamish opened the front-passenger-side door of his car.

'Ah, thank you! That's really kind,' Eugenie said as she ducked into Hamish's Jaguar.

Once Eugenie had settled comfortably in her seat, Hamish slammed her door shut and sauntered round to the opposite door, which he swung open and jumped through.

After closing his door and clicking his seatbelt on, Hamish declared: 'It's time to get going!'

-

The first ten minutes of the drive were spent in silence as Hamish battled the traffic caused by the seemingly-endless roadworks on the edge of Colchester. Once free of those, and in a 60mph stretch, he put his foot down. The car roared as its power was unleashed.

As well as having a fast speed limit, the road Hamish was on was twisty. This meant he had no choice but to slow down at times, and guide the car around sharp bends.

'This baby corners like she's on rails!' Eugenie cried on one of the tightest bends.

Hamish let out a gurgle of laughter. 'She's no Lotus Esprit, but I do love this girl,' he replied.

The mention of a Lotus Esprit made Eugenie gasp. 'You

got the reference? You've seen *Pretty Woman?*' she questioned.

'Yes, *that* popular thing *does* interest me. My sister loves it, and I spend a lot of time with her. It intrigues me, because it shows how good people can end up doing bad things,' Hamish replied.

Pretty Woman was a film Eugenie had watched so many times she'd lost count. Not once had she thought of it in the way Hamish did.

'I suppose it does. Vivian, bless her, has a heart of gold. She never meant to end up selling her body,' Eugenie agreed.

'I was thinking of Mr Lewis. His business strategy will have created hundreds of redundancies. Prostitution is of course a bad thing, but so is ruining people's livelihoods for personal greed. The ending shows that there's good in him somewhere though, and Vivian brings it out in him,' Hamish revealed.

'He's so handsome! And so in love with Vivian! I love the way he looks at her, and the ending, with the fire escape, is so romantic! Besides, Stuckey is far worse. Lawyers always seem to be bad guys,' Eugenie enthused.

As he didn't want to agree or disagree that lawyers were bad guys, Hamish said nothing more.

A few seconds later, Hamish wished he had something to say, preferably a question to ask, because he wanted to hear Eugenie's voice. Luckily for him, he thought of one.

'My sister wanted a Lotus Esprit when she was a teenager, because it appeared in *Pretty Woman*. She still does. She's very jealous of my Jag, even though it hasn't appeared in a film. Then again, I think she'd be jealous of everything.

She's always complaining about her car,' Hamish said.

'Oh, bless her. Is it that bad then? What has she got?' Eugenie asked.

'I'm afraid I don't remember the name. It's a big red people carrier, which seats seven. It has to. She has four children. That's the only reason she has a car like that. Otherwise, she'd have a nice car like me,' Hamish replied.

In the back of her mind, Eugenie felt like she'd recently seen a red people carrier with four children in it. She couldn't remember where though.

It irritated Eugenie that she couldn't recall where she'd seen a big red people carrier. In an attempt to remember, she gazed out the window and let her mind wander. A woodland flew by outside the car (technically, the *car drove* past the *woodland*, but that wasn't how it looked to Eugenie). Standing bare without their leaves, the trees looked sad and desolate to Eugenie. For a moment, she *felt* sad. Unhappy thoughts drifted through her head. One of them featured a red people carrier with four children.

The scenery outside the window changed to open fields. Eugenie's spirits soared.

'I saw your *sister's* car outside church!' Eugenie cried.

Hamish nodded. 'Yes, you did, so you know how ugly it is,' he replied.

Now she knew the car she'd seen belonged to Hamish's sister, Eugenie didn't think it was at all ugly.

CHAPTER EIGHTEEN

Around an hour after spotting Hamish out of the window of her flat, Eugenie spotted a simple building out of the windscreen of Hamish's Jaguar. It stood alone, surrounded by fields, with the sea as a backdrop. In spite of its nondescript appearance, Eugenie found her eye was drawn to the building.

The road Eugenie was being driven along ended, to be replaced by a gravel car park riddled with potholes. She was so focused on the building in the distance that she didn't hear the crunch of the gravel under the wheels, or feel the bumps as Hamish guided his car around the worst potholes. When Hamish swung the car hard left to park it, the building disappeared behind some trees, and Eugenie was once again aware of the rest of the world around her.

'We're here. Isn't it captivating?' Hamish asked.

'Isn't *what* captivating? I got distracted by a barn in the distance,' Eugenie replied.

Hamish smiled. 'That barn is what I was asking about. That's the chapel,' he revealed.

With the knowledge that the building she'd been transfixed by was the chapel, Eugenie wanted to see it again. To do so, she threw her door open, leapt out of the car, and dashed across the car park.

Although Eugenie hadn't told Hamish what she was doing, he knew. The first time Hamish had seen it, when his mother had told him that the pretty barn by the sea that she'd taken him to was actually a chapel made with the ruins of a Roman fort, he too had taken another look.

'It *is* breathtaking, or whatever you said! I want to see inside it!' Eugenie called to Hamish, who was leisurely getting out of the car.

When Hamish joined Eugenie, he put his arm around her. She felt a jolt of heat, which ended as abruptly as it had begun when Hamish promptly removed his arm.

'Erm, sorry. Let's get walking. That'd be good,' Hamish mumbled.

Before Eugenie could ask him why he'd put his arm around her, Hamish started walking.

Eugenie automatically followed Hamish to the kissing gate he was heading to.

-

After starting to walk, Hamish didn't stop. He plodded along at a steady pace. He didn't speak either.

Sometimes, silence bothered Eugenie. Not on her walk with Hamish though. She allowed the rhythmic synchronised crunching of their feet on the path to lull her into a trancelike state, in which she absentmindedly admired her surroundings. The open fields around her made her feel free, like she could do anything.

The open fields *actually* allowed the *wind* to do anything. It cut across Eugenie and Hamish with no consideration for how icy it felt on their faces.

'Sorry, I've been a bit inconsiderate. I didn't ask you if you minded walking in weather like this. It is *bitterly* cold,' Hamish said, breaking the silence that had fallen for ten minutes.

'It's fine, because I'm close to you,' Eugenie replied.

Hamish raised an eyebrow. 'I don't understand. How can being close to me keep you warm?' he asked.

When Eugenie realised her mistake, she blushed, and felt even warmer. She didn't know why, but whenever she was near Hamish, heat flooded through her. She had a feeling that if she told him that, he may feel uncomfortable around her. Hamish was waiting for an answer though, so she had to think up a lie, and fast.

'I mean that I don't mind being cold because I'm with you, visiting this great place,' Eugenie lied.

'I'm worth being cold for then?' Hamish questioned. A second later he shook his head and said: 'I mean this place that I brought you to is worth being cold for?'

'Yes! That's what I meant. This place is worth being cold for,' Eugenie swiftly agreed.

Having established that their destination was worth being cold for, Eugenie and Hamish continued ambling towards it.

-

With every step, the chapel got closer. It was eventually so close that Hamish was able to open the substantial wooden door with its wrought iron handle and say: 'Welcome to Saint Peter's Chapel.'

When Eugenie stepped inside, her footsteps echoed on

the cold stone floor. The noise ceased almost as soon as she'd crossed the threshold, as she paused, struck by the simplicity of the interior. The room she was in was the only room. Along the sides were a few rows of low, backless, wooden pews, and at the end was a stone altar with clean lines and three stones set into it. What drew Eugenie's eye though was the cross mounted on the wall above the altar.

The cross inspired Eugenie to wonder how someone could love humanity so much, they'd give up their life for it. She wondered if she could've done it. If she could've let herself be killed for the good of the world. Although she wished the answer was *yes*, in her heart she knew it was probably *no*. As she was not Jesus, she would never have such a decision to make.

While Eugenie would never have to sacrifice her life for humanity, there were other struggles that she had to bear for the sake of others. Standing in the chapel, she felt more able to accept that her mother didn't live near her. She even felt more pleased than she ever had before that her mother spent her time in Manchester helping thousands of people in need.

Thinking about the work her mother did for charity made Eugenie wonder what *she* did to make the world a better place. She'd often thought that dressing people up at Toothill's brightened up the world, for the clothes she dressed people in made them feel better about themselves.

As far as she knew, the biggest thing Eugenie did for the world was be bright and cheerful. Most days, it was natural to her. Occasionally, she found it an enormous struggle, but she never admitted that. Her sacrifice for humanity was bottling up her misery on those difficult days, in order to not drag people down with her.

'Sorry, I've just realised. We've been stood here in silence for five minutes,' Hamish said.

Hamish's words echoing off the cold stone floor and walls dragged Eugenie away from her thoughts.

'It's fine. I was thinking,' Eugenie replied.

'Yes, me too. About a couple of things, as it happens,' Hamish revealed.

From behind Eugenie and Hamish came footsteps. They both looked over their shoulder to see an elderly woman shuffling into the chapel. The pair exchanged a look, and both left the chapel.

Without saying a word, Eugenie and Hamish started making their way back to the car.

'What did you think about?' Eugenie asked Hamish.

'A couple of things,' Hamish replied.

Because she wondered if Hamish needed to share, Eugenie asked: 'Would you like to tell me either of them?'

While internally debating whether or not to share his thoughts with Eugenie, Hamish realised that the wind had calmed down.

'One of them, yes. I've forgiven my father,' Hamish said.

'What for?' Eugenie asked.

'For leaving Mum. I was furious with him when he did it. I'd just left home, and my sister had fallen pregnant with her first child. It was an emotional time anyway for Mum, and that's when he chose to tell her he didn't love her anymore. He told her at breakfast on Friday, was gone before dinner that day, and started divorce proceedings on the

Monday. Now I know though, that the anger doesn't do me any good. I can't keep it with me. I have to let it go, and understand that my father is human. For my own good, I have to forgive him. Nobody's perfect,' Hamish revealed.

When Hamish talked about his father, Eugenie was reminded of her own. She immediately banished thoughts of him. Ever since she'd been eight years old, when her mother had told her about him, she'd made a pact with herself not to think of him or talk about him. She had not forgiven him, and didn't intend to.

In order to not linger on the subject of fathers, Eugenie said: 'I love that, with just a look, we decided to leave the chapel because that lady needed her space.'

'We communicate well. We make a good team,' Hamish replied. After a few steps, he added: 'At least, I *think* so.'

'Oh, me too. Definitely! We're a great pair!' Eugenie instantly agreed.

-

Not long after agreeing that they were a great pair, Eugenie and Hamish reached Hamish's car. After Hamish had opened the door for Eugenie and she'd slunk in, he himself got in and drove his car back to Colchester.

CHAPTER NINETEEN

For most of the drive back to her flat, Eugenie could tell Hamish was deep in thought. She assumed his father was the subject of his thoughts. She wished that *she* was the subject of his thoughts.

The moment Hamish turned the engine off outside Eugenie's flat, he said: 'There's something I have to say to you, but it's something you may not want to hear. Would you be more comfortable if I told you here in the car, where you're right next to me; outside, where it's freezing; or in your flat, your own home?'

Before answering, Eugenie tried to guess what Hamish wanted to tell her. Nothing sprang to mind. For politeness, she decided she ought to invite him up to her flat.

'It may take you a while, so I can't have you hanging around in the cold. If you come upstairs, I can make us tea to sip while you tell me whatever it is you have to tell me,' Eugenie offered.

Hamish nodded. 'Thank you. I appreciate that. I just hope you don't end up choking on it,' he replied.

While wondering what Hamish's choking-worthy revelation was, Eugenie lead him up to her flat.

When Hamish entered Eugenie's kitchen-diner, a particular wall caught his eye. It made him smile.

'Could you not decide what colour to paint the walls?' Hamish asked, pointing at a wall with sixteen squares on it, all different colours.

Eugenie laughed. 'No, we like it that way. I wanted a bright, multi-coloured wall, so Holly had the great idea of buying lots of different tester pots. We did it last week, and I love it,' she explained.

'It's very you,' Hamish commented with a smile.

Unsure what to say about the fact that a wall with sixteen tester pot squares on was very her, Eugenie flopped down on her sofa.

When he saw Eugenie looking at him expectantly, Hamish realised it was time to say what he'd come up to the flat to say.

'I didn't *need* your help getting presents for my workmates, although I'm extremely happy about what you chose. As for today, yes, I thought you'd like the chapel, but our trip was actually for *my* benefit. Both things were just excuses to be with you. I'm admitting this now, because I've run out of excuses, but I still want to see you,' Hamish said.

In order to check that she wasn't dreaming, Eugenie pinched herself. She was delighted to find that it hurt.

'You want to see me? It isn't just me who feels a connection?' Eugenie questioned.

Feeling that he ought to be closer to Eugenie, Hamish sat on the sofa next to her. Her soft grey eyes gazed curiously at him. He could tell she was wondering what his next move was going to be. She wasn't the only one. Since pulling up outside Eugenie's flat, Hamish had been unsure what words were going to come out of his mouth, or what actions he was going to take.

'How I feel around you is so different to how I feel around everyone else. *You* are so different to everyone I've ever known. In the chapel, after realising I should forgive my father for leaving, I thanked God for bringing you into my life. You're a ray of sunshine,' Hamish replied.

Eugenie squealed. 'Oh, this is too good to be true! I've been desperately trying to keep in my feelings for you, but sometimes I've felt like I might burst. I've told Holly that you're charming, but I neglected to add that you're handsome, amusing, and a true gentleman. When you called me that day I was eating the scrummy cheese sandwiches Holly made me, my heart soared! I had an awful feeling that I'd never see you again. Now I know I will! This is great!' she enthused.

Although he knew he wanted to see Eugenie again, Hamish wasn't sure where.

'I feel that our next step is to go on a date, but where? What sort of thing do you like?' Hamish asked Eugenie.

When Eugenie thought of what she liked, a long list flowed through her head. One of the activities she thought of had been her go-to dating option when she'd been a teenager, so she chose that.

'I love *all sorts*. Let's go bowling. That makes for a good date,' Eugenie declared.

'I've never been bowling, so that sounds great. I can't think of a better person to share my first time with than you,' Hamish agreed.

Hearing that Hamish couldn't think of a better person

than her to share his first time bowling with inspired Eugenie to jump off the sofa and twirl around the room.

Seeing Eugenie jump off the sofa and twirl around the room, making her pastel pink hair fly, inspired Hamish to give her a quizzical look.

'I cannot *wait*! You're a charming gentleman, who goes to church, who's single, and you want to go out with me! I'm the luckiest girl in Colchester!' Eugenie cried.

Although he didn't have the energy or the inclination to twirl around the room, Hamish stood up, for he felt uncomfortable being the only one sitting down.

'*You* are a good Christian girl who's full of life, and I get to spend time with you. I believe *I'm* the lucky one,' Hamish replied.

Halfway through a twirl, it occurred to Eugenie that she'd forgotten something. She abruptly stopped turning and said: 'I said I'd make tea. I'll do that now.'

Hamish shook his head and started to walk towards the door. 'Don't, please. I'm going now,' he told Eugenie.

The pure joy that had burst out of Eugenie's soul when Hamish had said he had feelings for her vanished. It was replaced with a buzz of anxiety as she wondered what she'd done to make him want to leave.

'Oh, no! What did I do wrong?' Eugenie asked.

'Do wrong? What makes you think you've done something wrong?' Hamish questioned.

Try as she might, Eugenie couldn't work out what she'd done.

'I'm clueless. I don't know what I've done to make you leave,' Eugenie murmured, her voice quieted by sadness.

'Oh, bless you, Eugenie! You've not done anything. I want to go because I worry that, if I stay, you'll change your mind, or I'll spoil it in some way. I'm leaving to make sure I keep this perfect feeling that I've had since you said you felt a connection,' Hamish explained.

Pure joy flooded back through Eugenie. To show this, she did a single twirl and let out a cry of laughter.

As he opened the door to the world beyond Eugenie's flat, Hamish said: 'I'll text you about the bowling date. Goodbye, Eugenie.'

'Bye! I cannot wait to see you again!' Eugenie called as Hamish walked out the flat and down the stairs.

When Hamish disappeared from view, Eugenie slammed her door and ran to her bedroom, from which she could see Hamish's Jaguar out of the window. This allowed her to wave frantically as Hamish drove away.

Exhausted from celebrating that she had a date with Hamish, Eugenie fell backwards onto her bed and laid on it, staring up at the smooth ceiling. She tried to recall her calendar, to work out when she was free to go bowling with Hamish. This made her think about her Christmas Genie clients, because she had many shopping trips booked in the coming weeks that would prevent her from bowling. One particular client sprang to mind, as did a present idea for them.

'Kintsugi!' Eugenie cried, sitting up in bed.

Having had a brilliant idea, Eugenie pulled her phone out to make contact with someone who could turn her idea into a reality. She flicked through her contacts and started a new WhatsApp conversation with "Art Shop Suzi".

"Do you have a friend that does Kintsugi? I have a client

whose grandmother recently broke a precious vase. They still have the pieces. I can't imagine a better present than that vase, repaired with precious metals. Love, Eugenie x x", she wrote to Art Shop Suzi.

While waiting for a reply, Eugenie hugged her pillow tight to her chest and daydreamed about bowling with Hamish.

CHAPTER TWENTY

A few shoppers trudging their way along Colchester's Lanes noticed that, despite the relentless downpour, a pink-haired young woman was practically skipping along in her black ankle boots. They all thought her weird, because they didn't know that she had a date the next day with the man of her dreams. Had they have known that the practically-skipping woman had a date the next day with the man of her dreams, they'd probably still have thought her weird for showing her excitement so clearly when it was raining.

The pink-haired woman practically skipped to a cafe near the bus station, where she was meeting a client.

'I'm here to see Blessing. We're going shopping together. I'm Eugenie, the Christmas Genie,' the pink-haired woman told the man behind the counter in the cafe.

The man behind the counter, whose badge revealed his name to be Tyrone, nodded and yelled: 'Blessing! Get your arse out here! That present buying girl's here!'

'Just my arse? I think Eugenie needs more than my butt to go shopping with me!' a female voice called back.

Although Eugenie found this hilarious, the frown on his face suggested that Tyrone did not.

'Blessing! Get out here *now*!' Tyrone ordered.

A woman of around Eugenie's age, shaking with mirth, appeared from the kitchen.

Even though Blessing had done as he'd told her to, Tyrone still looked cross.

'It's chucking it down buckets out there! Where's your coat and umbrella?' Tyrone questioned.

Blessing shrugged. 'Forgot my coat, and I never use an umbrella. You should know that, Dad. I'll be fine though,' she replied.

The look in Tyrone's eyes communicated that he didn't believe Blessing would be fine, but his lips didn't move to say so.

'Hi! I'm Eugenie, the Christmas Genie. I'm here to take you shopping, like we talked about on the phone,' Eugenie said.

'Yeah, I know that. I'm Blessing. Nice to meet you. Shall we get going?' Blessing replied, holding the door open.

In order to "get going", Eugenie stepped through the door Blessing was holding open. Having a door held for her made Eugenie think of Hamish, who she was seeing the next evening.

Unlike Blessing, Eugenie had a coat. It saved her from most of the rain, and kept most of her body warm. As it didn't cover them, and she didn't wear gloves, her hands were cold and wet, but this didn't bother her much.

The brick surface of the Lanes had several puddles in it. Eugenie skirted around them, but Blessing splashed straight through them with a grin on her face. This put a smile on Eugenie's face.

-

After a minute of following Eugenie, Blessing said: 'Suppose I should ask you where we're going and whose present is first.'

'I thought we'd deal with your father first, as his is the simplest,' Eugenie revealed.

The idea of her father's present being the simplest made Blessing snort. 'Nothing about Dad is simple. He's a nightmare to buy for. When you ask him what he wants, he always says: "A nice, well-behaved, obedient daughter. Can you get me one of those?". He hates unnecessary things, which makes present buying impossible,' she replied.

The thought that she knew exactly what to buy for a man who was apparently "a nightmare" added a spring to Eugenie's step.

'It's not impossible, because I'm taking you to a place that sells something he wants,' Eugenie pointed out.

'What could Dad possibly want, except for me to do as I'm told?' Blessing questioned.

As if answering Blessing's question, a hardware store appeared in front of her, which Eugenie gestured for her to go into.

By a shelf of drills stood a large man with a large frown on his face.

'Oh, it's you. Is this to do with Helen's scheme?' the man by the drills asked.

'Yes, Clive. This is Blessing, a Christmas Genie client, and I'm here looking for a wallpaper stripper for her father,' Eugenie replied.

'A wallpaper stripper? Where did that idea come from? Who buys a wallpaper stripper as a Christmas present?'

Blessing questioned, staring at Eugenie.

Every time a client gave her a brief, Eugenie thought carefully about what they'd like. This meant that she could easily explain why she thought Blessing should buy her father a wallpaper stripper.

'You said he doesn't like unnecessary things. A wallpaper stripper is necessary if he wants to redecorate the flat above the cafe,' Eugenie explained.

Blessing snorted. 'Like he's ever going to do that! He *says* he will, but never gets round to it,' she said.

'Maybe if you buy him a wallpaper stripper, that will prompt him to do it,' Eugenie suggested.

As this seemed correct to Blessing, she didn't say anything.

Thanks to a sizeable yellow sign hanging from the ceiling, Eugenie knew where to find wallpaper strippers. She and Blessing made their way to the correct display.

Thanks to owning the shop, Clive knew where to find wallpaper strippers. He followed Eugenie and Blessing to them.

'Now, I'll help you girls out because, obviously, you don't know the first thing about these contraptions,' Clive said.

Blessing folded her arms. 'And why's that? Why do we "obviously" know nothing about wallpaper strippers?' she asked.

Something in Blessing's tone made Clive take a few steps back. He took a few seconds to work out how to put the reason why he thought Blessing and Eugenie knew nothing about wallpaper strippers into words.

'Well, you know. You girls don't look like you know anything about them, that's all. No need to get all huffy about it. I was just trying to be helpful. I didn't realise you couldn't do that these days either,' Clive replied.

As that answer wasn't satisfactory, Blessing questioned: 'What about me suggests I need your help?'

While considering how to answer that question, Clive fiddled with the top button of his green polo shirt. It didn't help him come up with a clever comeback.

'It's just that girls... not many people know as much as I do about power tools,' Clive answered.

To stop Blessing pushing further, Eugenie asked: 'So, what can you tell us about wallpaper strippers?'

'Some get the paper off better than others. Also, some work for longer, some take longer to be ready to use, and there are safety features that you don't get on all of them. There's quite a variety. It depends on your budget and what's important to you really,' Clive told Eugenie.

Many things that were important to her flashed through Blessing's head, none of which had anything to do with wallpaper strippers. One of her thoughts, she managed to relate to power tools.

'Safety features are important to me. I don't want it exploding in Dad's face, or him burning himself on it,' Blessing said.

'Are you sure about that? Would you really miss him bossing you about?' Eugenie questioned with a smile on her face.

'Yeah, actually! I'm sure I don't want Dad to die in a DIY accident! True, we wind each other up, but I love the man to pieces, and he's done such a good job for me and Shan! What you saw was banter. Beneath that, Dad, Shan, and I are tighter than tight!' Blessing snapped.

Clive chuckled. 'All right! Calm down, girl! Eugenie was joking. Can't you take a joke?' he asked.

Even before Clive had pointed it out, Blessing had known Eugenie was joking. Knowing they were said in jest didn't stop Eugenie's words offending Blessing.

The ring-ring of a distant phone drifted across the shop. Without excusing himself, Clive ran off to answer it. This left Blessing and Eugenie alone by the wallpaper strippers.

Knowing she had to say something, Blessing told Eugenie: 'I know you can't see it, but Dad means the world to me, and Shan and I mean the world to *him*. He's all I've had since Mum walked out when I was a baby. That's why the idea of him getting hurt isn't funny. It made me think of what life would be like without him, which reminded me that Mum isn't a part of my life. Even twenty years on, that's a sore point, that she left Dad to get on with it, and it scares me that Dad's all I've got, parentwise.'

'I'm sorry! I didn't think! I really hope I haven't upset you too much and you can forgive me!' Eugenie cried.

Blessing sighed. 'If you've not been through it, then you wouldn't think of it. I don't expect you to understand,' she replied.

'But I do! I've never met my father. When Mother told him she was pregnant with me, he didn't want to know. There's a man out there, related to me, who doesn't care a jot about me. He doesn't even know me. Just like your father is all you have, my mother is all I have,' Eugenie revealed.

The man who made her mother pregnant was someone

Eugenie never talked about. It shocked her that she'd told a complete stranger about him. To rationalise it, Eugenie told herself she'd opened up to Blessing to make Blessing feel better about opening up to her.

'Is it weird if that makes me feel better? I've always wondered what me and Shan did to drive Mum away. Your Dad didn't want to know you though, and you hadn't even been born. That suggests it's *them*, not *us*,' Blessing said.

Eugenie nodded. 'Oh, it's definitely not *us*. Some people aren't meant to be parents, but they don't realise that until after they've conceived. That's what Mother has always told me,' she replied.

As he wandered back from the counter, Clive asked: '*What* has your mother always told you?'

Most of the time, Eugenie could chatter without end, but Clive's question left her speechless. Answering it honestly wasn't an option, because Eugenie didn't want to tell a man like him something so personal, but she couldn't lie either. Lying was something Eugenie had promised herself, and her mother, and God, that she'd never do.

Noticing beads of sweat on Eugenie's forehead, Blessing told Clive: 'Her Mum said to always buy safe power tools. Safety is the most important feature.'

With safety in mind, Clive slipped one of the wallpaper strippers off the shelf and held it for Blessing to see.

'This one has a cool-to-touch tank and an anti-explosion valve, so it's good for that. If I got it as a present, I'd be chuffed,' Clive replied.

As it was being shown to her, Blessing read the spec on the wallpaper stripper's box. It made as much sense to her in English as it would've done in German, which was none at all.

In order to hide the fact that technical specifications were like a foreign language to her, Blessing said: 'It sounds perfect. I'll get it for Dad.'

So Blessing could buy it, Clive took his safest wallpaper stripper to the counter.

'Thanks for finding something for Dad. I love that I get to give him something he'll like and appreciate,' Blessing said to Eugenie.

'My pleasure,' Eugenie replied.

There were few things in life that gave Eugenie as much pleasure as her customers being happy. The joy she felt seeing Blessing smile as she took the wallpaper stripper from Clive pushed any thoughts of Eugenie's father to the darkest corners of her mind, where she kept them locked away.

CHAPTER TWENTY-ONE

The door to Bygones was one of those with a bell behind it that tinkled when customers entered the shop. It was in keeping with the rest of the shop.

As soon as the bell rang, Helen came rushing out of the stockroom that she was attempting to tidy.

'Good morning, Eugenie. I've heard that the Christmas Genie scheme is going well,' Helen said.

'Yes, this is one of my Christmas Genie clients, in fact. We've got a present for her father and her uncle, and now we're looking for something for her sister and her boyfriend,' Eugenie replied.

'What now? A vintage bookcase for Shan because she loves reading but never has enough space for her books? An old mirror for Aaron to use when he's preening himself for hours and hours while I'm waiting downstairs to go out?' Blessing asked.

There was something in Blessing's tone that suggested she was bored or dissatisfied. As Blessing was using the Christmas Genie scheme, which she'd invented, that bothered Helen. She felt responsible for Blessing's boredom or dissatisfaction.

'So, she's had me buy notebooks, for my writer uncle to jot ideas down in, and, get this, a wallpaper stripper for Dad, because he's gonna redecorate our flat. A *wallpaper stripper*!? Don't get me wrong, the people I'm buying for will love these things, so she's doing her job well, but, said in the style of Chandler Bing, could it *be* any more boring? I'm a girl. I wanna buy some pretty things, you know?' Blessing explained to Helen when she saw the look on her face.

After complaining, Blessing wondered if her words would offend Eugenie. When she heard laughter coming from beside her, she knew she hadn't.

'Stationery is *not* boring. Some people would say some notebooks are pretty. The ones we got for your uncle definitely were,' Eugenie pointed out.

Blessing shook her head. 'Well I'm not one of those some people. I bet whatever we're here for is something perfect for Aaron or Shan, but dull as dishwater,' she replied.

'I'm interested now. What *are* you here for, Eugenie?' Helen asked.

A smile spread across Eugenie's face when she revealed: 'We're here for jewellery. An eye-catching ring for Shantelle, because she loves to make a statement, and cufflinks for Aaron, who you say is very dapper and takes pride in his appearance.'

The smile on Eugenie's face was mirrored on Helen and Blessing's faces.

'For real? We're finally getting pretty things? I get to go jewellery shopping?' Blessing questioned.

Satisfied that Blessing was content, Helen said: 'Jewellery

is in the cabinets on the far right. I'll leave you to it.'

When Helen had walked off, Eugenie squealed and exclaimed: 'Let's go and buy pretty things!'

To get to the pretty things Eugenie was referring to, she and Blessing had to pass other things that could be called pretty. One of the pretty things, a vase, Blessing thought looked like Murano. To check if she was right, she paused to read the tag. The pretty vase *was* Murano, and the price on the tag that confirmed it was anything *but* pretty.

For the rest of the walk to the jewellery, Blessing discretely read the price tags on various items of various appearances, and found them all to be out of her budget. Before meeting, Eugenie and Blessing had spoken on the phone to discuss who they were shopping for and what they liked. Part of that conversation had been about how much Blessing wanted to spend. When she spotted a chest of drawers for £625, she wondered if Eugenie had misheard her.

By some glass cabinets that were considerably taller than her, Eugenie came to an abrupt stop. Gazing inside, Blessing noticed how much the diamonds in the rings on the middle shelf sparkled. She also noticed how many numbers were on the price tags beside them.

'Look, Eugenie, as much as I'd like to get Shan diamonds, and as much as she deserves them, I work in my dad's cafe. I can't afford stuff like this. I don't know why you've brought me here,' Blessing said.

'Oh, I know we can't have the diamonds. I just paused here to gaze longingly. The rings we're here to see are pretty too though,' Eugenie replied.

As if to show how pretty the rings she thought Blessing

should buy were, Eugenie moved one cabinet to the right and gestured at its contents.

The rings Eugenie gestured at were indeed pretty. There was one in particular that Blessing thought Shantelle would love. The cabinet it was in was so full that she couldn't see the price tags on anything.

'These are all still antiques though. Can I afford any of these?' Blessing questioned.

'Oh yes! As long as you don't take a shine to anything that's made of precious metals, or has rare gemstones, or is truly ancient, then it'll be well within your budget. Think of *Bargain Hunt*. Not all the jewellery on there costs a fortune, does it? If it did, it would be *Very Expensive Thing Hunt*,' Eugenie pointed out.

The way Eugenie made her point, and the knowledge that she could get her sister an antique ring, made Blessing laugh.

Now that she knew she could probably afford them, Blessing had a second look at the cabinet of rings. The first one she'd spotted still seemed like the best.

'Can I have that ring with the rectangular blue stone out, please?' Blessing asked Eugenie.

Showing great care and dexterity, Eugenie plucked the ring with the single emerald cut blue topaz stone on it out of the cabinet without disturbing all the other rings. Once she had it safely in her hand, she gazed at it, stroking the silver band.

'It's stunning! This is the sort of thing I pictured you choosing for Shantelle,' Eugenie commented.

When Eugenie handed it to her, Blessing took a closer look at the ring she'd chosen. That confirmed that she'd made the right choice.

'Shan's gonna love this. Thanks, Eugenie,' Blessing told her.

'Thank *you* for using the Christmas Genie service, and liking what I've chosen. Nothing makes me happier than making other people happy,' Eugenie replied.

Wanting to make Blessing happy again, Eugenie said: 'Let's get cufflinks for your boyfriend!'

Together, Eugenie and Blessing walked to the end of the aisle, where a glass-topped wooden display unit full of cufflinks and vesta cases was waiting for them. When she spotted some car-shaped cufflinks that she could afford, Blessing breathed a sigh of relief, because she knew she was going to be able to buy her boyfriend a present he'd like.

While thinking about how clever Eugenie was, Blessing wondered if she had a partner of her own. She wanted to know, but decided it would be rude to directly ask a stranger if she had a partner.

'There's a lot of pressure, buying for your partner, isn't there? Your present has to show that you know them well. I'm guessing you, as an expert in present buying, don't struggle with this,' Blessing said.

'I don't struggle to buy presents for my boyfriend, because I don't have one. I haven't had a relationship long enough for exchanging presents since I left school,' Eugenie replied.

Part of Blessing wanted to question how long you had to be with someone before you could exchange presents with them. She didn't ask that, because it would've sent the conversation along a tangent that didn't interest her that much. Another part of her was impressed that, without directly asking, she had learnt that Eugenie was straight and single.

'That surprises me. You're so bubbly, not to mention pretty, that you'd think men would queue up outside your house to date you. It just goes to show what idiots men are,' Blessing told Eugenie.

Eugenie blushed. 'Ah, thank you! That's very kind. I live in a flat, and I don't have a queue of men outside it, but *one* man recently asked me out on a date. A charming and handsome gentleman, not an idiot. I'm going bowling with him tomorrow, and I cannot wait!' she revealed.

'Oh, that's great! Best of luck with that! I hope you end up buying him a Christmas present!' Blessing cried. Sheer delight made her voice loud, but there were no other customers in the shop to bother.

Remembering that she was with Eugenie to shop, not to chat about boyfriends, Blessing turned her attention back to the display unit of cufflinks. She removed the car-shaped pair, checked them for damage, and then snapped their box shut.

'Right, I guess I'd better pay for these bits,' Blessing said, making her way to the counter.

At the counter was Helen, who'd been discreetly watching Eugenie and Blessing for their entire shopping trip. She smiled when Blessing placed her items in front of her.

'My, these *are* pretty things. I hope they make up for the wallpaper stripper and notebooks,' Helen commented.

'Oh, yeah, I'm happy now. To be fair, I was happy before. This is just the icing on the cake. Eugenie here is *the best*. I've had a great afternoon. If you can give her one, she deserves a pay rise,' Blessing told Helen.

'Thank you, but I wouldn't want one. All the participating shops club together to pay me for the hours I spend shopping with clients, minimum wage, and I earn commission on what clients buy. That's more than enough. This scheme is about getting people to use their local bricks-and-mortar shops more, and to get cash through their tills at a hard time of year. I don't want to take that money back out of their tills,' Eugenie replied.

Until Eugenie had explained it, Blessing hadn't really understood who paid her wages, or why the Christmas Genie service existed. Now that she did, she was even happier that she'd used the service.

'I get it. My dad owns a cafe. We need people to use little local places like this. They put food on families tables, and, they're usually better than the chains. Good on you for doing this,' Blessing said.

'It was Helen's idea. When I heard about it, I begged her to hire me. Luckily, she did,' Eugenie told Blessing.

-

Having paid for her gifts, there was nothing for Blessing to do but say goodbye to Helen and leave Bygones. Once outside, she thought two things.

Blessing's first thought was: *'It's miserable out here. Typical British winter.'*

Blessing's second thought was: *'Oh, no more shopping. Now I have to say goodbye to Eugenie.'*

To delay parting with Eugenie, Blessing studied the window display of Bygones. The sleet falling on her convinced her that, as much as she didn't want to, she had to leave Eugenie and go back to the cafe.

'This has been so much fun. Thanks again, Eugenie, and enjoy your date tomorrow,' Blessing said, managing not to use the word "goodbye".

'My pleasure, Blessing, and I'm sure I will enjoy tomorrow. Hamish is great. Goodbye,' Eugenie replied.

As she walked away from her, Blessing called out: 'Have a Merry Christmas.'

'You too,' Eugenie yelled back.

The joy of a satisfied customer, and the anticipation of her impending date with Hamish, propelled Eugenie at great speed along the Lanes to Toothill's, where she flew through a short afternoon shift.

CHAPTER TWENTY-TWO

What it lacked in architectural splendour, The Colneside Entertainment Centre made up for in the variety of its attractions. The top floor was entirely given over to a snooker club and sports bar. Below it sat an arcade, a bowling alley, a coffee shop, two newly-opened karaoke pods, and a steakhouse.

The karaoke pods could fit ten people, but, as she could only convince one person to sing with her, Eugenie's pod just had two people in it.

There were 80,000 songs available in the karaoke pod, and Holly used the touchscreen to find one of her favourites.

'It might not be the Spice Girl's version,' Holly told Eugenie when the song started playing.

'That doesn't matter! We know it well enough to ignore the words on screen and sing the proper lyrics. The ones about aeroplanes, a world tour, Tesco's tiny turkey, and babies,' Eugenie replied.

The karaoke pod was made for ten people. This meant that, if used by only two people, there was space to dance.

Dancing is a very broad term. Eugenie interpreted it as jumping around while playing air guitar.

Beside Eugenie, Holly shuffled a little bit from side to side while singing Mel C's lines.

-

As soon as the last word disappeared from the big screen on the wall, Eugenie and Holly burst out laughing. The laughter was amplified by the microphones they were still holding, but they were too busy laughing to notice.

'You know how to have fun, Eugenie. This is great!' Holly exclaimed.

Eager to have more fun, Eugenie was tapping away on the touchscreen.

'It's so good to see you letting your hair down. Let's keep it going with this one,' Eugenie replied.

When the opening line of the song Eugenie had selected appeared on screen, Holly wondered if she'd chosen a hymn. It then occurred to her that karaoke pods probably don't have hymns.

'What is this?' Holly asked.

A second after Holly opened her mouth, the speakers around her started playing a calypso beat. She only knew of one Christmas song that sounded like that.

'Oh, it's the Boney M one, isn't it?' Holly realised out loud.

As she was singing "The Boney M one", more commonly known as *Mary's Boy Child/Oh My Lord*, Eugenie was unable to answer.

Like she had when other songs had played in the karaoke pod, Holly sang along. *Unlike* the other songs, she thought about the lyrics of *Mary's Boy Child/Oh My Lord*.

She hadn't even entertained the possibility of Santa Claus coming to town, but she wondered if Mary's boy child, Jesus Christ, really *had* been born on Christmas Day, and if humankind *would* live forever because of it.

-

Despite spending four minutes and three seconds thinking about it, Holly wasn't sure if she believed the words she'd sung.

'Are you okay, Holly?' Eugenie asked, cutting into her thoughts.

'Ah, yes, sorry. I was miles away,' Holly replied.

Eugenie laughed. 'We're here to keep me occupied so I don't get all worked up about the fact that I'm about to date the best man I've ever met, but it looks like *you're* the one who needs distracting. Wherever you were looked dark. Your face was so serious,' she pointed out.

One of the few things Eugenie and Holly never discussed was religion. Ever since she'd met Eugenie, and Holly had realised how strong her new flatmate's faith was, she'd been careful not to bring it up. It worried her that their differences on the subject would drive them apart. To Eugenie, her faith was what she built her life around, but to Holly, it was an unanswered question that rarely entered her head. Eugenie was sure and steadfast, while Holly was questioning and ever-changing.

To avoid having to reveal what was on her mind, Holly said: 'On the subject of your date, isn't it soon? We only have time for a couple more songs.'

'But it's not date time yet! Let's make the most of being together,' Eugenie declared, cuing up another song.

-

Having dishonestly sang that they wished it could be Christmas every day, and that it was the most wonderful time of the year, Eugenie and Holly had to exit the karaoke pod. As she walked out of the soundproof pod, a wave of sound hit Eugenie, as did a wave of emotion as she realised it was finally time to date Hamish.

CHAPTER TWENTY-THREE

When Eugenie dashed up to the desk that swapped normal shoes for bowling shoes, many heads turned. This was partly because of the clip-clop noise her heels made on the floor, but mostly because of the squeal her mouth made when she spotted Hamish.

Upon hearing Eugenie, Hamish questioned: 'Is everything alright?'

'I can't believe it's finally time!' Eugenie cried.

Unseen and unheard by most of the people hanging around the bowling desk at The Colneside, Holly sidled up to Eugenie and Hamish.

'Treat her well, or you'll have me to answer to,' Holly told Hamish.

'Please don't take that personally. Holly cares a lot about me,' Eugenie commented.

Hamish looked from Holly's face, which had a slight smile on it, to Eugenie's, which bore a huge grin. To him, it was clear to see that Holly cared about Eugenie, and clear to see why.

'So she should. I'm sure *you'd* say the same to someone

who was about to date *her*. Holly can be assured though, that I'll be nice to you. You're so chirpy that I think it would be impossible to be anything *but* nice to you,' Hamish said.

This response *did* assure Holly, so she said her goodbyes and headed home.

With Holly gone, Hamish and Eugenie turned their attention to Ahmad, the man behind the bowling desk.

'Good evening. Let's have two games of bowling for the two of us, please,' Hamish said to Ahmad.

'You will need to wear the special shoes we provide. What sizes do you need?' Ahmad asked while typing on the computer till to his right without looking at it.

'Ah, the shoes! I'd forgotten that you have to change shoes! I'm a size four,' Eugenie cried.

'And I'm a nine,' Hamish added.

Armed with the information he required, Ahmad removed two pairs of red and white bowling shoes from the rack behind him.

'You can change shoes on that bench over there and then hand them to me for safekeeping. Payment is by card only,' Ahmad informed Hamish.

After Hamish had paid for two games of bowling for two players, he and Eugenie took the shoes Ahmad handed them and made their way to the bench.

The bowling shoes Eugenie slipped on felt cold on her feet. The sensation, combined with the fresh scent of the cleaning spray that had been used on the shoes, invigorated her. She jumped up off the bench, and then realised how different the bowling shoes were to her own shoes.

'They don't go with my outfit, and I'm really short now,' Eugenie commented, looking down at her feet.

'Shoes don't matter that much, do they?' Hamish questioned.

Eugenie tutted. 'Oh, dear! If that's what you think, then I'm not sure we're going to work out as a couple. I love my shoes,' she replied with a smile.

As Eugenie had been walking to the counter at the time, Ahmad heard the end of her sentence. He also saw the sparkly silver heels Eugenie loved when she placed them on his counter.

'These are wonderful shoes. You're lucky you have tiny feet. If these fitted, then I'd be trying them on while you were busy bowling,' Ahmad told Eugenie.

-

Having thanked Ahmad for his help, Eugenie and Hamish headed to the lane he directed them to.

Separating the bowling part of The Colneside from the arcade was a black metal rail with racks of brightly-coloured bowling balls behind it. Eugenie rifled through the balls until she found a pink one with a six on it, and an orange one that bore the number eight. She promptly took them to the ball return by the lane she and Hamish were to play on, and placed them next to the four balls that were already there.

When Eugenie turned away from the ball return to ask Hamish if he wanted to go first or second, she realised he was still by the rack of various balls, which he was staring at as if it was an exam paper. Wanting to be near Hamish, Eugenie dashed over to him.

'I can see they've got numbers on, but I don't know what

they mean. I've not done this before. How do you know what ball you want?' Hamish questioned when Eugenie joined him.

It was rare that someone asked Eugenie for help with anything other than shopping. As she didn't consider herself to be a knowledgeable person, this made sense to her. The idea that Hamish knew nothing about bowling, so she could teach him, made her feel like an expert.

'The numbers are to do with weight. Usually, heavier balls have larger finger holes. To work out what you want, pick a ball up, see if your fingers fit comfortably, and feel the weight of it. If your arm isn't falling off, it's probably the one for you. If, when you're playing, you find you don't like it, you can always come back and swap,' Eugenie explained.

'Ah, I see. Thanks for that,' Hamish replied.

Just because he liked the dark shade of blue it was, Hamish picked up a ball to his right. It felt like an extension of his arm, so he concluded it was the right ball.

Because he'd seen Eugenie put hers there, Hamish put his ball on the ball return.

By the ball return was a bright yellow keyboard on a pedestal, which Eugenie pressed a button on.

'Do you want to go first or second, and would you like to use your full name or a nickname?' Eugenie asked Hamish.

'I don't mind,' Hamish replied.

As Hamish didn't mind, Eugenie made the decisions herself. She entered "Eugenie" for player one, and "Hamish" for player two. These names appeared by a blank scoreboard on a screen suspended from the ceiling above the ball return.

Taking her pink ball from the ball return, Eugenie said: 'This game is simple.'

To demonstrate how simple bowling was, Eugenie kissed her ball and then hurled it at the lane. It landed with a thud and hurtled straight into the skittle to the right of the front one, knocking it and five others down.

Eager to take down the remaining four skittles, Eugenie rushed back to the ball return and snatched the orange eight ball. Like on her first throw, she brought the ball to her lips before sending it in the general direction of the skittles. When she saw the ball veer to the right, Eugenie wafted her hands to the left vigorously. Despite the wafting, the ball skidded past all the skittles.

As her turn was over, Eugenie returned to Hamish, who was sitting on a bench by the ball return, watching Eugenie intently.

'And that's how you bowl,' Eugenie told him.

'What is the kissing for, and why did you wave your hands at it?' Hamish questioned.

Eugenie laughed. 'I kiss the ball for luck, and the wafting is to encourage it to go to the left,' she explained.

'But the ball has already left your hand. Surely the waving doesn't affect anything,' Hamish pointed out.

'Not really, but it feels like it does. It's fun,' Eugenie replied.

With no more questions to ask, Hamish jumped up and said: 'Let's give this a go.'

To "give this a go", Hamish picked up his dark blue ball and carried it to the black line at the start of the lane he'd paid a reasonable sum to use. There, he swung his arm strongly in the direction of the skittles, releasing the ball right at the start of the upswing. It rolled straight down the middle of the lane and into the middle skittle. The ball's journey through the skittles knocked eight of them down.

'Wow! That's great! Well done!' Eugenie cried.

Hamish shrugged. 'It's just luck. All I did was throw the ball,' he replied.

'But you threw it well, and now you've got the hang of it,' Eugenie pointed out.

The ball return system made Hamish wait almost a minute to get his ball back. Once he had it, he used it to floor a ninth skittle, which made Eugenie clap.

'Fun, isn't it?' Eugenie said when Hamish returned from his successful go.

'Erm, yes, I suppose so,' he replied.

-

As bowling is a game where players take it in turns to throw balls, and the seating provided is quite a few paces from the lane, which is in a noisy room, Eugenie and Hamish couldn't hold a conversation.

Instead of listening to Hamish's voice, as she'd thought she would, Eugenie listened to the thud of bowling balls hitting wood on fourteen lanes; bleeps, bloops, and blaring music from the arcade; and the multi-tonal waves of conversation from the steakhouse that sat overlooking the bowling lanes. It was loud and chaotic.

The chaotic cacophony seeped into Eugenie's head, causing it to pound. Every time a bowling ball hit a lane, including Eugenie's own, it seemed to shake her brain.

On her final throw of the first game, Eugenie lobbed her ball down the lane, and didn't care when she saw it swerve into the gutter. The moment the ball disappeared from view, she trudged back to the bench and sank down onto it.

'Unlucky,' Hamish commented, his word penetrating the fog that seemed to have descended over Eugenie's mind.

When Hamish got up to bowl, Eugenie didn't watch him. She shut her eyes in the hope it would ease the growing pressure in her head. It did not.

Without giving it much thought, Hamish unleashed his ball on the skittles, which were all sent flying. When he did this two more times, the screen above the lane declared the game to be over, won by Hamish.

Noticing that Eugenie had her head in her hands, Hamish said: 'Sorry, it was really bad manners of me to beat you. I hope you're not too upset.'

'No, I'm not upset,' Eugenie mumbled.

'Are you sure? Is something else up?' Hamish asked.

It took all Eugenie's willpower to stop herself from admitting that she was in agony. Because telling Hamish about the explosion in her head might make him feel bad and cause him to end their date early, Eugenie managed to keep it to herself. No lie came to mind though to cover up the truth, so if she wasn't careful, it would end up slipping out anyway.

To stop herself from revealing how much pain she was in and ruining her date, Eugenie decided to put some space between her and Hamish. 'I need to go to the ladies,' she told him, getting up to do just that.

Thinking that Eugenie's demeanour was just due to needing to relieve herself, Hamish didn't comment on this. He just assumed that Eugenie would return in a few minutes, feeling better.

CHAPTER TWENTY-FOUR

The ladies toilets of The Colneside were cool and quiet. They offered respite from the chaos of the entertainment centre they served.

As there was only one set of toilets for all female visitors to the building, it didn't surprise Eugenie that there was already someone in there. That someone was at the mirror, tying her long blonde hair up in a bun.

Unsure what to do with herself, Eugenie leaned on the sink next to the lady tying her hair up.

'Are you okay? You don't quite look well,' the blonde lady said.

Although she didn't want to admit to Hamish that she didn't feel well, Eugenie was happy to tell the blonde lady. She was a stranger, and probably wouldn't be too upset or change her plans because someone she didn't know had a headache.

'My head is exploding! I'm on a date with the man of my dreams, and it's all going wrong,' Eugenie revealed.

'Sorry to hear that, Eugenie. Have you taken anything for it? I've got painkillers in my bag if you need them,' the blonde lady replied.

When the blonde lady called her by her name, Eugenie realised she knew her. Unfortunately, she didn't know the blonde lady's name, but she remembered her amazing blonde hair and serving her several times at Toothill's.

'Oh, that's so kind of you! I have nothing on me. If you don't mind, I'd love painkillers. I want this agony to stop so I can enjoy being with Hamish. This is my one chance to make him fall for me, and I can't do that with my head pounding. I can barely think straight,' Eugenie agreed.

The blonde lady put her white shoulder bag on the counter and fished through it. After rummaging for a few seconds, she pulled out a box of paracetamol, a box of ibuprofen, and a small bottle of water.

The second it was on the counter in front of her, Eugenie opened the box of paracetamol and yanked out the tray of tablets.

Continuing to search through her bag, the blonde lady said: 'That's not all I have in here. Do you need anything else, like a condom or a tampon?'

After gulping down two paracetamol with the aid of water from the small bottle she'd been given, Eugenie shook her head. 'I never go that far on a first date, and thankfully I'm not on my period at the moment. Painkillers was all I needed, thank you,' Eugenie replied.

While Eugenie swallowed ibuprofen, the blonde lady asked her: 'Apart from coming down with a headache, how's your date going?'

The lights in the room flickered. When they did, Eugenie briefly thought it was her eyes playing tricks because of her headache. She was reassured to see the blonde lady glance up at the lights, which confirmed that it really had happened and her headache wasn't so bad that it was causing visual disturbances.

'Hamish is wonderful! He's the perfect gentleman, and great company. For some reason though, I'm struggling to talk to him. We just seem to be taking it in turns to bowl, and we're hardly saying two words to each other. I think I've messed up another date,' Eugenie revealed.

'Perhaps it's the atmosphere? My best dates with my partner are either outdoors or in quiet places. We never have a good time at busy and noisy places like the downstairs here, except when we're with friends and part of a crowd. Don't worry too much. Stress will only make your head worse. If he's a nice guy, he'll be happy to try again somewhere else,' the blonde lady suggested.

As the blonde lady had asked about her date, Eugenie felt like she should ask the blonde lady something about her. There was something she wanted to know anyway.

'Are you still with the man you cooked dinner for in the green velvet dress you bought from us?' Eugenie asked.

The blonde lady smiled, which answered Eugenie's question before she'd even spoken. 'I'm delighted to say that I *am* still with Jude, who I bought that dress for. He's upstairs in the snooker room, in fact. We're doing most well. So well that my Christmas present to him is going to be a key to my house,' she revealed.

The idea of the blonde lady moving in with Jude filled Eugenie with glee. She showed her gleefulness by clapping her hands.

'That's so *romantic*,' Eugenie sighed.

'For all you know, next Christmas the man you're dating

will give you a key to his house, if he has a house,' the blonde lady said.

'I don't know where he lives, or what his job is,' Eugenie realised out loud.

'Then you have something to ask him when you go back to him. That should get your date back on track,' the blonde lady pointed out.

Just knowing she had questions to ask Hamish made Eugenie feel better. It gave her hope that the rest of her date would go well, and Hamish would agree to see her again.

Although she was enjoying talking to the blonde lady, now that she was feeling slightly better, Eugenie wanted to return to Hamish. That was difficult though, because she didn't know how to politely part from the blonde lady.

The door to the ladies toilets opened, letting in the cacophony outside and a tall ginger woman.

'Oh, sorry, Tamsyn. Were you wondering where I'd got to?' the blonde lady asked the newcomer.

'She was helping me. I have a headache, so she gave me tablets. She also gave me advice for my date, so now I feel much happier and more hopeful that I'll keep *this* man,' Eugenie explained.

Tamsyn smiled. 'I knew she'd be helping someone,' she said.

The pounding in Eugenie's head was a little quieter. The room was silent, so she was able to realise this. It was too early for the painkillers to have taken effect, so she knew this was just thanks to the blonde lady's words, not the contents of her handbag.

Feeling better made Eugenie think once again about returning to Hamish. She hoped that Tamsyn coming to check on the blonde lady would allow her to leave without being rude.

Before saying goodbye to the blonde lady and heading back out to Hamish, Eugenie looked at herself in the mirror. What she saw put a smile on her face, which made her look even more attractive.

'You are most pretty. Now go back out there and show your date that,' the blonde lady told Eugenie when she saw her looking in the mirror.

A feeling of pride and power flooded through Eugenie. Pride in her appearance, and the power to make a man fall in love with her.

'Thank you for your help, lady with the amazing blonde hair. I'll do just that,' Eugenie said.

Brimming with confidence, Eugenie marched towards the door. Just as she was about to open it, she felt the need to go back and say something else, so she did.

When she turned back towards them, Eugenie saw that both Tamsyn and the blonde lady were doubled over with silent laughter. They both stopped when they realised Eugenie had returned.

'Sorry, "lady with the amazing blonde hair" is not your name, is it? I don't know your name,' Eugenie apologised.

'It's not the name on my driving licence, but I'm happy for you to call me Lady With The Amazing Blonde Hair. If you wish to pay me such a compliment, who am I to stop you?' Lady With The Amazing Blonde Hair replied with a smile on her face.

Unsure how to respond, Eugenie stood silent and still.

'You are still pretty, and your date is still waiting for you,' Lady With The Amazing Blonde Hair pointed out.

As this was correct, Eugenie span round to head out of the room. She forgot that the bowling shoes she'd been forced to wear had very little grip, so she turned further than she'd meant to. After correcting that, she strode out of the quiet toilets, into the busy arcade, which was between her and the bowling alley.

CHAPTER TWENTY-FIVE

'You were gone a while. Did you get chatting to someone?' Hamish asked when Eugenie returned from the ladies.

On her walk back from the ladies, Eugenie had anticipated that question and formed an answer in her head.

'I *did* get chatting, to a lady with amazing blonde hair. I told her I had a headache and she gave me painkillers, and water to take them with. She's one of my customers from Toothill's. We chatted about my date with you, and her partner,' Eugenie revealed.

The enthusiasm in Eugenie's voice made Hamish smile. He'd come to expect that energy from her, and had been surprised to find it absent for most of their date. Now he knew she had, or *had* had, a headache, that made sense.

'She sounds nice. I hope the tablets she gave you clear the headache up,' Hamish said.

Many men Eugenie had dated in the past would've asked what she'd said when the blonde lady had asked how her date was going. A few had spontaneously asked Eugenie to rate them out of ten. It didn't escape her notice that Hamish had done neither of those things, and it made her like him even more. To her, it was a sign of his maturity and good manners.

'Thanks to her, my headache is mostly gone now,' Eugenie told Hamish.

'Glad to hear it!' Hamish replied.

Having explained her absence, Eugenie wanted to get back to the game of bowling that they were there to play. This time though, she wanted to intersperse the throws with conversation.

'Shall we get started on our next game? I've got an idea for this one. Before one of us goes up to throw, the other one could ask a question. On the return from the throw, we could answer it. Basically, the person whose turn it is gets asked a question before they go, which they answer when they get back,' Eugenie suggested.

'Yes, let's!' Hamish agreed.

As Eugenie was first to throw, Hamish was first to ask a question. 'What is the most important thing in your life?' he asked her as she picked up her pink ball.

While powering her ball at the helpless skittles, Eugenie wondered what *was* the most important thing in her life. The answer came to her just before her ball reached the skittles, which it knocked down all ten of.

Upon realising that she'd scored a strike, Eugenie couldn't help but squeal with happiness. She strutted back to Hamish. This style of walking was quite at odds with the shoes she was wearing.

'My faith is the most important thing in my life. I grew up with the church, and I can't imagine life without God. He's with me through everything, and I feel His support every day. I adore Him, and He is the pillar that I build my life around,' Eugenie told Hamish.

Hamish beamed. 'I've always wanted a date to say that. It's the centre of my life too. It's so rare that I come across someone else with the same faith as me. My ex was an atheist, and she never understood a huge part of me and my life. In fact, she laughed at my faith. To know that you understand is so nice. I'm a committed, God-loving Christian, and I love that you are too,' he enthused.

'I'm sorry for her that she didn't understand. She's missing out, not just on the love of God, but *your* love too. Poor woman,' Eugenie replied.

When he tried to answer, Hamish realised that he didn't have the words. The only response he could give was a smile.

As it was his turn to bowl, Hamish picked up a bowling ball. He didn't check if it was the one he'd used before, but it fitted his hand, so he assumed it was correct. Once he had the ball, Hamish turned to Eugenie, as if he expected her to do something, even though it was *his* turn to bowl.

Until she caught Hamish's questioning eye, Eugenie had forgotten she was supposed to ask a question. She'd been miles away, thinking about the fact that Hamish had said God-*loving*, not God-*fearing*. It perfectly summed up how she felt about God too. It didn't make sense to her that people feared God, and she was pleased to hear someone else seemed to be of the same opinion. Thanks to chatting to Lady With The Amazing Blonde Hair, Eugenie knew exactly what she wanted to ask.

'Oh yes, my turn with the questions. What do you do for a living, and where do you go home to once you've done it?' Eugenie asked.

Hamish laughed. 'That's two questions,' he pointed out.

Realising her mistake, Eugenie laughed with Hamish. 'Sorry, I'm just so eager to know all about you. I didn't mean to cheat,' she replied.

'Well, I'll answer them both, but only because you're sweet, and I'll make you wait until I've bowled,' Hamish said.

Being called sweet by Hamish gave Eugenie a flippy feeling in her tummy. She couldn't keep her eyes off him as he chucked his ball down the lane. It made her splutter with laughter to see it clip just one skittle.

When Hamish walked towards her to pick up another ball, Eugenie held her breath, eager to hear what Hamish's job was and where he lived.

As he knew Eugenie was waiting for him, Hamish took great care over each step, extending her wait and building her anticipation.

Just when Eugenie thought she might burst, Hamish revealed: 'I'm a lawyer. That allows me to live in a nice townhouse a little out of town.'

'A lawyer? But you're so nice!' Eugenie cried.

'Lawyers can be nice. It is our job to ensure our clients get justice. We help people in a setting where they can't help themselves. My firm, or rather, the firm that employs me, does a lot of legal aid work. It's very rewarding, and very nice,' Hamish told Eugenie firmly.

The passion with which Hamish spoke about his job mesmerised Eugenie. A daydream played in her head featuring him making a polite but powerful argument in court, which saved an innocent client who thought they were destined to end up behind bars. Even though it was just a dream, and Hamish wasn't presently her partner, it filled her with love and admiration.

Firmly in the present, Hamish made his way back up to the lane with a ball in his hand, calling to Eugenie: 'I'll get thinking about my next question for you.'

In a slight improvement on his first throw, Hamish's second throw caused three skittles to flop over. That gave him enough time to think of a question for Eugenie.

'How long have you been single for?' Hamish asked Eugenie.

'Ooh, depends what you mean by single. My last date was only a couple of months ago, but that didn't go anywhere. The last partner who lasted more than a few dates left me over two years ago. So far, no-one has fallen in love with me and become my boyfriend, so you could say I've always been single,' Eugenie revealed.

That answer surprised Hamish so much, it left him momentarily speechless.

When Hamish regained the power of speech, he murmured: 'But you're such a bright and sunny young lady, not to mention easy on the eye. How could any man lucky enough to date you let you go?'

'Really? Do you really mean that?' Eugenie questioned instantly.

'Yes, Eugenie, I do. I probably shouldn't say so. It's the modern way to play games and hide your feelings. I know that, but I can't do it. I can't help but tell you how I feel. Besides, I don't see the point in these games, and you don't play them either. *You're* more open than *me*. It's one of the many things I like about you,' Hamish confirmed.

At this point, Eugenie realised that all traces of her headache were gone. She had some peculiar feelings in her head, but they weren't pain.

'Playing it cool is not a concept I understand, or am capable of, so I feel like I must tell you that I'm delighted that you feel that way about me. I think you're a charming, clever, moral, and handsome gentleman. When I first saw you, I thought you'd make a great boyfriend, and all you've done since then is prove me right. I keep daydreaming about spending the new year, and maybe the rest of my life, getting to know you, and getting you to like me. You are something special, I can tell. My heart races at the thought of being near you, and my greatest fear right now is something going wrong between us. No man has ever stuck around in my life, and I am literally praying that you are different. That you can put up with me. Put simply, you're my dream man, Hamish, and I'd love my dreams to become reality,' Eugenie gushed.

The emotion in Eugenie's speech made Hamish yearn to have physical contact with her. He placed a hand on her shoulder, and noticed her let out a little gasp and look at the hand, as if it had healed a scar she'd had since birth. When she turned her gaze from his hand to his eyes, Hamish smiled at Eugenie. In silence, they told each other that their minds were on the same track.

Just to make sure he was understood, Hamish said out loud: 'I won't *put up* with you. I'll thank God for every minute I get to spend with you. I'll prove to you that a man *can* stay, and he can have the time of his life doing so.'

CHAPTER TWENTY-SIX

The gerberas in the bouquet Hamish handed to Eugenie gave it a bright and cheerful feel. Even under the artificial glare of the streetlights in The Colneside's car park, they looked good.

'I can't believe I nearly forgot to give them to you. It would've been a disaster!' Hamish said while Eugenie admired her flowers.

The moist softness of the flowers delighted Eugenie as she stroked the petals. When she put the bouquet under her nose and inhaled, she was reminded of a summer breeze, even though it was so cold that she could see her breath.

'I can't believe you bought me flowers! You really *are* a gentleman. Thank you so much!' Eugenie cried, still gazing at her flowers.

While Eugenie gazed at her flowers, Hamish gazed at Eugenie gazing at her flowers. There was something about the way Eugenie was enraptured by the beauty of the natural big round bursts of colour in her hand that Hamish found captivating.

While gazing at Eugenie, it occurred to Hamish that they

were both out in the cold, late at night. The moment could not last forever. It would have to end soon, and, most likely, end with them parting ways.

'As much as it pains me to say this, I think it is home time. How are you getting back? Are you driving?' Hamish asked.

'I can't drive. On one of my first lessons, back when I was seventeen, I killed a squirrel. It upset me so much that I couldn't bear to get behind the wheel again,' Eugenie revealed.

Although he had never before heard of killing a squirrel as an excuse not to drive, Hamish didn't find it hard to believe that it had put Eugenie off for life. It was very unusual, but very her.

'Oh, that's sad. If you don't drive, how are you getting home?' Hamish questioned.

'Taxi, I suppose. If it was light and warm, I'd walk. I love walking around town in the sun. Sadly, it isn't, but that's okay. One of the local firms knows me well, and I'm sure they won't take long to get here,' Eugenie replied.

Even before he knew the story of Eugenie and the squirrel, Hamish had suspected she intended to get a taxi. He had other ideas.

'If you're comfortable with it, I'd like to drive you home,' Hamish told Eugenie.

The grin on Eugenie's face told Hamish she'd accept his offer before she'd even moved her smiling lips.

'Yes, I'd love that! Please *do* take me home in your swish Jaguar,' Eugenie said.

As he opened the front passenger door, Hamish laughed.

'Swish?' he questioned.

When Eugenie hopped into the front passenger seat of Hamish's Jaguar, she was reminded of how comfortable it was.

'Yes, swish. You know, fancy and high-spec,' Eugenie explained.

Still laughing, Hamish shut Eugenie's door. Having done that, he skipped around the front of the car to get to the driving seat, which he eased into.

While clipping his seatbelt on and starting the car, Hamish thought about the route between The Colneside and Eugenie's flat. The most direct one went right through the town centre along streets lined with shut shops and restaurants that would be open for a couple of hours yet. At that time of night, he didn't expect too much traffic to be on them. Traffic wasn't his only consideration though. There was another, more roundabout route, that he thought might be of more interest to Eugenie. It would also take longer to drive, so they'd get more time together.

'I'm going to go around the houses to get you home. We should see some Christmas lights on the way,' Hamish told Eugenie as he pulled away.

-

The first light-up festive decorations Eugenie spotted were colour-changing icicle-shaped lights. They were in the downstairs windows of a narrow townhouse. These didn't evoke any emotion in Eugenie.

After Hamish turned a corner, a utilitarian 1970s detached house with a generous front garden came into view. Eugenie could tell the garden was a generous size, because it was full of bright Christmas decorations. There was a little reindeer made up of white lights on a frame, which was looking at an inflatable snowman which was a tad lopsided. Many smaller decorations stood on the lawn too, but Eugenie couldn't take them all in. Not to be outshone by the garden, the upstairs windows had lights depicting Santa Claus in them. The whole display over-whelmed Eugenie, and she couldn't see any personality in the decorations.

Further down the same street as the 70s house with the full garden was a little bungalow with a front door that opened straight onto the pavement. There were little twinkling white fairy lights tracing where the roof met the rest of the house. In keeping with the fairy lights, there was a silver light-up decoration in the shape of a present displayed in what looked like the bathroom win-dow. Crammed into the window next to it was a smaller present-shaped decoration, a Santa Claus that jerked from side to side in a poor attempt at dancing, a three foot pink artificial tree adorned with blue tinsel that sparkled in the gentle light emitted by the present-shaped decor-ation, and a Christmas card depicting a robin. The variety of the decorations suggested to Eugenie that the bunga-low was home to a family, all of whom had had a say in the decorations. As, to Eugenie, family and togetherness was what Christmas was all about, she considered the bungalow to have the perfect display of Christmas decor-ations.

'The decorations are so varied! To me, they represent the diversity of our community,' Hamish commented, glan-cing at a townhouse with just a Christmas tree in the win-dow while he waited for the third car he'd spotted that journey to pass the traffic calming measure up ahead.

'I've never thought of it like that, but you're so right! I guess that's why I love some house's lights, but not others, and I never appreciate the town's display,' Eugenie agreed.

-

When Hamish pulled up outside Eugenie's flat, she felt her spirits sink. Despite the car being stationary outside its destination, she made no attempt to get out of it.

'May I see you into your flat?' Hamish asked.

As this meant spending a few more seconds with Hamish, Eugenie replied: 'Yes! That would make me very happy.'

Holding the flowers he'd given her, Eugenie showed Hamish up to her flat. Demonstrating a lot of skill, she fished her key out of her pocket and opened the door with one hand, an elbow, and a foot.

When Eugenie and Hamish entered the kitchen-diner, they found Holly was already there, curled up under a purple and orange patterned blanket on the sofa.

Seeing the flowers in Eugenie's hand, Holly commented: 'They look nice.'

'I love them! It was so thoughtful of Hamish to get them for me,' Eugenie replied.

It made Hamish blush to hear Eugenie compliment him. He wasn't comfortable with praise.

Seeing the book in Holly's hand, Hamish asked her: 'Are you enjoying your latest read?'

'Yes. I'm at the bit all romance novels have, where there's a misunderstanding and the hero and heroine part, thinking it's the end for them,' Holly replied.

There was a pause while Hamish wondered whether to lie. He decided against it.

'I'm afraid I have no idea what you mean. I barely read, and, when I actually get time to pick a book up, it is never a romance. You could tell me they all have a scene where the hero and heroine meet in an unexpected place and I'd believe you. I just asked because I wanted to know you weren't bored while waiting for us to come home,' Hamish admitted.

Puzzlement crossed Holly's face. 'I have books. How could I be bored?' she questioned.

As Holly's question was an unanswerable one, Eugenie and Hamish remained silent.

It occurred to Holly that, as this was the end of their date, Eugenie and Hamish would want to discuss whether or not to have another one. If they had different answers, it could be a very awkward conversation. She felt it was definitely a conversation they didn't need to have in front of her.

'I'm off to the bathroom now, to get ready for bed. It was nice to see you again, Hamish. Thanks for bringing Eugenie home safely,' Holly said.

'My pleasure, Holly, and good to see you too. Goodnight,' Hamish replied.

Having said goodnight to Hamish, and told Eugenie she'd see her before going to bed, Holly slipped away to the bathroom to leave them to it.

Once Holly was gone, Eugenie and Hamish gazed into each other's eyes, wondering who would speak first. They both knew the question they wanted to ask, and they were both hopeful that they'd get the answer they wanted.

As much as Eugenie loved gazing into Hamish's hazel

eyes, she was desperate to know if she was going to get another opportunity to gaze into them. 'Can we go on a second date?' she asked.

'Yes, let's. You're so sweet that I can't possibly say no. It would be my pleasure to take you out again,' Hamish replied without hesitation.

Eugenie gasped. 'So it's happening? We're dating now? You like me?' she questioned.

With a smile on his face, Hamish nodded. 'I like you a great deal. So much so that, even though I'm not that keen on bowling, I've had a great night. I'm sure we'll have another great night when we go out again. If you don't mind, I'll choose what we do for our next date. When I've got a plan, I'll call you to make arrangements,' he told Eugenie.

'Perfect! I look forward to your call,' Eugenie agreed.

When the cuckoo popped out of the clock on the wall with the tester pot squares on, Hamish conceded that he had to go home.

'It is getting late, and I'm meeting with a client tomorrow morning. I'm afraid I must bid you farewell,' Hamish said, frowning.

With similar feelings to Hamish, Eugenie frowned too. 'I know I must let you go. Thank you for such a lovely night. It was my favourite date ever, despite getting a terrible headache in the middle of it. That's thanks to you,' she told Hamish.

Waving as he went, Hamish left the flat.

Just like the first time Hamish had been to and left her flat, Eugenie dashed to the window to watch him drive away.

Unlike the first time he'd been to and left Eugenie's flat, Hamish couldn't see Eugenie waving. He suspected that she was though.

When Hamish's taillights were out of sight, Eugenie traipsed back to the kitchen-diner. Already there was Holly, who was wrapped up in her dressing gown.

'He's wonderful! I've had such a lovely time with him. I know I've said that about several men, after several dates, but this is different. *Hamish* is different,' Eugenie enthused.

Holly nodded and said: 'Yes, I feel it too. This man actually *will* call you. I'd bet good money on it.'

CHAPTER TWENTY-SEVEN

The flowers on the table by the window brightened up the kitchen-diner and the mood of anyone who spent a few minutes in the room. As she was still buzzing from the date on which she'd been given the flowers, Eugenie didn't need brightening up.

It wasn't just Eugenie's mood that was buzzing. The vacuum cleaner was buzzing and humming while being pushed around the kitchen-diner by its owner.

Vacuuming was one of Eugenie's favourite jobs. It was simple, which meant she could daydream while working. On that day, Eugenie dreamed about wearing roller-skates and being pulled around town on them by small dogs with pale, curly coats. She wasn't sure why this idea was in her head, but it was, and it seemed like fun.

Just as Eugenie was imagining rolling through Fenwick while being stared at by their staff, her phone rang. As she was so deep in her daydream, she briefly thought *Wannabe*, which was her ringtone, was playing through the department store's PA system. When she remembered that song was her ringtone, she realised it was her phone making that noise.

When Eugenie slipped her phone out of her pocket, she expected to see Hamish's name on the display. It disappointed her to see that the caller's name began with an M, not an H. Upon reading the five letters after the M, Eugenie's disappointment was completely reversed.

'Mother! Hello! To what do I owe the pleasure?' Eugenie asked.

'Hello, darling. I have news for you. Good news,' Eugenie's mother replied.

When she heard she had good news, Eugenie knew it would either be about the man her mother had recently moved in with or that she was coming down for a visit.

'Tell me, tell me!' Eugenie cried.

'I've got someone to cover me next week at the food bank, so I'm coming down to see you and Victoria,' Eugenie's mother revealed.

Eugenie squealed. 'Oh, that's wonderful! I'm desperate to see you,' she said.

'And *I'm* desperate to see *you*, darling. One week won't make up for six months apart, but it's something,' Eugenie's mother replied.

'We can have turkey with all the trimmings together, and bake gingerbread, and sing along to cheesy festive songs, and all of that!' Eugenie cried.

Although she wasn't vacuuming anymore, daydreams played once again in Eugenie's head. These ones didn't have any roller skates or dogs in them. They featured herself, her mother, and her auntie, all laughing and smiling around the dining table in her flat. The daydream wasn't accurate, for the food in it was delicious, but none of the people who starred in it could cook.

'I'm not sure about the lunch bit, unless you've been taking cookery classes. Since Stuart moved in, he does all the cooking, thank goodness, and we both know Victoria will never learn,' Eugenie's mum pointed out.

This put paid to Eugenie's dream. It saddened her that, just because none of them could cook, they couldn't have a nice traditional lunch together. Eating out in a restaurant felt completely different to cramming around the modest, but private, table in the flat.

Cooking was a skill Eugenie had never mastered. Her mother had taught her the basics, but she'd had no natural skill to pass on to her daughter. All Eugenie had inherited was her mother's ability to turn food black. The only person she knew who *could* cook was Holly. Thinking of Holly and cooking gave Eugenie an idea.

'None of *us* can cook, but *Holly* can. The poor girl never gets to see her *own* family, except on a laptop screen. I'm sure she'd love to join us. If only her hours at work were different, she'd cook every day of the week. She's a culinary wizard, and she loves performing her magic,' Eugenie realised out loud.

'That's a great idea! I barely saw her the last couple of times I was down, and I'd love to get to know the girl you live with,' Eugenie's mother agreed.

'Holly would *love* you, I'm sure. Then again, *anyone* would love you,' Eugenie said.

After saying that anyone would love her mother, Eugenie realised it wasn't strictly true. There was one man who *hadn't* loved her mother. Eugenie's very existence suggested that the man had been physically attracted to her mother, but he hadn't *loved* her.

On her mother's end of the call, Eugenie could hear someone shouting: 'Elizabeth! The man from the church is here!'

'Sorry darling, but I have to go. See you next week,' Eugenie's mother said.

Eugenie sighed. 'You are a very busy woman,' she commented.

The person who'd called for Eugenie's mother called again.

'Yes, I am, Eugenie. I have to be though. They need me. That's why I transferred to be up here. See you next week, darling,' Eugenie's mother replied.

The next thing Eugenie heard was a bloop from her phone to tell her the call had ended.

'Goodbye, Mother. I love you,' Eugenie told her phone.

Eugenie felt an odd damp sensation on her cheeks. She prodded her face and realised the dampness was caused by tears falling from her eyes.

In response to the discovery that she was crying, Eugenie scoffed and told herself: 'Man up, Eugenie. Tears are pointless. Be positive. Mustn't grumble. At least she called you, and you get to see her next week. How dare you cry about missing her? At least she stuck around to raise you. Be grateful, not miserable.'

The wall with seventeen colours on it did not respond. Neither did the gerberas in the glass vase behind Eugenie.

In an attempt to not be miserable, Eugenie told her smart speaker to play Heart Radio, turned it up loud, and switched the vacuum cleaner back on.

CHAPTER TWENTY-EIGHT

Thanks to buttons all the way down it, Eugenie found it easy to take the navy-blue dress off the mannequin. Once she'd got it off, Eugenie handed the dress to the woman who'd asked for it.

'See, you're not being awkward, Lily. That was easy,' Eugenie said to the woman who was now holding the dress she'd asked for.

'Oh, I am glad. This dress is just what I'm looking for, and I was so disappointed when I couldn't find it in my size on the rail,' Lily replied.

As Lily turned to take the dress to the fitting room, Eugenie spotted a pair of black leather strappy open-toe stilettoes that were on sale. With a mental image of Lily wearing the heels with the dress in her hands, Eugenie snatched them off the shelf and chased her to the fitting room.

'Try these with it! They're twenty-five percent off when bought with any dress, and you did say you love a bargain. They should go perfectly with the dress,' Eugenie told Lily, thrusting the heels into her hands.

'Yes, I do. It's always more fun to buy something if it's

reduced. They'll finish the look off perfectly. Thanks,' Lily agreed, examining the shoes.

Once Lily had swished the curtain of the fitting room closed, Eugenie skipped over to the rail where she knew she could find the dress Lily was putting on in a different size. After flicking through the many dresses, she found the one she was looking for and whisked it off the rail.

Putting the dress on the mannequin was so easy that Eugenie was able to gaze out at the street while doing it. There wasn't much to see. The street had very little traffic and, thanks to the biting north-easterly wind, very few pedestrians on it. This meant that she spotted Helen well before the creator of the Christmas Genie service reached the door of Toothill's.

When Helen *did* reach the door, and pushed it open, a little bell rang to inform all those in hearing range that someone had either arrived or left.

'How lovely to see you!' Eugenie cried, to inform all those in hearing that she was delighted to see Helen.

Helen smiled. 'You too, Eugenie the Christmas Genie. I've come to ask you a question,' she replied.

'What about?' Eugenie questioned.

'Doing a newspaper article. My friend is a local journalist, and he needs a cheerful story for next week's paper. He knows about Christmas Genie, and wants to write a piece about it. It would mean interviewing you and I, and taking a picture of you. Obviously, I'd love this, because it would spread the word about my idea, but I'm not sure how you'd feel about it,' Helen revealed.

Although Eugenie tried to contain her excitement, it showed in her beaming smile. She couldn't think of a reason *not* to do it, but she *could* think of plenty of reasons *to* do it. Why wouldn't she want the world to know her name, what she looked like, and what she did for a living? Where was the harm in it?

'That sounds great! I'll do it!' Eugenie agreed.

Having secured Eugenie's agreement, Helen slipped her phone out of the pocket of her jeans. She tapped on it a few times to open her contacts app. Once she'd told it to add a contact, she handed it to Eugenie.

'Can you type your *work* mobile in there please so I can give it to my journalist friend?' she asked.

The blank boxes on screen were swiftly filled with the eleven digits of Eugenie's work mobile number. Once done, she typed her name in the box at the top and saved it.

When Eugenie gave Helen her phone back, she shoved it back into her pocket.

'Right then. I'll pass that on, and Oliver will be in touch shortly,' Helen told Eugenie.

Eugenie clapped her hands together. 'I do hope so,' she said.

The phone that Eugenie had typed her work number into started blaring out *Please Don't Let Me Go*. Helen read the screen and shook her head.

'I need to take that. Sorry,' Helen said as she used her left index finger to tap the green circle on her phone screen.

Once she'd answered her phone, Helen dashed out of Toothill's, onto the quiet street outside.

As she'd just received good news, and had the shop to herself, Eugenie decided to twirl around. The thought of what her aunt would say if she could see her inspired Eugenie to laugh and add some skips and hops between her twirls.

When Lily swished the curtain of the fitting room back to show Eugenie her outfit, she was treated to the sight of the shop assistant's pastel pink hair flying past.

'What's got you in such a good mood?' Lily asked.

Eugenie was so absorbed in her joy that she'd forgotten she was at work and had a customer. When reminded of her duties by Lily speaking, she promptly stopped prancing and went a shade of red that complemented an elegant dress she'd put in the window a few days ago.

'Oh, sorry. I just found out I'm going to be in the paper, that's all. It is a small thing, I know, but I like to celebrate *everything*! I find that dancing around about the joys of life, be them little or large, greatly improves your mood. The more you acknowledge your happiness, the happier you feel,' Eugenie explained.

Lily nodded. 'Sounds like a good idea to me. I'd be like that, if only I had the energy,' she said.

As Eugenie had nothing to say to that, silence fell. During that silence, she remembered what her job entailed.

'The dress and shoes really suit you! If you come to the mirror, you'll be able to see for yourself,' Eugenie told Lily.

As it was designed for trying on clothes in, the fitting room had a mirror of its own. This meant that Lily had already seen that the dress and shoes suited her. As pointing this out may upset Eugenie, Lily didn't mention it. She just did as she was told and stood in front of the mirror by the counter, which, like its counterpart in the fitting room, was there for people to look at themselves in.

When she'd set out that day to buy herself an outfit for her work's Christmas do, Lily had tried to picture what she was looking for. It had proved impossible for her to visualise the set of clothes that would look good on her and be suitable to wear around her colleagues, but she'd been able to imagine the feeling the right ensemble would give her. The outfit Eugenie had helped her pick gave Lily that feeling she'd dreamt of.

'Do you like it?' Eugenie asked.

The look on Eugenie's face reminded Lily of the expression her Labrador had had when she'd first seen him at the rescue centre she'd got him from. Had Lily have had to disappoint Eugenie, it would have crushed her almost as much as it would've done if she'd had to leave her now-beloved Lab behind.

'Yes, I love it. This is perfect,' Lily told Eugenie.

Eugenie clapped her hands together, as if she'd just watched the best play in history. 'Oh, I'm so pleased!' she squealed.

Buzzing thanks to the knowledge that Lily loved the outfit she'd picked for her, Eugenie tapped the details into the till and counted out the cash Lily gave her.

-

The buzz Eugenie felt remained throughout the afternoon, and followed her home to the flat. It stayed until, while turning chicken into charcoal, Eugenie realised that Hamish hadn't called her. It had been a week since their date at The Colneside.

CHAPTER TWENTY-NINE

People in kitchens often feel hot. This is partly because kitchens contain appliances that make food, and people, hot, but also due to the fact that they can be stressful. In some cases, they are stressful because of another person in them. Other times, the stress is related to the people who will eat the food prepared in them.

One Sunday, while cooking for Eugenie, Elizabeth, and Victoria, Holly was hot. She was hot because she kept putting things in the oven and forgetting to dodge the cloud of hot air that escaped every time the door was opened, and also due to the stress of having to cook for someone else's family.

As well as monitoring various side dishes, Holly kept an eye on the door to the flat, which would open when Eugenie got back from church with her aunt and mother in tow. She knew when Eugenie usually walked through that door, and that time had been and gone. This only added to Holly's worries. If Eugenie and co were too late, their food would either be burnt or cold.

'Why did I offer to do this? It's not like I have any experience of this. I don't cook for my own family,' Holly muttered to herself as she checked on her Yorkshire puddings.

On the stairs beyond the front door, Holly heard footsteps and chatter. She knew from the light and happy tone of the voice talking that it was Eugenie and her family. Dinner would not be ruined by lateness. In Holly's opinion, it may still be ruined by lack of skill.

Despite knowing Eugenie was outside the door, Holly didn't open it. This was to give the accurate impression that she was busy.

As soon as Eugenie turned her key and opened the door, she cried: 'It smells great!'

To see the food that smelt great, and the girl cooking it, Eugenie dashed into her flat. She was closely followed by Elizabeth and Victoria.

'Hi,' Holly said, waving a hand that was holding a spatula at the newcomers.

'Afternoon. After the Arctic conditions in church, this is like Rio,' Victoria replied, taking a seat at the dining table which Eugenie had laid before leaving.

After getting through the door, Eugenie dashed off to the loo, taking a quick glance at the food as she went.

Rather than sitting next to her sister, Elizabeth walked towards Holly, arms outstretched. 'Hello, darling! Nice to see you again, properly this time! I hear so much about you from my Eugenie. It makes me so happy that she lives with such a nice girl,' she enthused.

It was obvious what Elizabeth wanted from her, so Holly did not resist. She took a step back from her pots and pans so Elizabeth could wrap her up. Being hugged unleashed a wealth of feelings that Holly thought she'd locked up. Those feelings found their way to her eyes, which threatened to leak water. To prevent crying in front of people she barely knew, she redirected her emotions to her arms, which held Elizabeth as tight as possible.

It wasn't until Eugenie returned from the loo that Elizabeth and Holly stopped hugging. When they did, Holly announced: 'Dinner will be about ten minutes.'

-

While Holly plated up, the people she'd cooked the food for debated what the best Christmas carol was. Eugenie said it was *Away In A Manger*, because it is so sweet. Elizabeth suggested *Silent Night*, for its haunting simplicity. Victoria argued that it was *Ding Dong Merrily on High*, simply because it was funny listening to people get out of breath while singing "Gloria, Hosanna in excelsis".

When Holly served up, conversation dried up. No opinion on carols was more important than the food that was now on the table.

Silence remained for the length of time it took Eugenie, Elizabeth, and Victoria to chew and swallow their first mouthfuls. It was the most nerve-wracking few seconds of Holly's life. After realising that, Holly wondered if she'd had a boring twenty-six years.

'This is good. Evidently your inability to cook isn't infectious, Eugenie,' Victoria commented.

'This is more than good. This is the best turkey I've ever tasted. It's so succulent and flavoursome. Everything turkey usually isn't,' Elizabeth added.

Having had feedback from her guests, Holly looked to her flatmate to see what she thought, and saw she was shovelling another mouthful in.

In the few seconds she allowed her mouth to be empty

for, Eugenie told Holly: 'Can't talk. Eating the best food I've ever tasted.'

When Holly herself ate a slice of the turkey, she understood why Eugenie couldn't talk. The garlic and herb butter she'd put on it made her mouth water, which added to the juice from the meat.

While chewing a fluffy Yorkshire pudding, Holly thought: *'I really can cook. I've made them all happy. I'm a good family girl, though not for my own family.'*

CHAPTER THIRTY

The familiar green rectangular box with red logo on was pulled out from the TV unit by Eugenie. She dashed over to the dining table with it and plonked it down.

'Scrabble?' Victoria questioned.

'Yes! It will be fun!' Eugenie replied.

Leaning over to her sister, Elizabeth whispered: 'It will be more fun than Monopoly, which is what she'll want to play if you say no to this.'

As no-one told her not to, Eugenie opened the box and put the board out in the middle of the table. Unopposed, she placed a plastic rack to hold playing pieces in front of herself, Holly, Elizabeth, and Victoria.

'We got this, and a few other board games, given to us at the food bank. Even though they're not food, we put them out for anyone who wants them. They were gone within an hour, and someone came up to us to say how happy they were to have it. It is amazing what a difference a good board game can make to someone,' Elizabeth said.

'I think it's amazing what difference *you* make to people. Being helpful is your entire life, and, although it keeps you busy twenty-four seven, you never complain. Nothing gets between you and a stranger in need,' Eugenie commented.

Elizabeth shrugged. 'I need to put my corporate management background to good use. Otherwise, what was the point of spending all those years in soulless meetings?' she replied.

'Getting pregnant with her was one point,' Victoria pointed out, nodding at Eugenie.

Unnoticed by Eugenie, Elizabeth glared at Victoria.

It was news to Eugenie that her mother had met the man whose genes she had while working as a senior manager.

In preparation for the game of Scrabble she wanted to play, Eugenie removed the drawstring bag of letters from the box and shook it.

'I didn't just mean in your role as area manager at the food bank. Whenever I text or call you, you're always busy with something, and that can't just be your job. I know you do things for your church, and, knowing you, Mother, I guess you help any stranger you come across who needs you,' Eugenie said.

'I do always seem to be busy, yes. I can't help myself. Honestly, I like it that way,' Elizabeth admitted.

The small kitchen-diner was filled with the racket made by 100 plastic tiles being shaken vigorously. After a few seconds of this came a thud as the bag of tiles was placed on the table.

'Okay, let's get on with this. Why don't you start, Auntie? Take seven letters out of the bag,' Eugenie declared, shoving the bag to where her auntie could reach it.

By putting the bag in front of her, Eugenie made Victoria remove seven tiles from the bag. Then, she pushed it over to Holly. After taking her own set of tiles out, Eugenie finally handed the bag to her mother.

To get the game started, Victoria placed "VOLE" in the centre of the board.

'You could have put down "love". That would've been sweet,' Eugenie pointed out.

'Vole is more appropriate to my life. I see voles more often than I see love,' Victoria replied.

'But you're married! You have love for life!' Eugenie cried.

As neither Eugenie's mother nor her flatmate wanted to tell her that marriage didn't guarantee lifelong love, they didn't speak. They *did* share a look that told each other they were thinking the same thing. A look that silently said: 'Bless her.'

'Tell Paul that. Unless you call *love* only talking to me when he wants housework done, and sleeping in the spare room because my snoring keeps him up at night, then I don't have love,' Victoria snapped.

'Are things really that bad?' Elizabeth asked.

Until her sister questioned it, Victoria had thought she was making her situation out to be worse than it actually was. Elizabeth asking made Victoria realise that she wasn't overdramatising. When she tried to open her mouth to confirm that Paul wasn't interested in her anymore, and she was miserable, she found that she couldn't speak.

'Oh, my darling little sister! You need to talk to him,' Elizabeth told Victoria.

When she saw that Victoria's eyes were brimming, Holly took herself off to the bathroom. As she wasn't related to Victoria, she felt it would be rude, and a little bit strange, to watch her cry about her marriage.

'He won't listen. When I try to engage him, he finds an excuse to shut me down, or just walks away,' Victoria whispered.

'If that's so, then maybe it's a lawyer you should talk to, not him,' Elizabeth suggested.

The mention of a lawyer made Eugenie question if she'd been following the conversation properly. As far as she knew, Victoria hadn't accused Paul of a crime.

'This *must* be serious if you're suggesting divorce,' Victoria murmured.

As her aunt and uncle had taken vows before God, it hadn't occurred to Eugenie that her mother was suggesting they divorce. Thinking about divorce made her feel as miserable as her aunt looked. Because she was with her mother, aunt, and flatmate to celebrate Christmas early, she didn't think she could be miserable. As it was supposed to be a celebration, she also thought that her aunt couldn't be miserable either.

'On the subject of love, have I told you about Hamish?' Eugenie asked.

'Yes. Yes, you have. The charming young man who bought you flowers, called you sweet, and is going to call you for another date to follow on from your perfect one at the bowling alley,' Victoria muttered.

For the second time that day, Elizabeth glared at Victoria.

'I saw that you text me about him, but I haven't had a chance to read your messages properly. When is this date?' Elizabeth replied.

'Almost a fortnight ago now,' Eugenie told her mother.

'I meant the *next* one,' Elizabeth explained.

'He hasn't called me yet to arrange it. I'm still waiting. I have checked my voicemail service, and the answerphone here, every day, but there's nothing,' Eugenie replied.

When Elizabeth had skimmed the messages Eugenie had sent her about Hamish, she'd thought her daughter may have at last found someone who'd love her properly, and wouldn't run away. It had been a great relief to her. Considering the amount of time Hamish had been incommunicado for, Elizabeth was beginning to question that, and the relief was fading.

'Have you tried calling him?' Elizabeth asked.

As this was the first time Eugenie had considered calling Hamish, it took a moment for the possibility to sink in. Eventually she declared: 'That's it! Why wait for him? I'm going to call him!'

Before anyone could question her, Eugenie dashed to her handbag, which she'd put on the sofa, and fished her phone out of it. In a blur of fingers and thumbs, she unlocked the phone and opened its contacts. A big swipe up with her index finger put Hamish's number on screen, along with a picture of him gazing into the sea, which Eugenie had taken from Facebook and assigned to his contact profile on her phone. She jabbed the number and put the phone to her ear.

When Holly heard a phone ringing out, she assumed that Victoria had finished talking about her marriage. This meant she felt comfortable to return to the dining table.

After nine rings, Hamish answered. The only reason Eugenie knew he'd answered was that her dial tone stopped and she wasn't directed to a voicemail service.

'Hello, it's Eugenie!' Eugenie said.

'Yes, I saw. Do you need something?' Hamish asked.

One of the many things Eugenie loved about Hamish was his kind and calm voice. That wasn't the voice Hamish was speaking in at that moment though. Based on the way he'd just spoken, Eugenie would call his voice harsh and harassed.

'You... Erm... You said you'd call me,' Eugenie reminded Hamish.

There was a lot of background noise on Hamish's end of the line, including a couple of shrill, loud, and constant voices. Eugenie wondered where he was. It sounded like a cross between a warzone and the racket that escapes from the playgrounds of primary schools at lunchtime.

'Yes, I did. Is that everything?' Hamish replied.

'Well, yes. I just called you because you said you'd call about arranging a date. You said you enjoyed our last one, and you'd call about another one,' Eugenie confirmed, her voice wobbling.

Down the phone, Eugenie heard a thud and a smash, followed by crying.

'I'm busy, okay. if you just called to complain that I've not been in touch yet, then that's now done and you can go, okay. It's all kicking off here,' Hamish told Eugenie.

An obnoxious bloop told Eugenie that the call had been ended. She stared at the phone in disbelief. When the screen went black, she dropped the phone into her bag. With her hands now free, she pinched herself. The fact it hurt confirmed that what had just happened hadn't been a nightmare.

Despite the three sets of eyes on her silently asking what had just happened, Eugenie didn't reveal anything about her phone call. She plodded back to the dining table without a word.

'That didn't sound good. Are you okay?' Holly asked, taking Eugenie's hand.

'It sounded like he was rude,' Victoria commented.

While trying to work out how to describe her exchange with Hamish without bringing everyone's mood down, Eugenie slipped her hand out of Holly's. 'He was busy. I interrupted something. That's okay though. At least he remembers that he said he'd call me. I'm sure he will soon,' she told everyone.

'Has he been constantly busy for two weeks? This is not acceptable, Eugenie. If he's like this when you're dating, imagine what he'd be like as a boyfriend. If I was in your heels, I wouldn't find out. I'd let him know what happens when you break your promises. It's about time men got taught lessons like that,' Victoria replied.

Eugenie had hoped that her loved ones would make excuses for Hamish and justify his behaviour. When it became clear that their feelings were the same as hers, she felt her spirits drop.

Worried that if she opened her mouth, infectious sadness would pour out, Eugenie didn't answer her aunt.

'Maybe he just has a bad telephone manner. Many people, especially those of your age and below, aren't very good on the phone. If you go to see him in person, at work perhaps, then he might be nicer, and you can sort this out,' Elizabeth suggested.

'Yes! That must be it. I'm only working the afternoon tomorrow, so I'll go over to his office in the morning and have a lovely chat and everything will be fixed,' Eugenie instantly agreed.

It occurred to Holly that Elizabeth was wrong. It also occurred to her that to say so would offend and upset Eugenie. *'They've spoken on the phone several times to arrange Christmas Genie meet ups. He can't have a bad telephone manner. If Eugenie breezes into his office, he'll feel harassed, and probably be even worse to her. Poor girl. I really did think this one would stick, but obviously not,'* she thought.

'If he's like my Paul, he just won't listen. Cut your losses, Eugenie. He's just another man who wasn't what he seemed. Just be glad you didn't marry him, so you're not stuck with him,' Victoria muttered.

As if she'd suddenly remembered it was there, Eugenie tapped the Scrabble board in the middle of the table. Looking at Holly, she said: 'Your turn. You've had plenty of time to think about it.'

Holly, and the other people at the table, had indeed had plenty of time to think, but they hadn't spent it thinking about Scrabble. As Eugenie pushed them to, they turned their minds back to the game.

Across Victoria's "VOLE", Holly placed five letters of the word "IGNORE".

CHAPTER THIRTY-ONE

'Hello, MacNicol, Germann, and Associates. How may we help you?' a voice asked over the intercom by the door.

'Good morning! I'm Eugenie, and I'd like to see Hamish, please,' Eugenie replied.

'Oh, hello, Eugenie! You sound exactly how I imagined you would,' the voice on the intercom said.

Outside the offices of MacNicol, Germann, and Associates, Eugenie wondered why the woman on the intercom had imagined her voice.

Inside the offices of MacNicol, Germann, and Associates, the secretary wondered whether Eugenie could cheer their favourite lawyer up.

'Come on up,' the secretary told Eugenie.

The intercom Eugenie had been speaking through buzzed. She pushed the door next to it open and took the stairs behind it two at a time. As she did so, she noticed how worn the brown carpet under her feet was. It inspired her to wonder how many people Hamish and his colleagues had helped.

At the top of the stairs was a desk. Behind that was someone who Eugenie imagined was the person who'd been on the intercom, and a large room lined with shelves of files.

'Hey, nice to meet you, Eugenie. I'm Elaine, secretary here at MacNicol, Germann, and Associates, and I have the pleasure of working with Hamish, four other lawyers, and a paralegal. You'll find Hamish in the first office on the left. His mood is no better today than it has been for the last fortnight, so good luck,' Elaine said, getting up to shake Eugenie's hand.

Having shaken Elaine's hand, and thanked her for her help, Eugenie made her way to the first door on the left, and opened it without knocking. Behind it was Hamish, sat at a desk, hammering away on his computer keyboard.

'Hello! I've come to see you. Maybe you'd like to get a nice, warming soup at a cafe somewhere and we can talk about where to go for our next date,' Eugenie told Hamish.

When Eugenie spoke, Hamish jumped so high that his bottom left the seat of his plain black office chair. 'What are you doing here?!' he cried.

Even though he was now aware of Eugenie's presence, Hamish didn't stand to greet her.

While gliding along the High Street on the way to Hamish, Eugenie had dreamt of the moment when she surprised him at his office. In her daydreams, he been delighted to see her, he'd made her a cup of tea, and he'd chatted about a stately home he'd like to take her to. It surprised her so much that her dream hadn't come true, she couldn't speak.

'I told you I'm busy,' Hamish pointed out.

'That was yesterday,' Eugenie replied.

'Yes, I was busy yesterday too, and for the last two weeks

or so. It's non-stop right now. Why do you think I haven't called you?' Hamish told Eugenie.

'I thought that, like other men, you found me too much to handle. I thought you didn't want to see me again, but didn't know how to say that,' Eugenie explained.

Hamish scoffed. 'No. Why would I do that? I mean what I say. I really do want to go on another date with you, I really am busy, and, if you don't need anything, I really need you to leave me alone for a while,' he said.

While wondering why Hamish seemed so stressed, Eugenie noticed he had bags under his eyes.

'If you've been that busy for so long, then you need a break. Why not come out for lunch with me?' Eugenie suggested.

'Because I can't! I'm not busy for fun! I'm busy because there's so much to do. I cannot afford to go out for lunch. I've got stuff to do. That's why I need you to go, right now!' Hamish snapped.

Whenever Eugenie got angry, which was rare, she took a deep breath, and she kept taking deep breaths until she felt calmer. As Hamish was similar to her, she assumed he'd do the same.

When, after a few seconds, Hamish hadn't taken the deep breaths Eugenie expected him to take, she decided it was her mission to cheer him up. The first step of that was pointing out that he didn't need to be angry.

'What is worth being this worked up about?' Eugenie asked.

'How about my sister being run over by a drunk driver and breaking her leg, me having to help her look after her children because her partner is away in Europe on his lorry, and this all happening when work is mental? I've barely slept, Eugenie. I don't know how I'm still functioning,' Hamish replied.

It took Eugenie a few moments to process that long answer. Finding the positives took even longer.

'So, you're spending more time with your nieces and nephews, and your sister? That's good. I know you love them,' Eugenie said.

The look Hamish gave Eugenie made her shiver. In the moment that their eyes met, the room felt colder than outside.

'Good?! My sister's in agony, and there's a big difference between visiting my nieces and nephews for a few hours and having to live with them and make sure they don't destroy the house while their mother is at a hospital appointment!' Hamish cried.

As if he'd suddenly used up the last of his energy, Hamish let his head fall into his hands. 'I don't know how to keep going. It scares me that I'm just going to stop coping, and I've got people relying on me,' he whispered.

Never before had Eugenie struggled so hard to be positive. There was part of her that wanted to rush over to Hamish and silently hold him tight while he cried and told her about all the things that had happened in the last two weeks. It confused her that she wanted to do that, because she saw it as giving in to negativity.

As Eugenie didn't think giving in to negativity was an option, she tried to think of a helpful suggestion, or something she could help with.

'Surely doctors can put your sister on painkillers? Then she wouldn't be in agony, and, if their mother wasn't in agony, your nieces and nephews would be calmer,' Eugenie pointed out.

Hamish sighed. 'She's on everything they can give her. It's not enough, and what's she's on makes her feel sick,' he told Eugenie.

'Aren't there drugs that would work, that wouldn't make her ill? Haven't you asked?' Eugenie questioned.

'No, this is the best they can do,' Hamish replied.

As hard as she looked, Eugenie couldn't see a solution. That didn't mean she was about to admit that Hamish had good reason to be stressed.

'Think positive. Put a smile on your face and everything will be better. There's no point getting stressed and upset about it all. Hopefully, things will get better soon, and then we can go out together,' Eugenie said.

'Yes, because that's the most important thing in the world, our date(!) You don't care that I really am struggling right now. All that matters to you is that, for fourteen days now, I haven't called you. Well, if it bothers you that much, there's plenty of other men out there. Men whose sisters *haven't* been run over, who *aren't* snowed under with work, and who have much easier lives than me,' Hamish ranted.

The suggestion that she should find another man shocked Eugenie more than anything else Hamish had said in the last few minutes. She couldn't see what she'd done to upset him so much that he didn't want her anymore.

'I *do* care about you, very much. That's why I keep going on about our second date. I don't want another man. I want you. I really want a second date with you, and I think it's just what you need,' Eugenie told Hamish.

'If you genuinely care that much about me, why aren't you listening to me?' Hamish questioned.

That comment confused Eugenie. She could recall most of the conversation they'd just had.

'I *am* listening. Work is busy, and you're having to help you sister with her children because she had an accident, so you're a bit fed up at the moment. From the way you're talking though, you'd think this is the end of the world. So many people are worse off than you. They're getting on with life, so you should too. Chin up, Hamish,' Eugenie replied.

Hamish shook his head. 'I also told you to go. You didn't listen to anything else I said, at least not properly, but please listen to that. Please go, and leave me alone. Don't text, don't call, don't turn up at my workplace unannounced, and don't expect me to contact you any time soon. Walk out that door and leave me to muddle through this mess, please,' he begged.

'But I thought you liked me. I'm just trying to help you. Don't you want me anymore? Are we over? We have a chance together to make something beautiful. If only you could stop being so negative, you'd see that life's not so bad after all, and I'm worth your time,' Eugenie protested.

For the first time since Eugenie had walked into his office, Hamish stood up.

As he strode across the room towards her, Eugenie wondered if Hamish was going to hug her. Every step he took to close the distance between them built the anticipation within her. Warmth flooded through her body, as if she was a robot booting up a "Prepare to be touched by an attractive man" program.

With his gaze firmly on his plain black brogues, Hamish crossed his room to get to the door on the other side. He twisted the cold brass handle on that door and pulled it open. Standing by the way out of his office, Hamish lifted his gaze to meet Eugenie's, and nodded at the room beyond his office.

The disappointment Eugenie felt when she realised Hamish wasn't going to hug her was quickly topped by the disappointment of being shown out of his office without so much as a goodbye.

As she passed Hamish, Eugenie couldn't help saying: 'Goodbye. For what it's worth, I loved knowing you. Thank you.'

For the twenty seconds or so it took her to escape the offices of MacNicol, Germann, and Associates, Eugenie listened intently for the sound of Hamish's voice calling her name. All she heard was the slamming of a heavy door.

On her walk away from the offices of MacNicol, Germann, and Associates, Eugenie found her feet, and legs, and head, felt heavier than they had on the way there. Every step was a struggle, but a necessary one, for she had to get to Toothill's for her afternoon shift.

CHAPTER THIRTY-TWO

On her way home from Toothill's, Eugenie stopped off at a corner shop to buy a couple of microwave meals. This meant that, when she got back to the flat, she could just flop down on the sofa instead of having to slave over the stove.

The first thing Eugenie saw when she opened the door to her flat was her black corduroy sofa. All she wanted to do was curl up on it. As she dumped the ready meals she'd bought in the fridge so she could do just that, it occurred to her that not cooking because she didn't feel up to it was giving in to negativity. That was something she couldn't do.

Although it was the last thing she wanted to do, Eugenie dragged herself to the fridge and searched its contents for the makings of a meal.

-

In an attempt to ignore the memories flying around her head of the conversation she'd had with Hamish, and the comments her aunt had made when she'd told her about that conversation, Eugenie focused harder than she ever had before on the food she was cooking. This meant that, when Holly walked through the door, it was neither burnt nor undercooked.

'You have perfect timing. This is ready,' Eugenie told Holly as the receptionist hung up her coat.

'Thanks for that. You sound very chirpy. I'm guessing that your meeting with Hamish went well,' Holly replied.

The reason Eugenie sounded chirpy was because her meeting with Hamish *hadn't* gone well, and she was trying to cover up how much that'd upset her. Even though she'd spent hours hiding her misery from customers and, to an extent, her aunt, she didn't feel she could hide it from her flatmate if they talked about it.

'Let's not talk about that right now. I think I've actually done a good job with dinner, and I don't want it to get cold while we chat,' Eugenie said.

Suspecting nothing, Holly accepted this. She sat down at the table, which Eugenie had already laid, and tapped her tablemat with her cutlery.

Onto the tablemat Holly tapped, Eugenie placed a bowl of warm stew.

The moment it was in front of her, Holly put a mouthful of stew in her mouth. As soon as she'd swallowed that mouthful, Holly said: 'I'm glad you're happy to chat later. I can't talk now. I'm eating the best thing you've ever put in front of me.'

Knowing that she'd provided Holly with a good meal made it a little bit easier for Eugenie to pretend to be happy. *Eating* that good meal made it easier still.

-

Much to Holly's disappointment, she eventually emptied her bowl. Scraping the edges with her spoon failed to magically produce more stew.

With her food gone, Holly remembered that she hadn't yet heard about how Eugenie's visit to Hamish's work had gone. She was eager to hear about it, not only because she cared about Eugenie's love life, but also because her own day had been challenging, so she could do with the distraction that hearing about someone else's day provided.

'Thank you for that delicious dinner. While it goes down, why don't you tell me how things went with Hamish?' Holly asked.

In the few seconds she had to think about it, Eugenie realised that refusing to talk about Hamish would reveal her feelings. If she wanted to hide how upset she was about what had happened with Hamish, she had to talk about it.

'Oh, his lovely secretary sent me through to his office as soon as I got there. We had a chat, and decided to end things,' Eugenie revealed.

Holly's mouth gaped open. 'You ended things? Oh, Eugenie! Why? I thought you liked him, and I was so sure that he liked you,' she questioned.

To give herself thinking time, Eugenie took the dirty bowls and cutlery from the table to the sink. If Holly pushed too hard, Eugenie worried she might crumble, and drag her flatmate's mood down.

On her return from the sink, Eugenie worked out how to explain to Holly why she and Hamish had broken up without revealing her emotions. She remembered the conversation she'd had with Hamish word for word, so she could repeat it to Holly without saying how those words had made her feel.

-

While listening to Eugenie recounting her exchange with Hamish, Holly found herself having to bite her tongue to stop herself interrupting. When she'd found out that Eugenie and Hamish had agreed to split, Holly had assumed it was because Hamish was moving away, or had suffered a brain injury that had damaged his common sense. The real story was nothing like what she'd anticipated, and yet it wasn't a shock to her. When she recalled conversations she'd had with Eugenie, she could understand Hamish's feelings. Though she didn't wish to admit so to her friend, Holly could understand Hamish's feelings more than Eugenie's.

'It was clear he wanted rid of me, so I left. I did tell him I'd loved knowing him when I said goodbye,' Eugenie told Holly, ending her story.

Holly knew it was her duty as Eugenie's friend to explain why Hamish had got so cross with her. Contemplating how to tell Eugenie she'd done wrong felt like preparing to kick a puppy. Nausea rose through Holly's body. She ignored it, and focused on what she had to say.

'It sounds like Hamish is having a hard time right now. I know you struggle to deal with difficult feelings, even your own. You *don't* deal with them. You just brush over them,' Holly told Eugenie.

There was something familiar about Holly's words. 'Auntie said I ignore other people's hardships. She even suggested that I didn't listen to Hamish, and that was why he got so cross. I remember every word he said though. That's how I was able to repeat them to you. When people are unhappy, I cheer them up. I tried to cheer Hamish up, but he wouldn't let me,' Eugenie said.

The fact that a member of Eugenie's own family had said similar to her gave Holly hope that she may actually listen. That Eugenie would hear the words she had to say, and not just memorise them like she had her conversation with Hamish.

'I think what your aunt Victoria means is that there's a difference between listening to someone and hearing them. You may have listened to Hamish, but you didn't hear him. Far from cheering him up, you've probably made him feel worse,' Holly replied.

'But, I couldn't just let him wallow in misery. What good does that do? Negativity doesn't do anyone any good. It's my duty to drag others, and myself, out of pointless misery. If everyone could just put their little upsets into context, put them to one side, and get on with life, the world would be a better place,' Eugenie argued.

In an attempt to stop herself screaming at Eugenie for not listening, Holly zoned out on the conversation. The second she stopped concentrating on Eugenie, she remembered another conversation she'd had that day. One that Eugenie would probably call "a little upset". To Holly, that label was only half true. The thought that she couldn't share something that was bothering her with someone who was supposed to be her closest friend infuriated the usually-calm Holly. It wasn't the first time that day when she'd felt like losing her temper, but it *was* the first time she didn't stop herself.

The fury and disappointment that Holly had felt earlier in the day combined with the present irritation of not being properly heard by Eugenie to make her burn with rage. It exploded out in the words: 'Grow up, Eugenie! People get sad. It happens. You have to be able to accept and acknowledge that. All you do by ignoring it is make it worse, for yourself and others!'

The volume and tone of Holly's voice shocked both her and Eugenie. They stared at each other for a few seconds, as if acknowledging this.

'Holly, that wasn't very nice. I'm only trying to be helpful,' Eugenie said, feeling the need to break the silence.

'Well, you're *not* being helpful! The very reason I'm this het up is because I had an awful phone call at lunchtime. As my friend, I should be able to share it with you. If I do though, then you won't understand why I'm so upset. You'll just tell me that there are people worse off than me and I have no right to moan. Do you have any idea how that makes me feel? You pat yourself on the back for being a good girl and spreading happiness, but all you've done today is kick two people who were already down. *And*, when I try to explain it, you won't listen! You should be *ashamed* of yourself, Eugenie, not *proud*!' Holly snapped.

When Eugenie opened her mouth to defend herself, she found her throat felt closed up. Her whole face felt hotter, especially around her eyes, and her mind was hazy. She couldn't speak, or think, and the more she tried, the worse it got. Like when a thunderstorm breaks, Eugenie suddenly found tears flooding out of her eyes, and wails escaping her mouth. She was full-on sobbing.

'And now *you're* crying. Can't you see that, as unpleasant as this is, it's human?' Holly questioned.

The only answer Holly got was Eugenie's tears intensifying.

All Eugenie wanted to do was stop sobbing, but she had

no idea how. Her feelings were so intense. She felt that, without some kind of intervention, it could go on forever. Help was needed, but Eugenie felt that, as she'd infuriated her, Holly couldn't provide that help. Only one person she knew could.

To get herself help, Eugenie got up, still sobbing, and found her way to the front door.

'Wait, where are you going?' Holly questioned, getting up to stop Eugenie.

In between her sobs, Eugenie uttered: 'Need Mother.'

Unsure what to do, Holly let Eugenie leave.

By the time Eugenie reached the street outside her flat, her noisy sobs had turned to silent tears. The feelings that had caused them remained just as intense. It worried Eugenie that the smallest thing could tip her back over the edge. She didn't seem to have much control over herself at that moment in time.

Eugenie's mother's hotel was out of town, too far away to walk to. Eugenie used an app she'd used many times before to book a cab to it. She was grateful that modern technology meant she didn't have to speak to anyone.

Once her taxi was silently arranged, Eugenie stood in the street, hoping that the car she'd booked had its heating on.

-

From her flatmate's bedroom window, Holly kept an eye on Eugenie. She watched her until a taxi picked her up. Once Eugenie was out of sight, Holly searched Facebook for an Elizabeth Holland.

CHAPTER THIRTY-THREE

The hotel Eugenie's taxi dropped her off at was a small independent one. It reminded her of Bridge House Hotel, until she walked into the lobby and realised it wasn't as swish as Holly's workplace.

The staff of the hotel which wasn't as swish as Holly's workplace were very helpful. As Eugenie was able to tell them which room Elizabeth Holland was in, they allowed her to find her own way to it.

When Eugenie knocked on the door with the number 13 on it in brass, her mother opened it without greeting her. This was because Elizabeth was on the phone.

'Even when she's hundreds of miles from it, work keeps her busy,' Eugenie thought.

'No, you were absolutely right to call. You don't need to worry anymore though, because she's here, in one piece. I'm going to speak to her now, so I'll say goodbye,' Elizabeth told whoever she was on the phone to.

'Not work then. Someone who's worried about me? Who?' Eugenie thought.

As she searched for the button to hang up her phone, Elizabeth gestured at Eugenie to sit on the bed.

Eugenie did as she was directed to do. She sank down onto the king-sized bed and waited for her mother to tell her who had called.

When Elizabeth sat next to Eugenie, the bed creaked. This seemed to escape her notice. 'That was Holly. Apparently, you two had a row, and you walked out in floods of tears saying you needed me. She wanted to make sure you got here safe, but didn't follow you because she thought you needed space from her,' she revealed.

'Oh, I didn't expect her to care,' Eugenie murmured.

'Because you had a row?' Elizabeth questioned.

Eugenie nodded. 'I never meant to upset her though, or anyone. It wasn't my fault. All I do is my best to spread joy and love, and be helpful,' she claimed.

In twenty-three years, Elizabeth has never seen Eugenie so drained and lacklustre. It unsettled her. To comfort her out-of-sorts daughter, Elizabeth wrapped her arm around Eugenie and gazed into her dull grey eyes. The physical and eye contact brought a little smile to Eugenie's face.

'Why don't you explain to me what you have argued about with Hamish, Victoria, and Holly?' Elizabeth suggested.

The very reason Eugenie had gone to her mother was to tell her about all the disagreements she'd had that day. None of them made sense to her, and they were all weighing on her mind. She hoped Elizabeth could give her some peace by confirming that she'd done the right thing, and it was coincidence that she'd wound up three people in one day.

'Hamish was cross with me for visiting. He's been busy, which is why he hasn't called. He's having to spend more time with his nieces and nephews because his sister has had a little accident, and his work is always demanding. It's plain to see that it's getting him down. I tried to cheer him up, and show him that it's not as bad as he's making it out to be, but he couldn't see it. He got really angry, and showed me out without giving me a goodbye. Of course, I told Auntie and Holly about this, separately, and they both said I didn't listen to Hamish. Holly say that I've made Hamish feel worse, and her too, because she's had a bad day and doesn't feel like she can talk about it. Holly even claimed that ignoring misery makes it worse, for me and others. This is wrong though, I know it. Being miserable doesn't do any good. When I tried to point this out to Holly, she exploded at me. She's never done anything like that before. It shocked me so much that I burst into tears, and couldn't stop myself. That's why I ran out. I didn't want to inflict that sadness on her, or anyone. I came here because I knew you'd be able to fix me,' Eugenie blurted out.

Since a minute after answering Holly's phone call, Elizabeth has known she had to have a difficult conversation with Eugenie. Knowing it was coming didn't make it any easier though. She had to make a point that three other people had already made, and somehow get it through to Eugenie when they'd all failed. It wouldn't be easy, but it was necessary, for the good of Eugenie and all who knew her.

'*Acting* positive and happy when we're not doesn't *make* us happy and positive. Pretending to be happy when you're not is pointless, as is expecting others to hide their feelings. Accepting your feelings, even the ones you don't like, makes them easier to deal with. If you try to clamp down on and ignore your feelings, they'll eventually return, stronger than ever. Your attitude, to your own difficult feelings and others people's, isn't helpful. The best thing you can do is make someone feel heard, not make them feel that they can't express their true feelings,' Elizabeth told Eugenie.

Still, Eugenie was confused. 'But, I thought being bright and cheerful was a good thing? Negativity is bad. The clue is in the name. I'm an incurable optimist. Surely that's a good thing?' she questioned.

Elizabeth shook her head. 'Genuine optimism is great! That's not what we're talking about though. Optimism is being hopeful about the future and believing it will be better than the dark times life throws at you sometimes. It's a good thing, because having confidence that things will improve gets you through challenges. You don't have to ignore the fact that things are challenging in order to hope they one day won't be though. *That's* the difference. What I'm talking about is you disregarding the fact that life is hard sometimes. That makes people feel ignored and that you're not listening to them properly. It can also make them feel like they're a burden, because they're not bright and sunny all the time. Also, darling, you once promised not to lie. This, hiding your feelings and suppressing other people's, is *lying*, she explained.

As her mother told her where she'd gone wrong, Eugenie began to realise the impact her mistakes had had. Shame settled on her like a heavy and unwanted cloak.

'And I've been doing this to people. People in desperate need who I'm supposed to love and support. I really thought I was doing the right thing. I thought I had to not give in to negativity. I see now though, that there's a difference between giving in to it and facing it head on. It takes a lot of effort to ignore unhappy feelings, and now I know all that effort has only made people feel worse. The thought that I've hurt people like that makes me sick. I pride myself on being a good person, but really I'm anything but,' Eugenie muttered.

'It's not just other people this sort of thinking harms. When turned inwards, so you start ignoring your own feelings and pretending you're always in a good place, it harms you too. This will actually have done you more damage than your loved ones. This doesn't make you a bad person though. You're misguided, not malicious,' Elizabeth added.

'So many times, I've felt awful, and I've hidden it. I thought that wearing a smile would make me feel better, but, thinking about it, it never did. All those feelings are still there. They're bubbling away under the surface,' Eugenie realised out loud.

When she looked into her daughter's eyes, Elizabeth could see the emotions that were pushing to come out. Eugenie was like a bottle of fizzy pop that had been shaken.

All Elizabeth wanted was to take Eugenie's pain away, but she knew she couldn't do that. The best thing she could do was end her suffering. To do that, she wrapped her up in the tightest hug possible.

Being held close by her mother lifted the lid on everything Eugenie had been holding back. All the little upsets and major distresses of life came flooding out in the form of water from her eyes. The sheer power of releasing all her feelings made her shiver. A few hours ago, allowing herself to cry like this would've been unthinkable to Eugenie. Now it was all she could do, it didn't feel so bad.

-

While sobbing in her mother's arms, Eugenie lost all concept of time. She was completely unaware that fifteen minutes passed.

Unlike her daughter, Elizabeth knew how long Eugenie cried for. When she considered how long Eugenie had been bottling up her feelings for, it made sense to her.

When Eugenie stopped crying, Elizabeth asked: 'Do you feel better now?'

'Yes. I feel better in myself than I have for a long time. How strange. I'd have thought weeping like this would have the opposite effect,' Eugenie replied.

'There's nothing like a good cry to sort your head out. It's like a relief valve for your emotions. Good ones as well as bad ones, because you cry when you're deliriously happy as well as when you're desperately sad. Of course, there are times when you *can't* cry, because you're at work for example. If you *can* cry though, why *not*? It's the most wonderful thing,' Elizabeth said.

Now that she felt better in herself, Eugenie's thoughts turned to others. As he so often did recently, Hamish popped into her head. Thinking about their last meeting earlier that day made her blush. Then there was Holly, her beloved flatmate and closest friend, who she'd also upset. Eugenie longed for a time machine so she could undo the extra pain she'd caused them on top of what they were already suffering. As the TARDIS exists only in fiction, all she could do was apologise.

From that moment onward, Eugenie wanted to live her

life differently. She wanted to confront her own difficult feelings, and support others with theirs, instead of burying them. It would be her new year's resolution, but she wouldn't wait until January to put it into action. The only problem was, she wasn't sure how to change herself.

'What do I do? Most of the time, I really do feel happy. When I'm happy, I want to laugh, and twirl, and sing. I don't want others to feel that they can't be *unhappy* around me though,' Eugenie questioned.

'Oh, you can still be happy! As I said, optimism is a good thing. The reason so many people love you is because you're so sunny. It gets you through hard times. I don't remember who said it, but someone said something about laughing with people when they are happy and comforting them when they are sad. You adapt for what mood you, and those around you, are in. My best advice to you is to just be yourself. Have faith in your ability to read other people,' Elizabeth told Eugenie.

As Eugenie had no words of wisdom to offer in return, she stayed silent. It worried her that facing the harder emotions of life would be too much for her to handle, but she knew she had to do it, so she didn't say so.

Elizabeth knew the impact her words were having. She could imagine the thoughts going through Eugenie's head as she planned to change the way she dealt with emotions. From experience, she knew how daunting the prospect of altering your very self was. Thinking about Eugenie making significant changes reminded Elizabeth of how she'd felt twenty-four years ago when she'd realised that her life was going to change forever. She remembered how hard it was. She also remembered how she'd got through it.

'Keep in mind, Eugenie, that you don't have to do this alone. You are a much-loved young lady. You have support. If you ever need to talk to someone, there are plenty of people to listen. I'm just a phone call away, I'm sure Holly would do *anything* for you, even Victoria would listen to you if you were desperate, and that's without even mentioning the charities you can call on if need be. As well as all that, you have the greatest support of all. You have the love of God. He's always there. His love has got me through some of the biggest challenges I've ever faced,' Elizabeth pointed out.

'I think He sent me here. When Holly was cross with me and I broke down, all I could think was that I had to get to you. The urge to see you seemed to come from nowhere, and was my only clear thought. You have helped me more than I could have imagined. This has been literally life-changing. He may well have planned that,' Eugenie replied.

With a knowing smile, Elizabeth said: 'He is always there when you need Him.'

CHAPTER THIRTY-FOUR

The street was eerily quiet when the taxi dropped Eugenie off outside her flat. It reassured Eugenie that the street-lights were still on, and the taxi driver watched her enter the building.

When she opened the door, Eugenie was surprised to find the light on in the kitchen-diner. She'd have expected Holly to turn it off when she'd gone to bed.

Eugenie was even more surprised when Holly herself got up off the sofa and said: 'I'm so glad you're home safe.'

The second Eugenie saw Holly, all the guilt she felt about the last conversation she'd had with her came rushing back. 'Oh, Holly! I'm so sorry about the way I spoke to you. Mother explained how wrong it was, and how I made you feel. It makes me so sad to think I did that to someone. Several someones, actually. Hamish and auntie Victoria got similar treatment. I really am so sorry. I don't know how to make it up to you,' she blurted out.

Holly shook her head. 'It's me who should be sorry. I'm in such a mood today. It's not your fault, but I took it all out on you. All you were doing was trying to help,' she replied.

Tiredness caught up with Eugenie. It announced itself in the form of a yawn.

The yawn made its way to Holly, who covered it with her hand. It prompted her to look at the clock on the wall. *That* prompted her to think about what time her alarms were set for.

'We need to go to bed,' Holly said.

'Yes, we have work tomorrow. Thank you for staying up to see me get home. You didn't have to,' Eugenie replied.

As she plucked her book off the arm of the sofa, Holly told Eugenie: 'It's alright. It meant that I got to read some of my book.'

On account of the time, and all the neighbours being asleep, the flat fell silent when Eugenie and Holly weren't talking. This meant that, when Eugenie's phone announced it had received an email, both she and Holly jumped. They then both laughed about the fact that they'd jumped at a phone alert.

When the laughter subsided, Eugenie felt the need to show Holly that she understood what she'd done wrong. She thought it would help them both sleep. 'Tomorrow, after work, would you like to tell me about the bad phone call you had today? I promise to hear you. Not just to listen, but to properly take in what you are saying, and not tell you to stop being miserable or that there are worse things in life. I want to be a proper friend and comfort you,' she offered.

'Erm, yes. Sharing it would be great. Are you sure though? I know you really struggle with difficult feelings, and trust me, I have a lot of difficult feelings right now,' Holly questioned.

Eugenie nodded firmly. 'Yes! I have decided to stop avoiding and ignoring those more challenging emotions, and face them head on. In the last few hours, I have learnt how good that can be,' she confirmed.

Looking at Eugenie's red and puffy eyes, Holly could see she'd been crying. It seemed like that had done her good though. She wondered if her friend really *had* changed. Sharing the phone call she'd had from her mother, and how it had made her feel, would be a good test of that.

Thinking about the next day made Holly yawn again.

'Right, bedtime now!' Eugenie declared, walking towards her bedroom door.

Heading for her own room, Holly replied: 'Yes, definitely. Goodnight, fab flatmate. Sleep well.'

As she and Holly reached the doors to their respective rooms, Eugenie called out: 'You too, Holly. Love you.'

CHAPTER THIRTY-FIVE

'I'm glad you slept well, because I need you to go through this. It's our last delivery until the new year, so it'd better all be there,' Victoria told Eugenie, tapping a pile of boxes that had been dropped off before the shop had opened to the public.

The thought of looking through new clothes filled Eugenie with joy. She expressed this joy by tearing at the boxes as if they contained cake and she was ravenous and had a sweet tooth.

'I'll leave you to it,' Victoria said.

Dazzled by a dress covered in silver sequins, Eugenie ignored her aunt.

-

Although processing new clothes is an exciting and absorbing task, Eugenie always paid attention to what she could hear from the shop floor. It was an unspoken rule that, if Eugenie and Victoria were both in the shop, they kept an ear out for each other, and appeared by the other one's side at the first sign of trouble.

'Hi, Victoria. Is Eugenie here?' Eugenie heard someone ask Victoria.

'Oh my, it's you! How *dare* you show your face in here?!' Victoria replied.

The anger in Victoria's voice caught Eugenie's attention. Wanting to see who had angered Victoria so much with their mere presence, Eugenie edged her way to a point where she could just about see out onto the shop floor. All she saw was a customer with no hair who looked to be of around Victoria's age. He didn't look threatening.

'I want to see Eugenie. I want to see my daughter,' the customer told Victoria.

The revelation that the customer was her father froze Eugenie. She wasn't sure whether to run out and introduce herself to the man she'd wondered about all her life, or run away from the man who'd abandoned her pregnant mother.

Victoria scoffed. 'Your *daughter*? You have no right to call her that. You have no right to be here either. Get out, Jason! Do you think, after what you did to my sister, that I'll let you hurt my niece too?' she snapped.

Never before had Eugenie seen a face as disappointed as Jason's when Victoria refused to help. It brought a lump to her throat.

'I was so young. When Liz told me, I was terrified,' Jason said.

'Don't talk to *me* about being scared. I was *Elizabeth's* birth partner. That day, in the delivery room, I saw what fear truly looks like. *You* caused that, and then you didn't stick around to help. Don't you stick around *now*. It's too late. *Now*, you *should* run away, before I call the police to have you removed,' Victoria ranted.

A single tear rolled down Jason's cheek. When she saw it, Eugenie moved to where she could be seen.

When Victoria saw Eugenie out of the corner of her eye, she put a hand out to stop her getting to Jason, or Jason getting to her.

'Eugenie, my daughter! I'm Jason, your dad. Well, the man who got your mum pregnant. I suppose I don't suppose I deserve the title of "dad". I wanted you to know who I am. I wanted to see you. Your aunt won't let me stay though, so I must go. At least I got to see how beautiful you've become,' Jason called to Eugenie.

The lump in Eugenie's throat got bigger as she listened to the first words her father had ever said to her. It prevented her from answering.

'Out!' Victoria barked.

Jason was turning to leave before Victoria shouted at him. All her one word did was speed him up.

When Victoria caught the look in Eugenie's eyes as they both watched Jason leave, she knew exactly what she was thinking. 'Don't. He's scum. Just think of the situation he left your mother in,' she said.

'But he's my father,' Eugenie replied.

Slipping past her aunt's arm, Eugenie dashed out of the shop.

Once out on the icy bricks of the Lane outside Toothill's, Eugenie couldn't run.

As he was in trainers, not high heels, and he cared less about safety than Eugenie did, Jason *could* run.

To stop Jason running back out of her life, Eugenie called:

'Father! It's me, Eugenie! Wait!'

The words echoing off the buildings were exactly the ones Jason had hoped for. They caused him to stop and turn around.

Across the cold grey bricks of the Lanes, Eugenie took the few steps that separated her from her father.

'Why now?' Eugenie asked, as it was the first question that popped into her head.

'I can't tell you on this Arctic street,' Jason replied.

Eugenie needed answers. On the spot, she decided to see her father again to get those answers.

'Can I give you my number? If you call me after five today, we can arrange to meet somewhere so we can talk. If that's okay with you, that is,' Eugenie suggested.

From the way his eyes lit up, Eugenie guessed that it was more than *alright* for her to give Jason her number.

'Yeah, that's perfect! You're so generous, Eugenie. That, you get from your mum. Liz had the biggest heart I'd ever seen,' Jason replied.

The mention of her mother made Eugenie uncomfortable. She wasn't sure Elizabeth would approve of her meeting up with Jason.

Before guilt stopped her, Eugenie got her phone out and asked for her father's number. When he gave it to her, she called it. That meant he then had *her* number for later.

'You ran out without a coat, bless you! Having just found you, I don't want you to die of pneumonia. Actually, I don't want to die of anything. I'd best let you get back to Victoria,' Jason said.

For the first time ever, Eugenie laughed at a joke her

father made. 'As much as I want to ask you about anything and everything right now, I know you are right. I've got work to do, and I'm sure you do to,' she replied.

'Yeah, must be sensible. Cheerio, Eugenie,' Jason agreed.

'Goodbye, Father,' Eugenie said.

With a smile and a wave, Eugenie and Jason parted ways.

The heating in Toothill's welcomed Eugenie as she re-entered the shop. The scowl on her aunt's face did not.

'You can't have anything to do with a man like that! What are you thinking, Eugenie,' Victoria questioned.

'I have to know,' Eugenie told her.

That explanation wasn't enough for Victoria, but Eugenie had said all that she wished to say, so she took herself off to her boxes of clothes in the backroom. The clothes were to be her only company for the rest of the shift.

CHAPTER THIRTY-SIX

'One of many things I learnt yesterday is that I cook better when I pay attention,' Eugenie told Holly after she complimented her food for the second day in a row.

Holly laughed. 'I could have told you that! No wonder you burn everything if you're away with the fairies when you're supposed to be keeping an eye on the oven,' she replied.

Good food had created an atmosphere in the flat that was at least twenty degrees warmer than outside, where a layer of frost was already claiming the parked cars, pavements, and windowsills. It was so nice that Eugenie didn't want to spoil it by dragging up what had upset Holly yesterday.

To buy herself a few more seconds of happiness, Eugenie cleared the plates. On her way to dump them in the sink, she reminded herself that deep and emotional conversations were good, and would in time create even more warmth. It was like putting logs on a roaring fire. When you first put a new log on, the fire is less beautiful, but when it catches, it is better than ever.

Picturing a cosy fire in a wood-burning stove, Eugenie sat herself down across from Holly and said: 'If you feel like it, tell me about yesterday. I'm ready to hear you.'

'My mother called from Australia. It's the first time she's been in touch since my nephew was born. I thought, having not spoken to me for the best part of a year, she'd want to catch up. That wasn't the case though. I should've known. My mother only gets in touch when there's a task that needs completing,' Holly told Eugenie.

There was a strong note of bitterness in Holly's tone. It made Eugenie want to hold Holly. She took Holly's hand across the table. Holly had often held Eugenie's hand when she thought she was sad, so she guessed that she'd appreciate the gesture being returned.

'I'm sorry that she doesn't call just for a chat. What was this task that prompted her to finally get in touch?' Eugenie asked.

'Presents. Christmas and my birthday are both coming up. My mother wanted to inform me that she wasn't going to bother with presents and cards anymore, and neither should I. With us being thousands of mile apart, it apparently is too much faff to arrange to send a bit of cardboard with some nice words on it and something nice but unnecessary that can gather dust forever. When I argued, she thought I was being greedy, and that I was just cross because I've already arranged and paid for my presents to them. It's not greed though. That's not why it bothers me. I'm not a materialistic girl,' Holly replied.

It amazed Eugenie that a mother could treat their daughter like that. If her mother had moved abroad, not kept in touch with her, and then refused to even send her a Christmas card, she'd feel unloved, like she didn't matter.

Although Holly was a very different person to her, she imagined that she felt similar.

'In my new role as The Christmas Genie, I've seen how much presents matter. My clients have had different budgets, different requirements, and very different family situations, but the smile on a person's face when they see the perfect gift for their loved one is the same every time. It's nothing to do with the value of the item, and everything to do with what it will mean to the person they'll give it to. It's the thought that counts, or the lack of thought in your case,' Eugenie said.

When Holly didn't immediately answer, Eugenie wondered if she'd made a mistake. 'Oh, am I wrong? Have I completely misunderstood? I'm so sorry,' she questioned.

Holly squeezed Eugenie's hand and smiled. 'No, you've got my point perfectly. I'm so glad it's not just me who can see it. I know it's a small thing and, as Sally at work pointed out, some people don't even have mother's to send them presents, but it really upset me. My brother is a good man, he always has been, but *I'm* a good *woman*. My parents worship him, they moved to the other side of the world partly so they could be with him, but they won't even send me a card. They don't want me,' she ranted.

'Oh, Holly. I can't imagine anyone not wanting you. You're such a kind-hearted girl. I hear how upsetting this must be, and you've done nothing to deserve it. You are a lovely girl. *My* mother loves you, and so do I,' Eugenie told Holly.

'Thanks. Just being heard makes me feel better. Given time, the hurt will pass,' Holly replied.

For no obvious reason, Eugenie wondered if she'd put all the items for the fridge and freezer away when she'd brought some shopping home after work that day. When she pictured that shopping, she could remember putting everything in its place. There was one item that might need moving though, and moving very soon.

'Do you think some cinnamon biscuits would help the hurt pass?' Eugenie asked with a smile.

'Yes! I know they would!' Holly confirmed.

In order to help Holly, Eugenie skipped to the kitchen counter, where she'd left cinnamon biscuits and a few other treats. The packet of cinnamon biscuits were swiped off the counter and hurried back to the table, where Holly was waiting for them with outstretched hands.

When Eugenie returned to her seat opposite Holly, she noticed there was a huge smile on her flatmate's face. *'Wow, the biscuits must be magic. She hasn't even eaten them yet, and look how much happier she is,'* she thought.

'You're wonderful, Eugenie! Our row yesterday was six of one and half a dozen of the other, so you don't have to make it up to me, but you just did,' Holly told Eugenie.

'Ah, thank you! I'm glad you like the biscuits so much,' Eugenie replied.

When Holly opened the packet of biscuits, their spicy scent escaped and filled the little flat. After Holly pulled the tray out, two biscuits escaped, or, more accurately, were pinched.

To Eugenie, chewing the biscuit was like holding a Christmas party in her mouth. The warm sensation it released made her feel like it was Christmas already.

Once she'd eaten her first biscuit, which took a considerable amount of time, Holly said: 'These are *incredible*, but buying them isn't what makes you wonderful. You are wonderful because you are you. You who cares about her friends, who highlights and celebrates all the good in life like a ray of sunshine, and *now* you who hears her friend's struggles and comforts them.'

As her friend, Holly knew Eugenie would be desperately trying to find kind and sweet words to answer her compliment. 'I know what you're thinking, but don't worry about it. You paid me a lovely compliment earlier, when you called me kind-hearted,' she told her.

Holly knowing what she was thinking warmed Eugenie even more than the cinnamon biscuit had. Thinking of the cinnamon biscuit she'd had made Eugenie want more of them.

As she took another biscuit for herself, Eugenie said: 'Let's polish these off.'

CHAPTER THIRTY-SEVEN

It was only when Eugenie left church for the last time before Christmas Day that she realised how close it was. When she thought about how few days work she had left to do, it seemed even more real.

Her favourite day of the year being a week away left Eugenie in a daze. She wandered down the path away from church not paying much attention to her surroundings.

When Eugenie came across a person who deliberately blocked her path and said her name, she began to focus again. What she focused *on* was Hamish, standing right in front of her.

'Hamish!' Eugenie squeaked.

'Yes, that's my name,' Hamish replied with a smile.

The rush of excitement Eugenie had felt when she'd spotted Hamish was replaced by shame as she remembered how they'd parted. She found that she couldn't look at the face she had once desperately wanted to see.

'I'm sorry about what happened in your office,' Eugenie mumbled.

'So am I. I'm most sorry about the ending,' Hamish replied.

'Which bit?' Eugenie questioned.

'The part where you dumped me, and I let you,' Hamish reminded Eugenie.

Until that moment, it hadn't occurred to Eugenie that she'd dumped herself. Yes, Hamish had been rude to her and shown her out of the office, but he hadn't ended their relationship; *she* had.

'If I undumped you, would you take me back?' Eugenie asked.

'Yes, if *you* wanted *me* back. That day, and many days around it, are unclear in my memory, but I remember being an unmitigated and comprehensive ass,' Hamish pointed out.

Eugenie expressed the joy of fixing her relationship with Hamish with a slight squeal and a little shoulder wiggle. This made a few of her fellow churchgoers frown, but the only reaction she saw was Hamish's, which was a smile.

'Is it wishful thinking to take that as confirmation we're back together?' Hamish questioned.

'That's *exactly* how I meant it to come across. Why else would I be so happy? Yes, your behaviour was... Frosty and hostile that day, but I know that's not you. I also know that I made things much worse. If you really do want to try again, then I promise to *hear* you in future, and not brush your emotions or mine under the carpet,' Eugenie confirmed.

'As I'm not as sweet as you, I don't cheer or dance to express joy. That doesn't mean I'm not ecstatic though. That day was a one-off, I can promise you that. Never before have I ranted and raged like that, and it won't happen again,' Hamish replied.

The gravel path from the church's front door to the road was narrow, and completely blocked by Eugenie and Hamish chatting on it. A few of the people who had to walk on the grass tutted at them. Eugenie was so used to being tutted at that she didn't notice. Hamish was so captivated by Eugenie that *he* didn't notice.

A distant car horn made Hamish notice the world around him, including a clock on the church.

'I've got to go and make sure my brother-in-law doesn't use every pot and pan in the house to make Sunday lunch. May I invite you over one evening next week? I'll pick you up and drop you home in my swish Jaguar,' Hamish offered.

Eugenie laughed. As Hamish had mimicked *her* phraseology, she decided to mimic the way *he* spoke. 'Yes, let's!' she agreed.

With a smile of recognition, Hamish said: 'That's my phrase!'

Eugenie blushed and gazed at her boots. 'I thought it would be funny,' she replied.

'It *was* funny, and *endearing*. I'll let you off,' Hamish conceded.

Being called "endearing" gave Eugenie flutters all over her. It was something no man had ever called her. That one word confirmed to her that Hamish was unlike any other man she'd been with.

Although Eugenie wanted to spend the rest of the day with Hamish, she knew he had to get on. As he was too polite to end the conversation and leave her, she did it.

'While you make sure your brother-in-law doesn't make a mess of your sister's kitchen, I'll be having lunch out with Jason, my father. If I want to get there before him, I must go now,' Eugenie told Hamish.

'Your father, *Jason*? Am I right that there's a reason why you use his title *and* his given name?' Hamish questioned.

'Yes, but I can't explain now because we both have to go,' Eugenie pointed out.

'Oh, yes. I'd forgotten that I had to leave you. Alright then. Good luck with your father, Jason. I'll call you, and I will *actually* call you this time, so we can decide what evening I'll have you over for. Good day, Eugenie,' Hamish replied.

'Goodbye!' Eugenie called to Hamish as they both set off on their separate ways.

Like most December days in Essex, the air was bitingly cold that Sunday. Unlike most December days in Essex, Eugenie and Hamish felt warm inside as they traversed the varied streets of Colchester.

CHAPTER THIRTY-EIGHT

The carvery was soulless and corporate. It had meaningless maroon walls, plain wooden chairs, a boring beige carpet, and an array of diners, none of which created a warm and welcoming atmosphere. It wasn't somewhere Eugenie would usually frequent. That was why she'd chosen to meet Jason, her father, there.

As soon as Eugenie was sat down, she looked at the desserts section of the menu. None of them interested her, but she'd probably end up having one of them. One thing Eugenie would never change about herself was her instance on having dessert whenever she ate out.

When Eugenie put her menu down, she saw Jason striding towards her, arms outstretched.

'Hey, how's my daughter?!' Jason asked.

As if it was her answer, Eugenie stood to let Jason wrap her up in a hug.

While hugging Eugenie, Jason whispered: 'Maybe I should just call you Eugenie, and perhaps I shouldn't hug you. I know it is a bit soon, but I'm so excited to see you.'

To show that she was perfectly happy, Eugenie squ
tighter.

Just in case her father didn't get the message, Eugenie told him: 'However excited you are, I'm twice as excited. Call me whatever you like, and don't worry about hugging me. I'm an affectionate girl. I'd hug the world if it would let me, so I'll definitely hug my father.'

When Jason let Eugenie go, he gave her the biggest smile she'd ever seen on a middle-aged man's face.

Still smiling, Eugenie and Jason sat opposite each other.

Seeing that both Eugenie and Jason were sat down, a waiter dashed over to them. 'Hi, I'm Gerry. I'm your waiter here. What can I get for you?' he asked.

'Waiter? It's a carvery. Don't you go up and get what you want?' Jason questioned.

Gerry shook his head. 'No, sir. We offer table service here at Balkerne Carvery. You just sit there and we'll get your food, *and* the drinks, for you,' he replied.

'Oh. I've always thought that part of the fun of a carvery is going up there, having a look at everything, and trying to work out how much you can stuff in your Yorkshires,' Jason moaned.

'I can assure you sir, that all the produce we use is to the highest standard, and our portions are plenty big enough,' Gerry told Jason.

Unnoticed by Gerry, Eugenie and Jason shared a knowing smile.

-

As soon as Gerry had taken their order and was out of ear-shot, Eugenie and Jason burst out laughing.

sir" and table service nonsense? I am not
s is a carvery,' Jason questioned.

ments made Eugenie laugh even harder.
ne nerves she'd had. They were both at
s going well. There was nothing to worry
about.

There would never be a better moment to start deeper
conversation, so Eugenie started by asking: 'Why have
you chosen now to get in touch?'

Jason fidgeted in his seat. 'I saw a story in the paper about
a clever girl who was doing a service where they help
you buy presents. I see her surname is Holland, and she's
twenty-three. Whenever I see that name and age somewhere, I pay attention. As I read on, I get more and more
convinced that this is my daughter. Then, it mentions
Victoria Toothill, the sister of the girl I got pregnant all
those years ago. Then, I knew I'd got lucky. After years of
wondering where you were and what you were up to, I'd
found you,' he replied.

'You were looking for me? I thought you didn't want me.
The reason *I've* never looked for *you* is that I thought you
didn't want me. The second you found out my mother
was pregnant with your baby, you left her. You left *me*, before we'd even had a chance to meet,' Eugenie said.

While she waited for an answer, Eugenie wondered what
possible justification Jason could have for walking away.
Before she'd laid eyes on him, she'd thought that nothing
excused getting a woman pregnant and then leaving her
to get on with it. Now she was getting to know him, she
wondered if her father's words might fill the gap she'd
had in her heart her entire life.

'What you've got to understand is, I was young and

frightened. Imagine being younger than you are now, and someone telling you your whole world is going to flip upside down. What should have been a bit of fun turned serious. My brain just shut down. I couldn't compute the enormity of it. That's why I left Liz, and you. I couldn't cope with it all. Now, with the benefit of maturity, I can see that having a daughter is a great thing. It guts me that I wasn't there, but back when Liz gave me the chance to be part of your life, I was too young to appreciate it. Then again though, in a way I probably did you and her a favour, because she'll have raised you alone far better than we would have together,' Jason told Eugenie.

When Eugenie imagined herself in Jason's shoes, she could appreciate how he'd felt. She liked to think that she'd have done the decent thing and stuck around, but she wasn't *sure* she would've done.

'I understand. I know why you did what you did. At least you're here now, owning up to it. Now I know I *am* wanted,' Eugenie replied.

'I think that, in a way, I've always wanted you. Now I know you, I *definitely* want you,' Jason assured Eugenie.

Ever since her mother had told her about her father, she'd wanted to know why he hadn't wanted her. Now she knew that he'd been scared as a young man, and, as an older man, he *did* want her. It healed emotional wounds Eugenie didn't even know she had, or *had* had.

'I want you too. I want a father,' Eugenie told Jason.

Just as Eugenie was going to ask what Jason did with his time, Gerry the waiter appeared and put plates in front of them. As silently as he'd approached, Gerry backed away to serve another table.

'We should get this down us before it gets cold,' Jason said.

Knowing that to be sensible, Eugenie picked up her knife and fork and dug in.

-

Once Eugenie had used most of her glass of wine to get the dry and tasteless meat down her throat, Jason decided to open back up the conversation, by talking about the thing that had brought them together.

'The story I saw about you said that Victoria owned the womenswear boutique you work in. Is that right? Is it solely hers?' Jason asked.

Eugenie nodded. 'Toothill's is Auntie's pride and joy, and mine too. It is so fun and rewarding to work there,' she replied.

'So she owns it? That's her business?' Jason questioned.

'It is *undoubtedly* hers. Auntie and Mother own it fifty-fifty, because Mother helped her set it up, but it is her business. She dreamt it up, she runs it, and it is her baby,' Eugenie confirmed.

While considering how to open his next line of questioning, Jason chewed on a piece of beef. The beef was tough, and gave him a lot of thinking time.

'What's the family situation like these days? I remember Liz and Victoria's parents are dead, bless them, but is there anyone else? Do you have cousins? Did Liz find someone else and have more kids?' Jason enquired.

'No siblings or cousins. I'm an only child, and my uncle doesn't want children,' Eugenie replied.

For an excuse not to talk for a moment, Jason put roast potatoes, a piece of Yorkshire pudding, and a slither of beef together on one fork.

'You're set for life then, because surely the shop will be passed down to you one day. It's a good business too. One that, sure, you'll need help with, but you'll have so much money that you can afford to get help, or *give* help if you're feeling generous,' Jason pointed out.

'I don't really think about it much,' Eugenie said.

'Well, you should! As wonderful as you and Toothill's are, you'll need help with it all when the time comes. Don't stress about it though. I'm here now, and I'm sure I'll be able to help you,' Jason told Eugenie.

With a jolt, Eugenie realised the real reason Jason had got back in touch. Despair made its heavy presence felt as she groped around on the floor for her handbag.

'What are you doing?" Jason asked as Eugenie dragged her bag on her lap.

In response, Eugenie slid a note across the table.

The look on Jason's face told Eugenie that he still didn't understand.

'This is all the money you'll be getting from me. If Toothill's *is* handed to me, you won't get anywhere near it, except perhaps *physically* near to the shop. I should have known that was all you wanted,' Eugenie said.

'What? I never said I was after your money,' Jason protested.

It didn't escape Eugenie's notice that Jason made no attempt to explicitly deny he was after her money. All he denied was *telling* her that was what he wanted.

Weighed down by her newfound understanding of her father, and why Victoria hadn't wanted her to have anything to do with him, Eugenie dragged herself to her feet.

As she walked away from her father and out of his life once again, Eugenie called: 'Goodbye, Jason. Thank you for being so obvious.'

CHAPTER THIRTY-NINE

The warm air from the vents, combined with the effects of being within touching distance of Hamish, made the car journey from her flat to Hamish's townhouse very comfortable indeed for Eugenie.

When Hamish maneuvered his Jaguar onto his driveway and put the handbrake on, Eugenie sighed.

'Something wrong?' Hamish asked.

'I don't want to leave the car. I'm so cosy,' Eugenie replied.

Hamish smiled. 'Wait here a minute, as long as you don't mind. I've just had a pleasant idea,' he told Eugenie.

While Eugenie wondered what that idea could possibly be, Hamish gave her his car key, jumped out the car, and headed into the house.

Sitting alone in the car, Eugenie watched a man and a woman going along the street. The woman of the couple kept stopping to admire the lavish Christmas light displays Hamish's neighbours had put up. Her partner's breath was visible, and, when he pointed this out to the woman, she gave him a tight hug. In her imagination, Eugenie could hear the woman saying: 'Warmer now?'

Inside the once-heated car, Eugenie was perfectly warm. Not having the distraction of being cold meant that she was free to dream about how lovely her evening would be. What she and Hamish would do, she wasn't sure, but it didn't matter to her. It would be special because they'd be together.

When Hamish came rushing out of the house, Eugenie felt a rush of excitement.

Before Eugenie could, Hamish opened the front passenger door. Now that she was exposed to it, Eugenie could understand why the man on the street had complained about how cold the air was.

When Eugenie swung her legs onto the tarmac of Hamish's driveway to get out of the car, he offered his hand to help her up. As a healthy twenty-three-year-old, she didn't need a hand up. As someone very attracted to Hamish, she took his hand. For the few seconds she touched Hamish's soft skin for, Eugenie felt tingles in her fingers. Once Eugenie was upright, Hamish released her hand. The smile he flashed her as he did so suggested that he'd enjoyed it every bit as much as she had.

Gesturing at his house, Hamish said: 'Let's enter my not-entirely-humble abode.'

Even though it was dark, Eugenie could appreciate how grand Hamish's townhouse was. It wasn't its size that made it impressive, for it was narrow and terraced. There was something about the chunky frames and sils around the windows, and the unrendered dark bricks that made it clear that house was worth noticing.

As Eugenie stepped through the door and into the hallway, she admired her surroundings. The grey perfectly-painted walls, navy short-pile carpet, and glass drop pendant light, looked so good together that she let out a little gasp.

Behind the awestruck Eugenie, Hamish stepped in and shut the door. 'Swish enough for you?' he asked with a grin.

'It's so calming and elegant,' Eugenie whispered.

Hamish chuckled. 'My favourite room is the sitting room, for one reason and one reason only,' he replied, striding into the aforementioned sitting room.

The second she entered the sitting room, Eugenie knew why Hamish loved it so much. 'You have a wood-burning stove!' she cried, dashing over the aforementioned wood-burning stove, which contained a roaring fire.

'I had a feeling you'd like it. I came in before you to light it,' Hamish said.

To Eugenie, a wood-burning stove was the epitome of cosiness. Even if she'd have known that they are responsible for putting three times as many toxic tiny particles in the air as road traffic, which she did not, she'd probably still have loved them. It filled her with joy to watch the fire inside it burn.

Facing the wood-burning stove was a black velvet sofa, which Hamish lowered himself onto.

When she saw Hamish was sitting, Eugenie dashed over and plonked herself down next to him.

'Now that we've settled, do you mind me asking how things went with Jason, your father?' Hamish asked.

'Not at all. It is kind of you to ask. Sadly, it didn't go well.

I realised that he only got in touch because he saw that Auntie has a shop. He wondered if I'd get it one day, and if, when that happened, there'd be any money in it for him. As, if I ever did get Toothill's, I wouldn't give him a penny, I decided not to waste any more of his time and walked out,' Eugenie revealed.

'I suspected as much, but I hoped I was wrong. Despite his failings as a husband, I get on well with *my* dad, and I hoped you would too. It's his loss though,' Hamish replied.

The last part of what Hamish said made Eugenie melt inside. The way he'd worded another thing he'd said amused her. Once upon a time, she'd have made a joke out of it. Considering her chat with her mother on the day she'd upset three people in the same way, she wasn't sure she could. After giving it a little more thought, she decided that it was fine. Making one joke didn't mean she was hiding or ignoring her feelings. It just meant she wanted to shine a little light into what was otherwise a dark thing.

'How do you know if I get on well with *your* father? We're not at the meeting the parents stage yet, so I don't know him,' Eugenie quipped.

After a momentary pause while he recalled what he'd said and how he'd said it, Hamish roared with laughter. He laughed so hard that the sofa he and Eugenie were sat on shook.

Once Hamish had stopped laughing, Eugenie said: 'It is a shame that Jason doesn't really care about me, but at least I've met him now. I've dreamt of so many versions of my father. Now I've met the real one, I can stop thinking about him. I'm glad that I didn't tell my mother. It would have been more upsetting if I'd have had to admit to the woman he abandoned that I wanted to have lunch with Jason, and worse still to tell her he was only interested in money.'

In the hope it would comfort Eugenie, Hamish put his arm around her. After doing that, it occurred to him that he hadn't checked it was okay with her, so he removed his arm.

When Hamish put his arm around her, Eugenie felt comfortable and loved. These feelings disappeared with a jolt when he withdrew his arm

'Sorry, I don't know if I should have done that. It may be a bit forward to put my arm around you,' Hamish apologised.

Eugenie scoffed. 'No, silly! I loved it! It upset me that you stopped!' she replied.

Knowing that Eugenie wanted it there, Hamish once again put his arm around her back and rested it on her right shoulder. The smile he got in response made him smile too.

'I missed *Songs of Praise* for him. It's my favourite telly show,' Eugenie commented.

The smile on Hamish's face grew even wider. 'That makes me love you even more. It's *my* favourite programme *too*! Shall we watch it together on catch up? I don't mind seeing it again,' he offered.

It wasn't until Hamish suggested watching it that Eugenie realised how much it bothered her that she hadn't watched *Songs of Praise*. She felt like she'd missed out on seeing her friends.

As she watched Hamish navigate through the menus of

BBC iPlayer, Eugenie realised he'd said something that was even nicer than offering to watch *Songs of Praise* again. 'You said you *love* me! The fact that I like *Songs of Praise* makes you love me *even more*, so you *already* loved me!' Eugenie cried.

'Oh, it slipped out, didn't it? Please don't be scared off! I know it's early to say that word, but I've known since we met that you were something special. You alter my very heart beat, I'm sure, and your mere presence makes me feel warm and fuzzy inside. Please don't let my feelings put you under pressure! I'm not in a hurry, not at all! It's just that, at this early stage, I'm already confident that you and I have a magnificent future together,' Hamish babbled.

No words beautiful enough to answer Hamish came to Eugenie. Love surged within her though, that she had to find an outlet for. In a flash of inspiration, she thought of the perfect response.

Talking isn't the only thing you can use your lips for. Eugenie demonstrated this by gently placing hers on Hamish's cheek. The moment her soft lips make contact with his warm, smooth skin, was the most perfect moment of her life. She made the kiss last a few seconds, which allowed her to take in the light floral scent of his freshly-laundered jumper. When Eugenie withdrew her lips from Hamish's cheek, they were curled up in an a smile as gentle as her kiss.

'I love you too. I can't put it into nice words like you did, so I thought I'd tell you with a kiss,' Eugenie whispered.

'You are *so* sweet,' Hamish murmured.

The crackling of the fire, combined with Eugenie and Hamish's steady breathing, became the only sounds in the lounge. Peace washed over them both as they watched the flames in the stove lick at the logs.

The peace was shattered when Hamish cried: 'Oh, I nearly forgot!'

The panic in Hamish's voice set Eugenie's heart racing. 'Forgot what?' she questioned.

'To ask what takeaway you'd like, and get it ordered. Starving you isn't a good way of showing you my love,' Hamish replied.

The panic Eugenie had felt turned to excitement. 'Take-away? What a treat! You are spoiling me! Can we order from a chippy? I *love* fish and chips,' she asked.

'Yes, let's! My guilty pleasure is chip shop chips coated with cheese and dusted with table salt, so that's fine by me. We're not getting takeaway because I'm nice, though. I'm an *atrocious* cook, and I couldn't cope with the thought that I may accidentally choke or poison you,' Hamish admitted.

Eugenie laughed and said: 'I burn everything. We're going to make a terrible couple!'

CHAPTER FORTY

'Sandra Bullock is so *cute*! I *love* that film! Thank you for putting it on,' Eugenie said when *While You Were Sleeping*, which Hamish had put on after *Songs of Praise*, finished.

'Another of my sister's favourites,' Hamish replied.

Since Hamish had picked her up, Eugenie had wanted to ask about his sister. It has begun to worry her that she wouldn't get a good opportunity, so she was relieved when Hamish mentioned her.

'How is she, and your nieces and nephews?' Eugenie asked.

Hamish smiled. 'The pain in her leg is slowly easing as it heals. My brother-in-law returned from Europe a few days ago, and he's agreed some time off with his employer, so he'll be at home for her. The children are delighted that their dad is home for a while. Being a lorry driver earns him a decent wage, but it means he doesn't get much family time,' he told Eugenie.

'I love how close you are with your sister. It says a lot about who you are,' Eugenie said.

'She's my big sister. She's always been there, through everything. Now *I* get to be there for *her*, and the children,' Hamish replied.

While Eugenie was daydreaming about how lovely it must be to have a sister, Hamish's phone buzzed in his pocket. Instead of just whipping it out of his pocket to check who in the virtual world had just done something, he raised a questioning eyebrow at the person he was with in the real world. Eugenie nodded her approval, so he slipped his phone out of his pocket and unlocked it.

The room was lit with green light from Hamish's phone, so Eugenie knew Hamish was on WhatsApp.

'Oh, one of the partners at work has skidded in the ice. He's fine, but his beloved white Land Rover Sport isn't. It went into a fence,' Hamish told Eugenie.

The photo Hamish then showed Eugenie on his phone made her toes curl. The front of the car was a mangled mess of metal. She couldn't help but picture Hamish's Jaguar in a similar state.

'That was on a road near here. He came across a patch of black ice. It could happen to us too,' Hamish murmured.

'I thought that. I'd hate for you to get hurt because of me,' Eugenie replied.

'I'm prepared to drive you home, as slowly and gently as possible. It worries me though, that we may still get into difficulties. There is another option. You could stay here for the night. By morning, it should be better. I could drop you home then, if you like,' Hamish offered.

This wasn't the first time a man had suggested to Eugenie that she stay the night with them. As much as she loved Hamish, she didn't want to do the thing that he hadn't mentioned, but was probably on his mind. It was difficult to find a way of saying that without offending him.

Seeing the conflict on Eugenie's face, Hamish told her: 'I

have a spare room. I wouldn't ask you to sleep with me.'

After saying that, it occurred to Hamish his words may not have come across as he'd intended them to. 'I mean I'm not asking you to sleep with me *tonight*. You are *extraordinarily* pretty, and energetic, and I am in love with you, so I probably *will* ask you to sleep with me in the future. It just seems too early to do that now,' he explained.

Eugenie laughed. 'I understand. Don't tie yourself up in knots. I feel the same. A kiss on the cheek by the fire is enough... For now,' she said.

Knowing that Eugenie felt the same as him both reassured Hamish and made him blush.

To distract himself from some of the thoughts in his head, Hamish asked: 'Will you stay?'

Eugenie nodded and said: 'You are a true gentleman.'

CHAPTER FORTY-ONE

When Eugenie woke up on Christmas Eve, she hoped it would be every bit as good as the day before it. After making her toast, Hamish had driven her into Colchester town centre. There, she'd worked a short shift at Toothill's. During the shift, Helen had popped in just to thank her for helping grant hundreds of present wishes as the Christmas Genie. The scheme had put some much-needed cash through the tills of the little businesses along the Lanes, got them publicity, and, most importantly, had spread happiness throughout the town and beyond.

Keeping yesterday's joy with her, Eugenie left her bedroom to wish Holly a happy birthday.

As expected, Holly was in the kitchen-diner. She was on the sofa, reading a birthday card. When Eugenie got closer, she saw that Holly was crying.

'It's from my brother. Even though Mum said that we wouldn't do presents and cards anymore, he still wants to. He's even remembered that I like separate cards and presents for my birthday and Christmas. There's another card for tomorrow, and two parcels, one of which has a message on saying not to open it until the twenty-fifth,' Holly explained, knowing Eugenie would wonder why she was crying.

'Oh, Holly! That's wonderful!' Eugenie cried.

Holly smiled. 'Told you he's a good man,' she said.

'And you're a good *girl*. This is no less than you deserve,' Eugenie replied.

'That's debatable,' Holly pointed out.

As Eugenie didn't want to get into a debate about what Holly deserved, she ignored her comment.

The parcel Holly's brother had sent for her birthday was at her feet. She snatched it off the floor and began to open it.

While Holly was distracted by the present from her brother, Eugenie snuck off to get her own present, which she'd stashed under her bed.

Outside her door, Eugenie could hear Holly laughing. When she returned to the kitchen-diner and saw that she was holding a brand-new teddy bear, she could see why.

'When I was a small child, I used to ask for a cuddly toy every birthday. I asked so often that my family stopped asking me what I wanted and just automatically bought them. My parents stopped buying me teddies when I turned seventeen, but my brother didn't. Every year, he sends a cuddly toy,' Holly explained.

'Oh, wow! I just thought you collected them. I never knew that it was a family tradition from when you were little,' Eugenie cried.

'Well, now you do. I'd prefer to share my bed with a nice

man instead of more than thirty cuddly toys, but I do really love teddies,' Holly replied.

Holding out an item that was loosely covered in wrapping paper, Eugenie said: 'It isn't as special as what your brother sent you, but I hope you'll still like my present.'

When she took the present from Eugenie, Holly couldn't help but smile at how badly wrapped it was. It made it very easy to open, which she liked. She was eager to see what Eugenie had bought her.

The present itself made Holly smile even more than the quality of the wrapping. 'Bookmarks! Handmade bookmarks by the look of it!' she cried.

'They *are* handmade! Suzi, who owns an art shop, makes them. Do you like them?' Eugenie asked.

'They're perfect, Eugenie. No wonder you did so well with the present buying service. You have a talent, and I'm so glad to be on the receiving end of it,' Holly replied.

The reason Eugenie had enjoyed doing the Christmas Genie service was that she got to see the look on people's faces when they saw a gift that they knew their loved ones would adore. Seeing a similar look on the face of someone *she* loved gave Eugenie even more joy.

It suddenly occurred to Eugenie there was something she'd meant to say as soon as she saw Holly, but she hadn't. To rectify this, Eugenie said: 'Happy birthday, Holly!'

'I think it actually *will* be a happy birthday,' Holly replied.

To properly celebrate the anniversary of Holly's birth, she and Eugenie stood and embraced each other.

CHAPTER FORTY-TWO

A loud rhythmic buzzing roused Eugenie from her deep slumber. She mumbled something about a nice dream being interrupted as she opened her eyes. When she realised the buzzing was an alarm, she grabbed her phone off the bedside table to silence it. It was then that Eugenie saw "25 Dec" in the top corner of her screen. That was enough to make her fully come to with a squeal. She no longer cared that her nice dream was interrupted. It was Christmas Day!

When Eugenie threw her prepared clothes on and dashed out into the kitchen-diner, she was met by the scent of hot buttery toast.

'I knew when you alarm was, so I thought I'd get breakfast done for when you got up,' Holly, who was responsible for the hot buttery toast smell in the room, told Eugenie.

'Yay! Thank you! Merry Christmas, Holly!' Eugenie said.

'Same to you, Eugenie,' Holly replied.

-

Eating toast didn't take more than a few minutes. Excitement made Eugenie ravenous, and food doesn't last around ravenous people.

'Will you leave for church soon?' Holly asked as she cleared the plates.

On Christmas Day, Eugenie always lost track of time. She checked her watch to see if she would indeed leave for church soon. When she got her answer, Eugenie wondered something else. Something her watch couldn't tell her.

'I will. Would you like to come too?' Eugenie asked.

Every Christmas they'd lived together for, Holly had bid goodbye to Eugenie as she'd left to go to church and then wondered what to do with herself. It had never occurred to her to go to church with Eugenie. As far as Holly knew, church was for deeply religious people who had memorised The Bible and lived their lives by strict rules. It was clear that she was wrong, otherwise Eugenie wouldn't be suggesting that she go with her.

To answer Eugenie, Holly went with her gut instinct and said: 'Why not, as long as you don't mind me tagging along?'

'Thank you! It will be fun!' Eugenie declared.

Holly wasn't sure it would be *fun*, but she didn't say so.

-

The church loomed tall over Holly as she approached it. She felt as if it was saying: 'Why are you here?'.

The inside, with its rows of stark wooden pews all facing the altar, was even more imposing. It took Holly a great deal of effort to follow Eugenie down the aisle. With every step, Holly reminded herself that God, if He existed, was a kind and loving being. His followers were too, Eugenie and Elizabeth were proof of that. There was nothing to fear. The only person judging her was her.

Feeling a little more self-assured, Holly lifted her gaze from the tiled floor. It fell upon three women, all of whom were looking in her direction and frowning. Still looking at Holly, one of the women whispered something to her companions. The whispered comment made all three of them laugh. Holly averted her eyes from them and focused on Eugenie, who was making a beeline for a particular pew and the people occupying it.

'Hamish, and family! How lovely to see you. Merry Christmas to you all!' Eugenie cried as she reached the people she'd had in sight.

In the quiet church, Holly caught the sound of three people tutting and muttering.

'Merry Christmas, Eugenie! This is my sister, my brother-in-law, and their children. Sister, brother-in-law, and your children, this is the woman I'm courting,' Hamish replied.

'My name isn't "Sister". My name is Laura. Nice to meet you, Eugenie. I've heard a lot about you,' Hamish's sister said.

'I introduced you like that so Eugenie knew how we're connected. If I'd have introduced you as "Laura", it wouldn't have made any sense, would it?' Hamish pointed out.

Eugenie laughed. 'You can tell you're brother and sister, and it's Christmas! This girl with me is my flatmate and best friend. Her name is Holly,' she told Hamish, Laura, and their family.

As soon as she was introduced, Holly felt pressure to say something clever. A thoughtful observation would do the trick, but she didn't have one to make. Relief struck Holly as she noticed Hamish's attire and knew exactly what to say.

'Yes, I'm Holly. Merry Christmas to you all. I'm loving the jumper, Hamish,' she said.

All of Hamish's family, adults and children alike, laughed. Holly wondered what mistake she'd made. Had she mispronounced a word? She didn't think she had.

'Ah, this beauty? The snow-capped cottages, complete with Christmas lights that actually light up, which you have to remember to take out before you wash it. I lost our annual Christmas Eve game of Monopoly last night, so the honour of wearing it fell to me,' Hamish revealed.

'Oh, I see. Well, *I* like it,' Holly replied.

Apart from the vicar, who was fiddling with a microphone, Eugenie and Holly were the only people standing. A few people who were sitting stared at them.

'Would you like to join us? The children can budge up,' Laura asked.

'Yes, that would be lovely! Thank you!' Eugenie agreed.

As directed by Laura, Eugenie and Holly took a seat on the wooden pew. Holly found herself on the end, which pleased her. The idea that she could leave without having to move anyone else was comforting.

-

When the service began, Holly found herself moved by the vicar's words. They were surprisingly relevant, and believable.

After speaking for a few minutes about the story of Christ's birth and drawing parallels with modern life, the vicar announced the first carol. It was called *Once In Royal David's City*. Holly had never even heard of it.

When the man on the organ started playing, everyone around Holly rose. Everyone except her. She was happy to sing sitting down. She knew it wouldn't sound as good, but that didn't bother her.

Across the church, Holly could see the three women she'd noticed earlier looking at her. They muttered to each other, and she caught the words "won't stand" and "disrespectful".

'We all rise for hymns and carols,' Laura whispered to Holly.

'I didn't know. I'm so sorry,' Holly replied.

Laura gave Holly the warmest smile she'd ever seen and said: 'It's alright. How would you?'

When everyone around her started singing, Holly realised that she couldn't sing along, for she didn't know the words. Being the only silent one in a room of around 100 people made Holly feel more isolated than she ever had in her entire life. She got the sense that everyone knew she wasn't singing. A few people in the neighbouring rows kept glancing at her with puzzled expressions.

By the second verse, Holly couldn't stand anymore. 'Don't worry about me. This just doesn't feel right,' she whispered to Eugenie.

Before Eugenie could question it, Holly stepped out of the pew and strode off down the aisle, her escape route. She got through the doors and into the for-once-welcome frosty air of outside.

'I know you're thinking of following her, but don't do it. She doesn't want a fuss. Now she's outside, she'll be fine,' Laura told Eugenie.

As she was singing, Eugenie just answered Laura with a grateful smile.

-

With every minute she spent in church with Hamish's family, Eugenie fell deeper and deeper into the Christmas spirit. Watching the children of the congregation answer religious quiz questions to win chocolates from an advent calendar was a particular highlight.

The last carol of the service was *Ding Dong Merrily on High*. When the chorus came round, Eugenie belted it out at the top of her lungs. As a soprano, it was comfortably within her range, so she could give it her all. This put frowns on a few faces, but she didn't care. To her, it was unthinkable to give anything less than her best.

In Eugenie's own pew, her enthusiastic singing made people smile. The biggest grin belonged to Hamish.

The chorus was difficult for Laura. Instead of singing the second one, she whispered to Hamish: 'I can see that you love her, and I can see why. Good choice.'

'It wasn't a *choice*. How could I *not* fall for her?' Hamish murmured in reply.

Lost in her singing, Eugenie had no idea Hamish and Laura were talking about her.

-

At the end of the service, Hamish, his family, and Eugenie, all trudged up the gravel path.

When she and her companions reached the road, Eugenie

knew it was time to part. Parting from Hamish was the last thing she wanted to do though.

'Hamish, would you like to come home with me? Holly's cooking a version of Christmas lunch, and it'll be delicious. We couldn't get a turkey for two. Even if you come, we'll still have too much food,' Eugenie offered.

Hamish looked at Laura, his brother-in-law, and his nieces and nephews, who were preparing to go home to celebrate Christmas as a family. 'Oh, I can't. It's Christmas. I've got to be with family,' he replied.

Laura scoffed. 'A pretty girl offers to have you over for Christmas lunch and you say no? What are you thinking? You've done more than enough for us. Go have lunch with adults,' she ordered Hamish.

To one side of Hamish was Laura's stern face. On the other was Eugenie's, whose grey eyes seemed to be begging him to go home with them.

To seal the deal, Laura leant in close to Hamish and, in a mock-whisper loud enough for Eugenie to hear, said: 'Besides, if you play your cards right, one day *she* will be family.'

In some of her frequent daydreams, Eugenie had imagined herself marrying, or married to, Hamish. It was a fantasy though, and one she thought wouldn't come true. The fact that Hamish's own sister thought it would happen gave Eugenie hope for the future. Being Laura's sister-in-law was almost as exciting a prospect as being Hamish's wife.

The look on Eugenie's face decided it for Hamish. 'I'd be delighted to dine with you and Holly,' he told her.

Eugenie squealed. 'You've just made my Christmas!' she

cried.

So Hamish couldn't change his mind, Laura bid him and Eugenie farewell and then herded her husband and children into the car. At the insistence of his wife, Hamish's brother-in-law pulled away as soon as everyone's seatbelts were on.

'Shall we get to my cosy flat so Holly can cook us dinner?' Eugenie suggested.

'Yes, let's!' Hamish agreed.

As she strolled along the frost-covered streets of Colchester with Hamish, Eugenie wondered how Holly was.

CHAPTER FORTY-THREE

Once she had escaped from the church grounds, Holly felt like a weight had been lifted. The sense of freedom she felt was like nothing she'd ever experienced. The idea that she could do anything, go anywhere, and think whatever she wanted to think, thrilled her. She chose to go through the town centre to get home.

It was eerie to see most of the shops on the High Street shut, and to be able to walk along the pavement without having to dodge someone every five seconds.

After passing a seven-foot-tall statue of a woman mid-stride, Holly crossed the road and veered off the High Street onto one of the many alleyways that connected it to the Lanes.

Ahead of her on the lane, she could see someone sitting huddled up in the doorway of a closed shop. The thought of someone sleeping rough on Christmas Day upset her. At least they weren't alone though, for a man had stopped to talk to them. With nothing better to do, Holly decided to join the man.

As she got closer, Holly realised that she knew the man

who'd stopped to talk to the rough sleeper, and she could guess why he'd done so. It was Darren.

'Oh, wow! This is Holly! She's the receptionist at the hotel that used to let me have a room on the cheap sometimes. Holly, this is Brian,' Darren told Brian, the rough sleeper, who Holly had guessed was an old friend of his.

'Ah, yes! The one you have a crush on,' Brian replied.

It was inconceivable to Holly that anyone, let alone Darren, had a crush on her. Brian must be joking, so she forced herself to laugh.

Darren's face went as red as the berries on female holly bushes. 'How embarrassing,' he muttered.

It confused Holly that Darren looked so uncomfortable. It was just a joke. It may not be funny, but it wasn't so bad that he had to react like that. His discomfort was so acute that it transferred to her.

In an attempt to put Darren, and herself, at ease, Holly made herself smile and said: 'It's okay. There's no need to be mortified. Look, I'm smiling.'

For a brief moment, Darren and Holly's eyes met. He broke eye contact almost instantly, and blushed even harder. In those few seconds, Holly's heart fluttered wildly, as if it was trying to escape her chest and get to *his* heart.

'But you were just being kind because it's your job, and you take a pride in your work. You didn't mean for me to have feelings for you. I'm the last person you'd want to fall for you. Now you have to politely reject me, which will be excruciating for both of us,' he murmured at the floor.

Realisation hit Holly like an avalanche. Darren really *did* have a crush on her. Now *she* was the one blushing.

'Look, I get that a nice girl like you wouldn't want nothing to do with me. It's okay. You can say it,' Darren told Holly.

'What if a nice girl like me *does* want something to do with you? What if *I* have a crush on *you*? Can I say *that*?' Holly questioned.

'Erm, well... I don't...' Darren stammered.

'As his friend, let me translate for him. That means: "Hell, yeah! Can I have your number?",' Brian said.

When Darren burst out laughing at his friend, Holly thought: '*Mmm, what a nice laugh. So deep and rich. I like that.*'

After his laughter faded, Darren stood stock-still, in silence. It was clear he had no idea what to do. Holly imagined it had been a while since he'd told a girl he liked her. It had a been a while since she'd admitted feelings for someone too. The shared awkwardness only deepened her attraction to him.

Luckily for them both, Holly had an idea of how to proceed with Darren. 'Would you like to walk around town with me? I was wandering aimlessly before I came across you, so we could wander aimlessly together,' she suggested.

'Great idea!' Darren agreed.

-

Once they'd said their goodbyes to Brian, and Darren had agreed to return later, Darren and Holly walked down the alleyway together.

As he watched Darren and Holly stroll out of view, Brian called: 'Bye, bye, lovebirds! Don't do anything I wouldn't do.'

'Brian is fun,' Holly commented to Darren.

Darren grinned. 'Yeah, he is. We met on my second or third week on the streets, and clicked instantly. Both of us had been addicted to stuff, were now fighting those addictions, but had started fighting too late and ended up being chucked out of our homes anyway. His was drugs. Coke, I think. Such a good bloke. He helps all the newbies, and is delighted for us when we move on to better things,' he replied.

When they reached the end of the alleyway, without a word to each other, Darren and Holly turned left. They both noticed they were in sync, and shared a smile about it.

Thinking back on what Holly had said about Brian reminded Darren of when he'd first met her in the hotel. 'See, this is what I first liked about you. You saw me as a person, just as you saw Brian as a person today. You treat us with respect, just like you would anyone,' he told her.

Holly frowned. 'Yes, that's because you *are* people,' she pointed out.

'But people don't treat us like it! Now I've got my flat, and a job, I get treated so differently to what I did a few months ago. I'm the same man though. I've not changed, but people's perception of me has,' Darren replied.

The way Darren and others who had been in the same situation as him were treated made Holly more upset than she could put into words. As she couldn't express her feelings on that subject, she focused on something else.

'Congratulations on getting a job! How are you finding it, and the flat, and everything?' Holly asked.

'It's cool. The job is just a few hours a day in a little cafe. Same people who got me the flat found it for me. I'd forgotten how good it feels to be safe behind a locked door. My favourite thing though is having my own shower, that I can use twenty-four seven. Yeah, I'm still *so* tempted to have a little flutter, but I know it just isn't worth it. I've got all this now, and there's no way I'm letting it go,' Darren told Holly.

The pride in Darren's voice made Holly want to cry. Whenever they'd spoken in the past, he'd always talked as if he was worthless. That was clearly no longer the case, and she couldn't be happier for him.

'Well done on not gambling. I can't imagine how hard that is, but you're right that it isn't worth doing. I could have guessed you'd love having a shower. You always did care about your personal hygiene,' Holly replied.

It touched Darren that Holly remembered how much being clean mattered to him, but he didn't know how to express that.

'Enough about me, how about you? How come you were wandering around Colchester, alone, at Christmas?' Darren asked.

'I made the mistake of going to church. Eugenie, my friend who lives with me, is a Christian. Going to church is what makes Christmas, *Christmas* for her. This morning, she invited me, and I couldn't think of a reason not to tag along. I made a mess of it though. I sat when I should have stood, I couldn't sing, and goodness knows what other transgressions I made. All my mistakes were spotted by these three old women who were muttering about me. I thought Christians were supposed to be friendly and not judge you, but apparently not. Never in my life have I felt so out of place. I thought I may be Christian, but it seems not. I had to get out, so I left. Eugenie is the only person I have to spend Christmas with. She's still at church, and I don't want to go home yet, so that's how I ended up wandering,' Holly explained.

'Just because all these people follow the same religion, it doesn't mean they're all the same. The judgy women don't represent Christians any more or less than you, or your friend. They had no right to pick on you. How are you supposed to know what you're supposed to do?' Darren replied.

The passion with which Darren made it clear that three people don't represent an entire religion seemed personal. 'Are *you* a Christian?' Holly asked.

Darren scoffed. 'No. When I look around me, I see no sign that there some nice guy in the sky who made all this and looks after us. How can there be a god when we've got innocent people on the streets, with no escape route in sight? I'm not talking about myself, or even Brian. We are responsible for what happened to us. I mean those brave men and women who risked their lives and left their friends and family to fight for what is right, only to come back here and be so messed up by what happened to them out there that they can't live life anymore. So many rough sleepers are ex-military. What god would allow such selfless people to suffer like that?' Darren ranted.

'God allows the actions of man. He didn't do this, we did. It is our doing, and we have to sort it, not Him,' Holly told Darren.

After the words left her mouth, Holly realised how much passion she'd spoken them with. Her religious views were every bit as strong as Darren's, and she'd only just realised.

'I offended you, didn't I? If you're offended by me saying there is no god, doesn't that suggest that you *are* a Christian? The church you went to may not be for you, but you clearly believe something,' Darren pointed out.

'I do, don't I?' Holly murmured, the realisation that she was religious still sinking in.

'Nothing wrong in that. It's not for me, as you've gathered, but good luck to people who want to believe. It's not like it does any harm, and it can do a lot of good. I'm pleased for you that you're beginning to work out what's right for you. It's a hard thing, to find stuff out about yourself,' Darren said.

As they passed another couple, who were both sporting garish Christmas jumpers, Darren and Holly gave them a wave. The other couple waved back frantically.

When all he could hear was footsteps, Darren realised he may well have bored Holly. 'I've banged on about some serious stuff, like addiction and religion. That probably wasn't great for what is technically a first date. Sorry about that,' he said.

Holly shook her head. 'Don't apologise. I like deep conversation. I wish we Brits were more comfortable with it,' she replied.

Somewhere over Holly's left shoulder, bells tolled to inform everyone in earshot of the time. The time which was a lot later than Holly thought.

'Oh dear, I really should be getting back. It's not that I want to leave you, but I'm supposed to be doing lunch. We need to exchange numbers and then I'll go,' Holly announced.

As he got his phone out to do as Holly suggested, Darren told Holly: 'I get it. Don't worry about it. What time we've had, I've loved.'

-

As she exchanged digits with Darren, Holly worked out when she could next see him. To show she was keen, she wanted to meet again as soon as possible.

'My workmate Sally is holding a New Year's Eve party. I'm invited, and Eugenie is coming too. Sally is a person who says: "The more, the merrier." Eugenie will probably bring Hamish, her new man. Would you like to come with *me*?' Holly asked.

Darren grinned. 'Yeah! What better way to see the year out? Thanks!' he agreed.

The enthusiasm with which Darren accepted her invitation made Holly delighted that she'd given it. It wasn't even lunchtime yet, and already this was the best Christmas she'd ever had.

CHAPTER FORTY-FOUR

'Don't tell my sister, but that was the best Christmas lunch I've ever had. It was exquisite, Holly,' Hamish told his host after polishing off the last slice of garlic butter turkey on his plate.

With a smile, Eugenie and Holly told each other that they had the same thought. In unison, they cried: 'Her name is Laura!'

As intended, Eugenie and Holly made Hamish laugh.

Under the table that Eugenie, Holly, and Hamish were all sitting at was the Christmas present that Holly's brother had sent. Holly used her foot to drag it towards her.

As she picked up the present from her brother, Holly said: 'I'm going to take this to my room to open it. Do what you like. I'll be a while.'

With the kitchen-diner to themselves, Eugenie and Hamish rose and gravitated to the middle of the room. As he looked around himself, Hamish noticed something was lacking.

'You haven't put decorations up,' Hamish commented.

'It's not what Christmas is about for me, and Holly doesn't care about decs either way. I noticed that *you* didn't have decorations up either,' Eugenie pointed out.

'I feel the same as you about decorations. I do wish though, that you'd put mistletoe up,' Hamish replied.

When she realised what was on Hamish's mind, anticipation found its way to Eugenie's tummy and bubbled away.

Even though she knew the answer, Eugenie asked: 'Why do you wish I'd put mistletoe up?'

Taking a step towards Eugenie, which closed the gap between them to mere millimetres, Hamish murmured: 'I wish you'd put mistletoe up so I had an excuse to kiss you.'

'You don't need an excuse to kiss me. In fact, I'd say you need an excuse *not* to kiss me,' Eugenie told Hamish.

Time slowed down as Hamish reached behind Eugenie and slotted his fingers into her hair. With gentle pressure from the hand behind her head, Hamish encouraged Eugenie's lips closer to his own. She willingly obeyed. Just as Eugenie was wondering how much longer she could wait, Hamish's lips locked with hers. Her eyes fell closed and she lost herself in the softness of Hamish's lips. So lost in his lips was she that she'd forgotten Hamish had his hands entwined in her hair. That is until he stroked his fingers along her scalp. The additional sensation made her moan with pleasure.

When Hamish withdrew his lips from hers and untangled his fingers from her hair, Eugenie opened her eyes and found that, while he wasn't touching her, he was still close enough to keep her heart racing.

'I couldn't think of an excuse not to kiss you,' Hamish

whispered.

'Um, well, I can't think of... Of words,' Eugenie stumbled.

Hamish laughed. 'Was it that good for you too?' he asked.

'Yes,' Eugenie confirmed.

When she was being kissed by Hamish, all Eugenie's logical thoughts were replaced with a feeling of pure bliss and connection. Him remaining so close had kept her in that state. It was as if her brain was a computer and he was emitting a jamming signal to prevent normal function.

Since ending his kiss with Eugenie, Hamish had had a slight smile on the lips he'd used to thrill her. The corners of his mouth took a sudden downturn when he realised he'd forgotten to do something. 'Oh, goodness me! I may not need an excuse to kiss you, but I ought to have an excuse for completely forgetting to buy you a present. Sorry,' Hamish said.

The upset in Hamish's voice and on his face gave Eugenie the shock that was needed to restore the power of rational thought. A memory came to her that should reassure Hamish she couldn't care less that he hadn't handed her a gift wrapped in garish paper.

With a smile that showed just how contented she was, Eugenie told Hamish: 'As I said to Holly about a month ago, all I wanted was to eat turkey with a lovely new boyfriend. You've fulfilled my Christmas wish.'

The End

ACKNOWLEDGEMENTS

I'll start by thanking you, for reading this. Without you, I wouldn't publish my books.

Inspiration comes from many places. I must thank the BBC, for inspiring major parts of Eugenie's character. Their television show Songs of Praise showed me how broad Christianity is, and is what convinced me that she'd be Christian. An article by BBC Bitesize introduced me to the concept of toxic positivity, something I'd experienced a lot but didn't know the name for. When I was trying to think of a major character flaw for Eugenie, this article came to mind. It is what I based some of her flaws on. It can be found at https://www.bbc.co.uk/bitesize/articles/z64yn9q .

Even for small things, like what flowers Hamish buys Eugenie, how Holly makes turkey tasty, or the safety features of wallpaper strippers, I need inspiration and information. For their websites that helped me with little bits of the story, I'd like to thank Visit Colchester, Explore Norfolk UK, The Beach Guide, Parcel Brokers, Warburtons, 1st Dibs, Screwfix, Singpods, M&S, Talking Flowers, and Cafe

Delites. Additional thanks are due to Lily King and Heidi Swain, for writing great books for me to make reference to.

For me, part of what transforms a 60,000 word document on my tablet into a book is the cover. To turn this document into a book, I asked Matt Jackson to design me a cover. As well as being a good friend and stunning photographer, he is a talented artist. I couldn't be happier with what he produced. I owe you a pint. Actually, I owe you several pints. Thank you.

The last part of this book flowed out while I was in a caravan, gazing at the sea. This is partly thanks to my friend Nikki, who convinced me to have a week away.

There are many things I could thank my mum for. In this case, I shall thank her for being the best book friend a writer, and a son, could wish for.

This is the second book I've published. When I put my first romance novel, Cue Romance, out into the world, I wasn't sure how well it would be received. The answer was: "Very well." Thank you to all of you who gave me feedback and left reviews for other readers to see. It is much appreciated. In particular, thank you to Tru and Kerri, for making time to read Cue Romance even though it isn't the sort of thing you'd usually read.

In conclusion, without you readers, I wouldn't have anyone to share my stories with, so thank you very much for your support!

SOCIAL MEDIA

I like to interact with my fellow readers and writers. I can be found on Facebook and Instagram.

Like and follow my Facebook page, **Michaela Trueman - Author.**

Follow me on Instagram, **@michaela_trueman_author**

I'm also on Goodreads and Amazon's Author Central. If you enjoyed reading this book, or even if you didn't, please, please, please leave a review on Amazon or Goodreads. Positive or negative, long or short, reviews help me, and your fellow readers.

BOOKS BY THIS AUTHOR

Cue Romance

Their eyes meet across a snooker table... or so Jude thought. In reality, Cecilia, the stunning blonde who's caught his eye is looking at the ball she wants to pot. She hasn't even noticed Jude, but he's noticed her.

Cue Romance is a tale of fun, friendship, and love under a mostly-sunny and sometimes seagull-filled Essex sky.

EXCERPT FROM SPRING 2022 BOOK

Here's an excerpt from my next book, which I plan to publish spring next year.

As she parked her boyfriend's Dacia Duster outside Mr Wight's flower-adorned cottage, Emma-Leigh wondered if Mackenzie would be home, like she had been a week ago.

Just in case Mackenzie was home, Emma-Leigh knocked on the door. It was swiftly opened by Mackenzie's grand-dad.

'Hello, young Miss Layton! In case you're wondering, I'm home deliberately to see you. There's something I want to talk to you about,' Mr Wight cried when he saw Emma-Leigh, who was unmarried and had Layton for a surname.

'Is something wrong with my cleaning?' Emma-Leigh asked.

'Wrong? Perish the thought! Your cleaning is perfect, and it's not what I want to talk about anyway. My enquiry isn't strictly professional,' Mr Wight replied.

The idea of an enquiry that wasn't strictly professional made Emma-Leigh uneasy. Mr Wight's words were ambiguous, and their meaning could be very awkward. When she considered the character of the man saying the ambiguous words, she dismissed her discomfort.

'What is it about then?' Emma-Leigh asked.

'Mackenzie, who I've sent out for a few bits. She's new to town, and I thought she could do with someone to show her around all the young person things. You're the only young person I know really, so I wondered if you'd mind taking her out someplace,' Mr Wight said.

Never one to turn down an opportunity for a new friendship, Emma-Leigh replied: 'I'd really like that, if Mackenzie wants to be taken out.'

-

While Mackenzie was out shopping, Emma-Leigh managed to clean the upstairs bathroom and dust the rarely-used office. She was pouting while she cleaned a mirror on the landing when Mackenzie appeared behind her, making her jump.

'Granddad asked me to speak to you. Apparently, I made quite an impression on you last week, and you want to show me around town,' Mackenzie told Emma-Leigh.

'Did he?' Emma-Leigh questioned. A second after speaking, she cottoned on. 'Yes, he did. I asked him if I could take you out. That's right,' Emma-Leigh lied.

Mackenzie frowned. 'Considering that I was tired and snappy, I doubt I made a good impression on you,' she said.

'But you did! I really want to take you out. I could show you what we young people do in Colchester,' Emma-Leigh argued.

Much to Emma-Leigh's surprise, Mackenzie started roaring with laughter. The hearty tone of Mackenzie's laugh didn't seem to match her speaking voice or her small size. The contrast was so strange that Emma-Leigh didn't think to question what Mackenzie was laughing about.

'Granddad asked you to show me around town, didn't he?' Mackenzie questioned.

'Yes, he did. I'm a terrible liar,' Emma-Leigh admitted.

'I have no idea if you're a terrible liar. I just know my granddad, and I know that's exactly the sort of thing he'd do,' Mackenzie replied.

Based on the little she knew about Mr Wight, Emma-Leigh also thought it was exactly the sort of thing he'd do. It was well-meaning, but ill-judged.

'I was happy to take you out, and I think it would make your granddad happy,' Emma-Leigh said.

'I suppose I'll let you show me around town then. I know very little of this place, so it would be useful, I guess,' Mackenzie agreed.

'You don't have to,' Emma-Leigh replied.

Mackenzie shrugged. 'I might as well though. As you say, it'll make Granddad happy,' she said with a smile, and a twinkle in her hazel eyes that Emma-Leigh hadn't noticed a moment ago.

-

Once she'd finished cleaning, Emma-Leigh went out into the garden. Out there she found dead plants, Mr Wight typing on a Sony Vaio laptop, and Mackenzie drawing on an Apple iPad. While Emma-Leigh was trying to work out what the black lines on her iPad screen were, Mackenzie sent it to sleep.

'I'm finished, Mr Wight,' Emma-Leigh announced.

'That's great. Thank you,' Mr Wight replied.

Looking at his granddaughter, Mr Wight asked: 'Have you young ladies made plans?'

'Not yet, but that's okay,' Mackenzie replied.

'I have plans. All I need is your number so I can arrange a time with you,' Emma-Leigh said.

'And what are those plans? What are you going to do with me?' Mackenzie asked.

Thinking of her plans made Emma-Leigh's eyes sparkle. 'I'm going to take you to the best part of Colchester!' she cried, her excitement evident in her voice as well as her eyes.

Printed in Great Britain
by Amazon

77283160R00154

OLIVER REED: WILD THING

by Mike Davis and Rob Crouch

This text was developed at the
Jack Studio Theatre with director
Kate Bannister

First performed as 'An Evening with Ollie Reed' at the
Dumfries and Galloway Festival, May 2011

Premiered as 'Oliver Reed: Wild Thing' at the Gilded Balloon
as part of the 2012 Edinburgh Festival Fringe presented by
Arrow Media, Skullduggery and Seabright Productions

Published by Playdead Press 2013

© Mike Davis and Rob Crouch

Mike Davis and Rob Crouch have asserted their rights
under the Copyright, Design and Patents Act, 1988,
to be identified as the author of this work.

A CIP catalogue record for this book is available from
the British Library.

ISBN 978-0-9574491-9-0

Playdead Press
www.playdeadpress.com

Arrow Media, Skullduggery and Seabright Productions present

OLIVER REED: WILD THING

by Mike Davis and Rob Crouch

Ollie   **ROB CROUCH**

Director   **KATE BANNISTER**
Stage Manager   **JULES RICHARDSON**
Costume Design   **DAVID SHIELDS**
Lighting Design   **KATHERINE LOWRY**
Sound Design   **JOE CHURCHMAN**
Set Construction   **KARL SWINYARD**
Costume Maker   **ALEX MacARTHUR**

General Manager   **SEABRIGHT PRODUCTIONS**

Production Acknowledgements

Helen Barford (Producer, Dumfries & Galloway), Rachel Brown-Williams and Ruth Cooper-Brown (Fight Directors), Claire Darcy (ASM, Edinburgh), Mill Goble (Stage Manager/ Technician, Edinburgh previews), Judy Gordon (Dance Choreography), Tony Nandi (Jack Studio Theatre Stills), Damian Robertson (Stage Manager / Technician, Guernsey), John Sanders (Additional Stills), Kris Snaddon (Set Construction / Stage Manager / Technician, Dumfries & Galloway), Austin Spangler (Fight Director, Spring Tour 2013), Jane Williamson (Stage Manager, Edinburgh), Michael Woodruff (Stills and Video)

With thanks to Roger and Maxine Windsor

www.olliereedtheplay.co.uk

KATE BANNISTER | Director

Kate has been artistic director of the Jack Studio since 2005. During this time she has produced 150 performance events at the venue, including new writing, revivals, musical theatre, comedy and film. Kate instigated the annual Write Now Festivals and other new writing programmes including Writers' Hub and Write Here. Selected Jack Studio productions include *The Ghost Train, Borderland, Anthem, Around the World in 80 Days, Secrets from the Long Grass, Chocolate Bounty, The Legend of Sleepy Hollow, Agamemnon, She Stoops to Conquer, Fighting, Women of Troy, Jane Eyre, The Hound of the Baskervilles, Can't Pay? Won't Pay!* Kate was awarded best venue director, Fringe Report Awards 2011, for her work in developing new writing at the Jack. Further productions include: *Hamlet*, Associate Director for Blue Apple Theatre (Winchester Theatre Royal), *The Miracle* (Broadway Theatre), *Orion* (Wilton's Music Hall), *Amah* (Tara Arts); *A Fans' Club* (New Wimbledon Theatre). Selected design credits: *Pass the Baton* (Theatre Royal, Stratford East), *The Smilin' State, A Mother Speaks* (Hackney Empire), *Five Guys Named Moe* (English Theatre, Frankfurt), *Preacherosity, My Matisse* (Jermyn Street Theatre), *Purlie, The Ballad of Little Jo* (Bridewell Theatre), *Question Time* (Arcola Theatre).

JOE CHURCHMAN | Sound Design

Joe began her career designing sound for broadcast animation and documentaries at one of Soho's leading post-production houses. She has worked on programs for all the major channels including the BBC's BAFTA award winning animation series *Yoko! Jakamoko! Toto!* Since becoming freelance Joe has sound designed a wide variety of projects such as; a site adaptive theatre performance of '*The Yellow Wallpaper*' at The Royal Festival Hall, Dorling Kindersley's new generation Apps for Apple iPad2, eBooks and interactive games. She has also created sound and visual installations that have exhibited in a number of London locations.

ROB CROUCH | Ollie & Co-Writer

Rob studied Theatre Arts at Goldsmiths. Recent acting credits include: Theatre: *Around the World in 80 days* (Tour), *Moll Flanders* (Perth Festival Theatre and tour), *Homeland* (Theatre 503), *Apple Pie* (Tricycle Theatre), *Three Hard Blasts* (Arcola), *A Fan's Club* (New Wimbledon Theatre), *Ubu Disco, Burke and Hare* (Edinburgh Festival), *Arsenic and Old Lace* (Strand Theatre, West End), *Bouncers, King Ubu* (both Jack Studio theatre). Film/TV includes: *Lead Balloon, The Retreat, England, My England, The Boss, Sugar Girl, 8.3 Minutes* and *Taylors Trophy*. Online: *Fifty Shades of Grey, Not Barking but Howling* and *The Movement for Gloom*. Radio: *Burke and Hare*. Rob is half of sketch duo Clarkson and Crouch (co-writing and performing in their shows *Away with the Fairies* and *Neighbourhood Watch)* and co-creator of comedy drama podcast *The Paranormalists*. He is also artistic director of Donkeywork, dedicated to mounting productions in non-theatre spaces and Brute Farce theatre, producing new versions of classic stories for small and midscale touring.

MIKE DAVIS | Writer

Mike is an Emmy-nominated television producer/director. He has worked for some of the UK's leading television production companies (Darlow Smithson Productions, Wide-Eyed Entertainment and Impossible Pictures) and Europe's largest visual effects studio (Framestore). Recent credits include *Stephen Hawking's Universe, March of the Dinosaurs* and *Secret Universe: The Hidden Life of the Cell*. As part of the creative team Crocanapple with Rob, Mike has co-written, directed and produced the successful podcast drama series *The Paranormalists*. This is his first play.

KATHERINE LOWRY | Lighting Design

Katherine is a freelance lighting designer and stage electrician based in London. She graduated from the University of East Anglia in 2007 with an honours degree in English Literature and History, and is currently studying a diploma in Electrical Engineering. Katherine has lit extensively for the Maddermarket Theatre Company in Norwich. Credits include: *Medea; Citizenship; The Musicians; The Miracle; The Exam;* and *A*

Dream Play (all for the Youth Theatre). *Hayfever; Top Girls; The Killing of Sister George; Death and the Maiden; Ira Levin's Death Trap; Lady Windermere's Fan; I Am A Camera; Toad of Toad Hall;* and most recently, *A Christmas Carol* (all for the Main Company). Katherine has also lit *Mid-----Night's Dream* (The Space); *Aloft of Dragons* (Dragon Hall, Norwich); *Le Theatre de Decadence* (UK tour); *Bodies Unfinished* (The Jack Studio) which received an Offie nomination for Best Lighting Designer 2011; the original production of *One for the Road: An Evening with Ollie Reed* (The Jack Studio); *The Last Day* (Waterloo East); *The Devil Doesn't Drink Cava* (The Jack Studio); *Emoticon* (The Jack Studio); and *Summer* (The Jack Studio).

JULES RICHARDSON | Stage Manager (Spring Tour 2013)

Jules studied Technical Theatre and Stage Management at the City Literary Institute in London, graduating in 2009. Since then she has worked all around the UK and internationally on a variety of work — drama, opera, children's theatre, musicals, comedy, dance and physical theatre. Jules has recently enjoyed working at London's Barbican Theatre and internationally with *Translunar Paradise*, (Theatre Ad Infinitum), visiting Colombia and Brazil in addition to extensive European travel with the company. In 2012 she worked on Vignette Productions' *La Cenerentola*, a highly technical production performed in a barn in rural Surrey, set in a 1950s sitcom that included a live broadcast to the audience and advert breaks for scene changes. Also in 2012 Jules toured the UK with the stage adaptation of Nick Butterworth's well-loved children's book, *One Snowy Night*. She is a regular at the Edinburgh Fringe Festival where she often works on four or five shows per day, ranging from drama in the morning (*Hand Over Fist* by Dave Florez) to improvised musicals (*The Showstoppers*) in the evening with some physical theatre (*Translunar Paradise*) and ventriloquism (*Nina Conti —Dolly Mixtures*) in between. Other recent experience includes *The Lady of Burma* (Theatre Royal Brighton), *Sexing the Cherry* (Southbank Centre) and *Terror 2011: Love me to Death* (Soho Theatre).

DAVID SHIELDS | Costume Design

David's production credits include *The Sunny Side Of The Street* (Jermyn Street Theatre), *Boys Plays, Sleeping Beauty* and *Sleeping with Straight Men* (Above The Stag Theatre), *The Ghost Train, Bloodline, Secrets from the Long Grass, Around the World in 80 Days, Skinhead* (Jack Studio), *Bash* (Barons Court), *One Flew Over The Cuckoo's Nest* (Lost Theatre), *Rent* (Greenwich), *Remains of the Day and 1888* (Union Theatre), *Song & Dance* and *Carmen Jones* (European tours), *Oh! What a Night* (Blackpool Opera House), *A Christmas Carol* (Nottingham Theatre Royal), *Dick Whittington* (Bristol Hippodrome), Anthony Minghella's *Cigarettes and Chocolate, Lonely Hearts* (The Old Fire Station), *Money to Burn* (London), *Chess* 10th and 20th anniversary productions for Oslo Spektrum, *Dido and Aeneas*, (Guildford). Costumes for Jose Carreras' *Amore Perduto*, (Dortmund). The Scandinavian productions of *Jesus Christ Superstar, Hair, Fame, Grease and Saturday Night Fever, Mannen Fra La Mancha* (Det Norske Teatret, Oslo.) *Naked Flame* and FRA winner of best farce, *Naked Flame – Fire Down Under*, UK tours. *The Hobbit* (Queens Theatre London and UK tours), *Diamond and Shamlet* (Kings Head), *Saturday Night Fever* (UK tours, London, Johannesburg, Madrid and Spanish tour) directed by Arlene Phillips and Karen Bruce. *Instant Magique* and *Crescendo* (Royal Palace Kirrwiller France). Also 13 World touring productions for *Holiday on Ice*. David has also designed the sets for *Strictly Come Dancing The Professionals Tour,* and *Ice Age Live A Mammoth Adventure*, Arena World Tour.

THE JACK STUDIO THEATRE

The Jack Studio is a vibrant performance space situated in southeast London. The Studio offers a diverse theatre programme throughout the year, with seasons of innovative revivals and dynamic new writing. The Jack also runs an annual new writing festival, Write Now, and several writing workshop programmes. The Jack is also home to film, cabaret and Scratch Nights.

Kate Bannister (Artistic Director) and Karl Swinyard (Theatre Manager) produce and programme theatre at the Jack, creating all in-house shows. In 2011 Kate and Karl were Best Venue Directors in the Fringe Report Awards.

The Brockley Jack Theatre Ltd
Box Office 0844 8700 887
Registered Charity No 1143158

410 Brockley Road
London SE4 2DH

www.brockleyjack.co.uk

SEABRIGHT PRODUCTIONS

Seabright Productions is a theatre production and general management company based in London's West End. As well as being one of the busiest presenters of UK tours on the small and middle scale circuits, recent London production and management projects include *Our Boys* (Duchess 2012), Olivier-nominated *Potted Potter* (Garrick 2011/3, world tour 2012/3), and *Potted Panto* (Vaudeville 2010/11), multi-award-winning improvised musical *The Showstoppers* (Ambassadors 2011, Criterion 2011, Southbank 2010/11/12), *Hit Me* (Garrick 2010), *Barbershopera* (Trafalgar Studios 2010/11), *The Fitzrovia Radio Hour* (Trafalgar Studios 2011, Ambassadors 2012), *The Terror Season* (Southwark Playhouse 2009/10, Soho 2011/2), and *Dirty White Boy* (Trafalgar Studios 2010).

Producer James Seabright's book 'So You Want To Be A Theatre Producer' was published in the UK in 2010 and in North America in 2011. James has produced and promoted over 150 productions at the Edinburgh Fringe since 2001, winning various awards including The Herald Angel and The Scotsman Fringe First. He co-founded the Festival Highlights producers' alliance in 2003, which has since grown to be the largest independent promoter of shows at the largest arts festival in the world. James has twice been the recipient of the Stage One New Producer Bursary (2002 and 2004), is a member of the Society of London Theatre, and has been a guest speaker at RADA, City Lit and at the Masterclass series run by Theatre Royal Haymarket.

Assistant Producer:	**JAMES QUAIFE** *Stage One Apprentice*
Associate Producer:	**KAT PORTMAN**
Press Representative:	**SUSIE SAFAVI**
Producer:	**JAMES SEABRIGHT**

Office:	Palace Theatre, Shaftesbury Avenue, London W1D 5AY
Telephone:	020 7439 1173
Fax:	020 7183 6023
Email:	office@seabrights.com
Web:	**www.seabrights.com**

ABOUT THE PLAY

This is an excerpt from an interview with Rob Crouch on
OliverReed.net. To read the interview in full, go to
www.OliverReed.net/press.

Stars such as Oliver could always talk in their own voices: they
were never just trotting out press releases and toeing some kind
of party line. I think this made it easier for us because all the clips
and interviews had an authentic voice that we could tap into. The
key was this voice — I tried really hard to get that right first off.
Something that Mike and I had in mind when we wrote the script
was that we wanted it to be structured like a drinking session. We
talked about the stages of drunkenness and each episode was
developed to represent one of these stages. So I worked on the
voice and I worked on being drunk! I don't want it to be an
impersonation though. The play is just that, a play, it's not a piece
of stand-up or the theatrical equivalent of a tribute band, so in
some ways the character is only our version of Ollie. Everything
was carefully researched but we're not claiming that this version
is some kind of definitive truth.

The play re-imagines the last hours of Oliver Reed's life, in The
Pub in Valletta, Malta. We wanted the setting to be The Pub but
also, in a sense, every pub that Ollie had ever drunk in and, at
the same time, a pub that represented his life. The notion of 'the
pub' — a place where he felt you could be yourself and be with
your mates — was central to Ollie's life and we wanted the
setting to represent this.

Ollie exuded real danger, which is rare enough, but he also came
across as a perfect gentleman, this is a pretty potent mix. He was
also a fantastic actor. In his best films he is every bit as good as
a Brando or James Dean. The fact that he made only a handful
of movies that lived up to his talent perhaps means that people
were always left wanting more. And the fact that one of these
movies was his final performance adds piquancy to that.

For me it's interesting that he never worked on stage — creating
a theatrical version of a performer who never worked in a theatre
was one of the many challenges we faced. He was a craftsman,
he was serious about his craft, but he never tried to elevate it to
levels of some kind of rarefied artistry. He always had the attitude

that acting was a job, he was bloody good at it and it was something he was lucky to be paid well to do.

This honesty is attractive and, for some, encourages nostalgic comparisons with modern celebrities. The lack of airs creates a sense of accessibility, a sense that anyone could have a drink with him. He didn't feel he was better than anyone. This harks back to another ideal; a man is as good as he is in the pub, not on the film set or in the public eye. It's a great leveller. And it is about being a man: Ollie's brand of no-nonsense masculinity is one that many mourn the loss of.

He was never going to break down and cry on Uprah and ask for anyone's sympathy. He was in control of his public persona because he didn't seem to care about it. There is a theory that he was sometimes not as drunk as he seemed on the various chat shows that he appeared on, I think this is nonsense — just watch the clips — but I think he was in control because he knew what was expected and was prepared to deliver it, whatever people thought.

Of course whether Oliver Reed cared or not about the opinions of others is a matter for speculation. And while his boozy antics inspire many to raise a glass and say 'Good on you Ollie!' there are as many people for whom they represent the criminal squandering of a great talent.

There is no doubt that at times he must have been enormous fun to be around and at times impossible to live with. Writing and performing a play about Ollie is certainly not about passing judgement on any of this — we're just seeking to present a complex individual in all his glory (and ignominy), asking people make up their own minds and hoping that they are have fun while they are doing it.

Rob Crouch

OLIVER REED — A BIOGRAPHY

Writer Mike Davis introduces the life of Oliver Reed.

Robert Oliver Reed was born in Wimbledon in 1938. From the off it seemed Reed was destined to be an actor... and a hell-raiser. A destiny coursing through his veins — his grandfather Sir Herbert Beerbohm Tree was a larger-than-life Victorian stage star, his uncle Sir Carol Reed a leading film director and he was alleged to have been the descendent of the fearsome Peter the Great, Tsar of Russia.

Despite this, acting was a career Reed seemed to resist for as long as possible. A child of the Blitz and a broken home, young Oliver was shunted between parents and grandparents for much of his childhood. He rebelled at school (later to discover he was dyslexic) and only really excelled in athletics. After a stint in the army he took various menial jobs; bouncer, cab driver, hospital porter, before his devilish good looks secured him some modelling, and eventually film and television, work.

Reed's film career, when it took off, was impressive, over 100 films in five decades. After a run of monster roles in Hammer Horrors, that established his dangerous, gothic image, Reed began a long-running relationship with major British directors Michael Winner and Ken Russell and became a huge movie star in the 1970s. Box-office hits like *Oliver!*, *Hannibal Brooks* and *The Three Musketeers*, along with his off-screen exploits, made him a household name. It was only his stubborn refusal to kowtow to Hollywood bigwigs and leave his beloved Surrey mansion (see millstone) Broome Hall that prevented him from becoming a bigger international star. Though Reed made some unfortunate decisions late in his career, often picking up the cheque to play the part of just another heavy, its easy to forget how accomplished an actor he was and what a powerful screen presence he could command (when he wanted to); Grandier in *The Devils*, Crich in *Women in Love*, KIngsland in *Castaway* and finally, brilliantly, Proximo in *Gladiator*.

Though Reed became infamous for his boozy antics, never away from the tabloid front pages in the Eighties or ever seemingly sober on chat shows in the Nineties, he was no drunken fool;

fiercely intelligent, highly amusing, easily bored and able to disarm with a gentle, shy, nature-loving side. He married twice, first to Kate Byrne in 1960, and then, after a long relationship with Jacquie Daryll, he married again in 1985 to the much younger Josephine Burge. Despite the age-difference they would remain inseparable until his death. He had two children, Mark, with his first wife Kate, and a daughter Sarah, with Jacquie.

When Oliver Reed suffered a massive heart attack in (appropriately) a Maltese bar, in 1999 while filming *Gladiator*, it brought an end not just to the life of one of Britain's truly great characters but, arguably, the age of the British Hell-raiser; men that were outrageous, uncompromising and truly original.

Mike Davis

MEETING MARK REED

Writing a play based on a real person was always going to carry responsibilities and from the very beginning people would come up with first (and second) hand tales of their experiences of Ollie. We met a charming gentleman who sat next to him at school after a show in Chichester and plenty of old drinking buddies have cropped up. Mark Lester, star of *Oliver!*, saw the show in Edinburgh: we end the show with the song *Consider Yourself* from the film and it was playing while we chatted about his 18th birthday in Budapest (during the filming of *The Prince and the Pauper*) and the scrapes that he and Ollie got into. All this extra detail has been worked into the show as we've gone along.

Perhaps most importantly, Mark Reed (Ollie's son) came to see a very early performance at The Jack Studio, when the show was still in development. Here is a transcript of our first, slightly nerve-wracking exchange:

From: Michael Davis
To: Mark Reed
Subject: AN EVENING WITH OLLIE REED

Hello Mark,

Hope you don't mind me dropping you a line. I understand that you have become aware of our one-man show through the guys working on an upcoming radio 4 play 'Burning At Both Ends' — who saw it during a preview run and that you have booked tickets for Friday.

It's an intimate studio space but if you'd rather come along anonymously we understand. Our play is respectful and fun and still at a relatively early stage but it's lacking in first-hand insight so it would be great to meet you and talk further. Look forward to hearing from you.

Kind regards,

Mike Davis

From: Mark Reed
To: Michael Davis
Subject: RE: AN EVENING WITH OLLIE REED

Hi Mike and thanks for your email. Frankly, I had hoped to slip in under the RADAR but clearly that's not going to be the case. Being 50ish seats, I'd probably have been sussed anyway!

I would be more than happy to have a chat with you guys either before the show, after, or both. You talk about it being an intimate studio space – I truly hope that having 'first hand insight' and my wife sitting there is not a problem for Rob. I'm there out of pure curiosity, not judgment and behind the scenes I'd be happy to be give honest feedback and the sincerest steer.

Best wishes,

M

From: Michael Davis
To: Mark Reed
Subject: RE: AN EVENING WITH OLLIE REED

Hi Mark,

Thanks so much for your e-mail. We really do appreciate it. I think Rob is a little daunted... but excited too. We're really proud of the play. Though it would of course be great to chat to you on the night we'd love to take you out for dinner the following week and talk the show through in a bit more detail. But only if you'd be up for that. And let's get through next week first! Looking forward to meeting you and thanks again.

Cheers,

Mike

From: Mark Reed
To: Michael Davis
Subject: RE: AN EVENING WITH OLLIE REED

Well done to each of you.

That was so much better than anticipated. It's so very clear to see the work that has gone into it.

Most impressed – it captures not just the history of the man but more importantly, his very spirit. It's factual, fun and superbly entertaining, an insight into Oliver Reed. You did justice.

Do ring or email and we will catch up, but as before, I'm more than happy to give you steer and support as needed.

Best wishes from us both – fuller feedback to follow.

M

We would like to thank Mark for the time he has spent with us and for his continued support for the show.

In Search Of A Legend, a mini-documentary that we have since made with Mark Reed about life with his father can be seen on our YouTube channel: www.youtube.com/olliereedtheplay.

Mike Davis and Rob Crouch

olliereedtheplay@gmail.com
twitter/olliereedplay
facebook: Oliver Reed Wild Thing

This text went to press before the end of rehearsals and so may differ
slightly from the play as performed.

OLIVER REED: WILD THING

by Mike Davis and Rob Crouch

*The action takes place in 'The Pub', Valletta, Malta on the
2nd May 1999 between the hours of 10am and 2.30pm.*

*The set represents The Pub, a typical English pub abroad.
There are 2 chairs, a stool and a bar covered with knick-
knacks, including a collection of trophies There is a coat
stand where various coats and hats are hung.*

Early morning sun floods the scene.

A loud blast of rock n' roll.

OLLIE *enters in a gorilla suit*

OLLIE:
Mumble mumble mumble

(*Pulling the mask off...*) I SAID ... what do you have to do
to get a drink around here?

Ah, The Pub. The pub — my drama class, my school, my
psychiatrist, my doctor, my everything. Always has
been.

Do you remember when I was on that chat show...
Aspel? One of the guests, Clive James... Clive Jameson...
Aussie fella, anyway, he said...

"Tell me, Oliver why do you drink?"

I mean, what an arse. Why do you drink? Why do you
think? For the effect. And as I replied at the time —
"Because the finest people I've ever met in my life have
been in pubs."

And that includes you, you rotten lot.

If 'who you really are' can be compared to a room in
your house, a favourite room stuffed with all of your
most treasured possessions, my room would be the bar
of a great British Pub: prints of Country Life, knick-
knacks on the walls, packs of Big D nuts behind the bar
concealing a wonderful pair of JUBBLIES.

Right. Quiet. Quieten down.

SHADDAP!

That's better. I have something to say.

I am like a bird, freed from the cage, nothing to drink for a week — then on Sundays I go mad.

I promised Ridley I wouldn't drink during filming. You see, I've BEGUN to get myself the reputation of being a bit of a... Richard Harris, a Peter O'Toole, a Richard Burton. But they were the senior ones and I was still practicing in the nets when they were out there batting. Though you could say I've been smashing it over the boundary rope ever since. The last of the great SHIT-KICKERS.

It's a beautiful morning isn't it?

Could you assist me, madam?

OLLIE *appeals to an audience member for help removing his gorilla suit*

You know, the last time I wore the monkey suit was on the Michael Parkinson interview. Smells a bit. But I thought it appropriate — I've always been seen as the scruffy, unshaven, drunken gorilla. Oooo-oooo.

I'm making a movie called... *Gladiator* and I play PROXIMO!

OLLIE *quotes lines from* Gladiator

Begins clapping

"Gladiators... I salute you."

I think it's going to be a hit. And I haven't had a hit in a while.

WHO SAID THAT?

Almost turned it down too.

My agent calls me up, as they do. And says, "Ridley
Scott wants you for a movie and they're going to send
you a script". So when I open the envelope that comes
through the door WHUUMPH the first thing that falls
out is a little note. "The sending of this script does not
constitute an offer". So I think... FUCK 'EM.

My agent phones me up again and says, "Ridley wants
you to read. Come on Oliver, you need the money, you
need the prestige, your life needs a final act." And I say,
"I don't READ, if he wants to see my work then there's
things that he can run, he can see my last movie..."

Then I think, well, if he really wants me to read then I
suppose I get a free trip to London and I can go see a
show. So I say, "I've never read for anyone before, I
think I might have read for Richard the third, years and
years ago. But for Ridley I'LL READ".

So I go in there and he's smoking a big cigar and says,
"Do you remember when we met thirty one years ago
when you were making *Oliver!*?" and I say "NO, I don't
remember". Then he says, "Are you going to read?" and
I say "Yea, sure". Then he says, "Better than that I've got
a studio set up downstairs" and I say, "A STUDIO? I
don't KNOW these lines and I can't READ because I've
got these spectacles" and he says, "Pretend they're
Roman spectacles".

So I just read and do a bit of bullshit. And a few days
later he calls and says... you did very well. With

4

Gladiator the world is going to RE-DISCOVER Oliver Reed.

And not before time.

Where the hell is Paul?

It's gone 10 o'clock. What's he playing at?

Paul! Paul, where are you?

(*to a member of the audience*) What's your name sir?

AUDIENCE MEMBER:
<NAME>

OLLIE:
Right <NAME> you are Paul the barman of 'THE PUB' in Valletta, Malta... can you do the accent?

You have a very important duty to fulfil. You are to furnish us with drink. Beers all round. Can't you see, these chaps are parched.

OLLIE *hands beer to* 'PAUL', *indicting that he should hand them out.* OLLIE *grabs a bottle for himself.*

(*to 'PAUL'*) Give one to that fellow there. Has anyone ever told you that you have something of Alan Bates about you? No? Funny that.

Ah, first of the day...

My part is nearly in the can. Just a few more days and then I head home. SO... cause for celebration.

5

OLLIE *drains the bottle in one and collects another from the bar*

The young blood in this picture is an Aussie called Russell Crowe. Finest actor of his generation — or so HE'S been saying. Got himself a reputation as a bit of a hell-raiser. So I am passing on the baton, as it were, gladiator to gladiator.

Our weapons are beer and whisky, the tabloid press our baying mob. Ave Caesar, morituri te salutant — Hail Caesar, we who are about to die salute you.

Cheers!

OLLIE *raises then drains the second bottle*

Young Crowe likes a drink and a scrap I'll give him that. But stick him in a room with a real man like Robert Mitchum and he'd be eaten alive. I saw Mitchum on set once in a terrible state. Michael Winner is directing, he says...

"Do you know you drank a whole bottle of gin at lunch?"

Mitchum replies...

"It wasn't the bloody gin, it was the whisky I chased it down with."

If the likes of us 'Wild Ones' went around kissing babies in prams, saying "I believe in the church" and doing good, then I wouldn't be giving the public what they want. That's not what the public expects from Oliver Reed. You want me to get drunk, get into a fight and fall

6

off the edge of a dustbin, and do all the things you read about in the papers. And while I admit that I make a nuisance of myself, in my own time...

(*to* 'PAUL') Nobody asked you, Paul!

But never on the film set. For me it's not even about the drinking — it's always been about the pub.

My life is a series of pubs. I remember my very first one. It's during the war. I'm three or four years old. I'm serving drinks to my mother's special friends... mostly servicemen. You know the type —

"That's Oliver, Marcia's boy. What a funny fellow. Like a little gypsy. Have you noticed, he goes around calling his mother by her first name? It's positively bohemian. Oliver! More drinks here..."

OLLIE *salutes*

Yes sir!

Well, as their cocktail waiter it's my bloody right to have a taste.

Session numero uno. — 3 sneaky sips of gin —

"His mama's awfully good-looking though, what? Tell me old boy; what's the story with the boy's father? Are they still even married?"

A quaff of champagne (most of which came back up through my nose) —

"Fellow's a conchie, eh? No wonder she doesn't want anything to do with him."

And a GULP of pale ale —

"And now the little chap's up on the table making a racket. Quite the centre of attention, isn't he?"

And I was. Nothing's changed. As I grow up I do anything to get noticed. I had to; I was the class dunce.

My schools became a hat stand of caps — 13 in total and they were all a certain type of quack-quack school, it was all "amo amas amat". But they taught me to speak English properly and that in every new playground when sides are picked for games, certain boys are left until last.

"You chaps take the four-eyed twit and we'll have the bladder of lard."

"No. We'll have Fatso and you can have pongo and cockeye."

By observation rather than instinct, I became the bully.

Let's play Cavaliers and Roundheads. What do you mean you don't know how? The Cavs are the goodies and the Roundheads the baddies. The Cavs always win. I am always a Cav. I'm Jack the Lad, Bully Boy Reed. I've got swagger.

I'm starting to feel a personality creeping up and I'm beginning to wear my dunce's cap like a crown.

8

While others swot away, I am pounding the running track. All doubts swept away. Pad, pad, pad go the feet. Flash, flash, flash, goes the mind. I can see my future before me. I am a world champion. I am a movie star. I am Top Cat. I am the greatest. I am true blue British and will take on anyone.

I am Oliver Reed.

Sports day, 195?, I clear up. Win the lot.

During the below OLLIE *collects trophies from the bar*

Glorying in the monotonous drone of the principal endlessly repeating "Won by Oliver Reed". Revelling in the politely clapping English garden as I bound up to collect another cup. Basking in the cheering and backslapping of my peers — carried on their shoulders back to the pavilion. It's all blue heaven.

As Captain of Athletics it is my duty to preside at the school dance. There's Enita Skidmore, Carol Pengelly and Mary 'one in a million' Smith, delicately perfumed and gowned. The last bus leaves at 11 but I think "screw the bus". I'll stay on with my beautiful princesses. But when midnight strikes my Cinderellas are plucked away. So I pick up my bag of pumpkin cups and walk home.

OLLIE *puts trophies in a bag*

By the Victoria Cafe, near Wimbledon Bridge, two policemen step out of the shadows.

"Hello, hello hello and where might you be going at this time of night?"

"Lingfield Road, my Gran's". I put down the bag and the cups clank.

"And what have we got here."

"Cups."

"We'll just have a looksee shall we?" And one of the policemen takes one of the cups out of the bag and stands it on the pavement. It glints in the moonlight. "Ve-ry nice, ve-ry nice, and where might I ask did you get these beauties?"

"Won them. Today at Ewell Castle sports."

"I think you'd better come along with us, no silly buggers now."

Of course, down at the station, it doesn't take Sherlock Holmes to figure out that the name sewn into my school cap matches the name on the cups that I had won the previous year. They laugh and congratulate me...

Which is more than my father does when I proudly take them round to his flat the next day. He never understood what winning in a physical sense was all about. What it meant for the dunce to breast the tape as champion in athletics. The only reason I was good, he says, is because of my size.

"If you want to be an ape, by all means continue running round the field, making noises like an ape. But it won't get you anywhere in later life. So don't bring your tin cups round here to try to impress me."

Would it have killed the old bastard to praise me just a little? To try to understand? I pick up my bag of cups and take them round to his mother's house. And Granny May calls in the maid and the gardener and says, "Look what my clever grandson has won."

I firmly believe that we are the product of everything that has gone before. As I left short trousers behind, I began to realise that if you shake the branches of my particular family tree then a fair few monkeys fall out. But for me, the origin of the Reed species was always shrouded in secrecy.

I never met Granny May's other half, Herbert Beerbohm Tree; he died before I was born. But I think we would have got along — that's why I often find myself having conversations with him, when I'm in my bath.

What do you think of the show so far, Herbert?

Charming... Well, you'd know.

This, ladies and gentlemen, is Herbert Beerbohm Tree. The eminent actor knighted for his contribution to the theatre, founder of RADA, builder of His Majesty's Theatre —

What? No they do not wish to hear your Hamlet, sir.

Herbert was something of a crumpet bumper just like me. My grandmother was one of his many mistresses. My family name, Reed, started with Granny May and the six bastard children she had with Tree — six! She chose the name to give a veneer of respectability to their illegitimate brood.

11

And why Reed? Because, as she would joke; "I am but a REED at the foot of a mighty TREE." and he never did leave his wife...

There are other things Herbert and I have in common. He was a dunce and a prankster just like me. He never read a bloody thing, for fear it would cramp his style. Myself, I have barely read more than the *The Wind In The Willows* and *Winnie The Pooh*, and the occasional film scripts that land on my mat. Or at least my part in them.

Well would anyone read *Venom* all the way through? Or *Condorman*? The feathered fart.

A drink

Not exactly Hamlet, eh, Herbert?

To my surprise and delight there was an even bigger and a good deal uglier fish tugging at the end of Granny May's bastard line. Things changed for me forever when I found out that her great-grandfather, my great-great-grandfather, was none other than Peter the Great, the Tsar of Russia.

NO, I'M NOT MAKING THIS UP!

Here's a historian's description of him, tell me if you think he sounds like anyone we know...

"Drunk, pop-eyed, making dreadful faces, roaring, slashing about at random with his sword, he was a fearsome host. Any man he liked, he embraced — eh Alan — any woman he unlaced..."

12

Yeah, yeah he shed more blood than any other
European monarch, personally chopped off the heads of
200 mutineers...

I've never gone that far. Even after 126 pints. But for a
dyslexic (as it turned out, ladies and gentlemen), a
young whelp with a vivid imagination, suddenly it all
makes sense. I am a lost prince. A boy out of time. Now
in History lessons I ride wheel cap to wheel cap against
the Romans with my pagan Queen. I kneel with Drake
and his admirals as he presents the spoils of the
Spanish Main. I am also Robin Hood and Dan Dare. As
an actor, I'm still playing this game of 'let's pretend'
and I've kept that child's curiosity about where I come
from and who I am.

Then my beloved Granny dies and there's nothing to
keep me at home anymore.

I'll never forget her last words...

"I'm quite tall, Oliver. I hope they make the coffin long
enough."

A toast — THE PAST — and GRANNY MAY!

I'm 17. I decide to run away. Pedalling furiously across
Wimbledon Common on my bicycle, tears streaming
down my face as my father gives chase in his green
Rover shouting:
"Come back gypsy boy! You'll end up just like your
mother!"

I am drawn to the West End. It's like a different planet. I
go around staring at EVERYTHING. Cop-dodging con-
men with their collapsible card tables, Teds in

13

fluorescent socks, gleeful Caribbeans in zoot suits, Maltese gangsters, pimps, prozzies, punters and plain-clothed policemen. All life is on display and I soak it up.

My acting school was, and always has been, life in the raw. Everyday life is my favourite theatre. People are my favourite actors. If I want to play a drunken labourer, I go to a public bar or workingmen's club and watch. Or a quack-quack club to observe a gentleman piss artist in stiff collars, pinstripes and bowler hat.

This is Soho in the mid-Fifties. Still a virgin I haven't got a clue. I'm accosted by everybody — from the Salvation Army to elderly gentlemen in public lavatories asking whether I'm Grenadiers or Coldstreams...

I wander into a Soho strip club, down a sticky staircase off of Brewer Street. And somehow, I get involved in a brawl, heaving out two West Ham fans who have got a bit lively with the girls up on stage. So they offer me the role of bouncer — I go from no sex to being paid five bob to watch girls take their clothes off...

It's a strange, moist world of warm champagne, beehives and old men in macs.. Of cockney slang and secret codes that go right over my head; Teddy Bears, 'vibes', 'going down'... then BANG a police raid. And my adventures in Soho are over as quickly as they began. I am up and out the lavatory window in a FLASH.

"THIS 'ERE SHOWER IS A DISGRACE TO THE QUEEN'S UNIFORM. BARF 'EM AND GET THEIR 'AIR CUT! BUNCH OF BLEEDIN' TONY CURTISES. MOVE IT! MOVE IT! MOVE IT!"

After boarding school National Service is a way of life that I am fairly familiar with and I revel in the Sergeant Major's shouting and swearing and blaspheming: being a right bastard in other words. So soon they make me a Corporal.

He reveals a tattoo on his upper arm

And that's not bird shit on my shoulder. It was never going to be pips though. Once they discovered I could barely read and write I wasn't exactly considered 'officer class'.

When the tour ends they get us completely rat-arsed, shove us in the back of a dumper truck and then tip us squaddies, vomit and all, into heap on Civvy Street.

According to my father, I'm destined to become either a burglar, or an actor.

I'm not sure which he thought was worse.

But I don't want any part of grandfather Tree's Royal Academy of Dramatic Arse. I don't mix well with actors. People like me prefer the company of artisans.

One of Beerbohm Tree's bastard offspring was quite a big shot in the movies but determined to make it on my own, I wait as long as possible before approaching my uncle, the famous film director, Carol Reed. Then, one wretched December day with just a single shilling left in my pocket, I think... FUCK IT.

Uncle Carol lives in a beautiful house in Chelsea. But this is to be no free meal ticket. The old sod turns me down.

15

UNCLE CAROL *pours a large glass of whisky*

"What you need to do is put yourself about a bit at the Ritz Grill or join a few good clubs.

"And, my boy, if you're really not interested in treading the boards then the best advice I can give you is to spend as much time as possible at the cinema. If you think a film is bad, watch it over and over until you're convinced you know why it is bad. The same with good films: only when you are sure you know why a film is good should you seek to emulate those finished performances."

He's absolutely bloody right of course. And it is films I'm interested in. Now I dream of being a MOVIE STAR.

But the cinema is still full of chaps like dear old Jack Hawkins...

"Steady number one." "Dear boy" — all of that — medals on their chests and Brylcreem in their hair. There's no place for an ape like me. So it's 'Don't Call Us, We'll Call You' and I'm driving a minicab and doing the rounds of casting directors and advertising agencies giving out copies of my photograph.

And here's my first wife, the lovely Kate.

We are both up for a Cadbury's commercial. They're looking for a clean-cut couple. The chocolate's melting under the lights and we stand there sticky and laughing... Turns out she is too beautiful for the girl next door and I am too much of a gorilla to be the boy who lived next door to her... so we are perfect for each other.

Except she is engaged to someone else.

Not for long though.

I was considered extraordinarily good-looking at the time. Even though that may be hard to believe now.

Despite this, I earn a living playing monsters, a bunch of Hammer Horror films follow....

"Virginia, I love you. I know I turn into a monster at night. But I love you."

My big break (that wasn't it) comes in a film called *The System*, directed by dear old Michael Winner, then one of Britain's hottest young directors.

"He was very good at being still, which is the essence of stardom: not to do too much."

OLLIE *stares at the audience*

Ha! Still got it.

"Right at the top of the picture, a train's coming into the station and Oliver's there on the platform - you hit a close up of this wonderful face in a big way. The audience was always very knocked out by that opening image. I was convinced he would become a major international star. And he wanted it very much too."

...and I did, I wanted it very much. Champagne!

OLLIE *turns to the bar*

Watch it MATE... or I'll bite your jugular out.

17

You again? What do you want? Fuck off.

Glass smash, OLLIE *screams in pain*

Thirty six stitches. Christ... That's it. Career over.

(*As* BILL SIKES)

BULL'S-EYE COME 'ERE. COME 'ERE BULL'S-EYE!"

Yes! Uncle Carol finally gives me a part in a movie. An actor playing the part of a burglar — my father must have been so proud.

Maybe, just maybe, it's *Oliver!* that makes me a star. Hammer Films gave me my start and Uncle Carol gets me noticed, but my early career was dominated by two directors who, at the time, were seen as pretty much the best in the business.
Michael Winner gave me my bread and Ken Russell gives me my ART, my finest performances are in Ken's films.

He first chooses me for the part of Claude Debussy, the French composer, for a BBC television drama about his life.

"What about my scars?" I say.

"Your scars? Oh, never mind about those. I'm not bothered about them."

Which I think is wonderful of him... until he says...

"Anyway, you'll be wearing a beard."

18

I worry awfully about working with a TV director having broken into the movies and his scripts are very, very arty at a time when I am becoming a commercial actor.

Take *The Devils*, most of it was originally written in Latin, pages of the bloody stuff were cabled everyday. I told Ken: "I can't spell, I can't add up and despite the efforts of a succession of school masters, I can't understand sodding Latin." I ended up writing my lines down and hiding them all over the place - stuffed into bread, floating on the top of holy water, tucked 'twixt the cleavage of nuns. It drove Ken crazy, I was supposed to be praying and I'd have one eye open all the time

But I won a Silver Mask at Venice for that one.

Ken wanted to shave my eyebrows off and I made him get them insured for half a million quid in case they didn't grow back. The whole set was covered in shaved, naked flesh.

Ken Russell was big on nudity.

Pause

Another one of his films became known for one particular world first — Alan, it is time...

No, you're quite right, let us delight their ears and not their eyes.

OLLIE *hands* 'ALAN' *a copy of D H Lawrence's Women In Love, encourages him to read the description of the wrestling scene.*

Ladies and gentlemen, Alan Bates... the second best actor in *Women In Love* and joint winner of the race to be first full frontal male nude in the movies.

Never read this book myself but the wife told me it was good.

The wrestling scene was my idea. Ken's script had me and Alan splashing around a lake in the middle of the night and naturally, I was worried about the effect that the cold water might have on my... physique.

My missus Kate points out that in the book they wrestle in front of a fire so she and I turn up pissed at Ken's house one dinnertime to persuade him to change the scene. To demonstrate my grappling prowess I threw him around the dining room a bit. He soon got the message. And a classic was born.

Don't worry, he got his own back, he nearly killed me on a number of occasions.

Ken later tells me that in the South American version of *Women In Love*, the censor cut out the entire wrestling match. So you go from me locking the door to me and Alan lying panting, naked on the carpet. It became known as 'The Great Buggering Scene' and filled cinemas there for months.

In London, in the Sixties, you still had solid chaps like Roger Moore poncing about in duffel coats and drinking lemonade through a straw. I was just another scruffy actor and nobody wants to know. Then I turn around and spit beer at the next fellow and get into a ruck and, suddenly, the press want to know all about me. So I build a reputation as a fast gun and that's very hard to

20

live down. It's this violent image that makes me irresistible to women and a magnet for men — who want to fight me.

Lucky for me gorillas are in. And I am King of the Swingers.

A female critic writes "He is the Gothic hero, in the living, lusting flesh, he smoulders: a mobile furnace."

Everybody wants a piece of me. Wherever I go flashbulbs pop. Barely a day goes by when I'm not in the newspapers. Usually on the front page. Downin' the sherbie and shaftin' the girlies. I am one of Britain's few true international stars.
In the early Seventies I have three hit movies playing in the West End at the same time.

I'm at the top of my game. No one can best me. EN GUARD!

OLLIE *fences with unseen foes*

Cavalier, musketeer, what's the difference?

Orson Welles says: "Oliver is one of those rare fellows who has the ability to make the air move around them".

Then WALLOP! King Kong takes Manhattan. I'm promoting a movie called *Burnt Offerings* that I starred in with Bette Davis and I'm invited onto the couch of the great American chat-show host, Johnny Carson... HEEERE'S JOHNNNY!

Paul, I'm going to have to ask you to be Johnny. I have your lines here. It's just reading from a few cards.

That's all they do on TV. Are you going to do the accent? Come and sit here.

Hands 'JOHNNY' *cue cards*

Away we go, from the top of the first card please...

JOHNNY:
Ladies and gentlemen, please welcome Oliver Reed.

OLLIE *comes and sits down*

JOHNNY:
Nice to have you with us.

OLLIE:
Thanks for having me.

JOHNNY:
How are you?

OLLIE:
Quite extraordinary.

JOHNNY:
That's what I hear. You and Miss Winters have never worked together?

OLLIE:
Ah, Shelley Winters, we need a Shelley Winters... Madam, the lovely lady in the front row, will you oblige? Ladies and gentleman, Shelley Winters! Two-time Oscar winner and star of *A Place in the Sun* and *Alfie*...

By this time, somewhat past her best. Unlike you madam. Here's a glass of water, should you need it.

22

OLLIE *hands* WINTERS *a glass of water*

From the top of the card please, Johnny.

JOHNNY:
You and Miss Winters have never worked together?

OLLIE:
No, we haven't.

WINTERS:
I'm intimidated by the British.

JOHNNY:
Why is that? You know most Americans seem to be
intimidated by English people.

OLLIE:
That's because, most of them, we've made love to.

WINTERS:
I would have remembered.

OLLIE:
You've forgotten.

No, I don't know why it is. I think it's a myth. I think it's
very polite.

I think America is an amazing country simply because
it's made up of a mosaic of European culture. They
came and they made a happy place of it. Some of them
behaved themselves and some of them, particularly the
ladies, got quite loud. The women in England are quite
good. They're always in the kitchen so you can't hear
them when they shout.

23

Who is that lady that shouted? Shakespeare wasn't a bird, madam! And neither is Johnny Carson.

JOHNNY:
So you think that's where women should be?

WINTERS:
Yes, do enlighten us Oliver, why is that?

OLLIE:
I really think that most women are happy in the kitchen.

Because they are feeding their children and looking after their man. And I think a man's place is to look after her, to protect her and provide her with a little warmth.

I really do believe that. SHUSH... QUIET WOMAN...

I love women: I wine them, dine them, make them laugh, hold the door open, and give them a slap on the arse when they need it. But really they are only good for scrubbing floors and shagging.

WINTERS *pours her drink over* OLLIE'S *head*

Ladies and gentlemen: Johnny Carson and Shelly Winters!

I have been smothered in whisky, AND IT IS WHISKY. I can taste it. But I'm not indignant because this is indicative of the bad manners of a lot of chauvinist ladies...

Anyone else?

24

I know; cheeky monkey aren't I? But I discovered a long time ago that the best way to get flames to rise is to poke the fire. Consequently, the room warms up. I happen to prefer a warm room to a cold room. So, if I find the embers dying down, I'll give the fire a DAMN good poke.

Even if it is on the most popular television show in the world.

Especially if it's on the most popular television show in the world.

I hate being bored, you see. And I hate to bore myself.

Time for a whisky — to drink.

Goes to the bar and pours himself a whisky

They never understood me in America; they want their Englishmen to sound like me but look like David Niven. But I love American actors, and I worked with the best of them — Richard Widmark, Chuck Heston, Orson Welles (not Jack Nicholson though, he's a balding midget). And the roughest, toughest movie star of them all — Lee Marvin. This giant of a man was a marine, a warrior. In World War 2 he was one of the few surviving members of his Company. Awarded a Purple Heart no less. We ended up making a movie in Mexico, *The Great Scout and Cathouse Thursday*. We became great friends. And boy, could he booze.

Another whisky

Now I don't have a drink problem. But if I did, and doctors told me I had to stop, I like to think I'd be brave enough to drink myself into the grave.

Isn't that what you would expect? At the very least?

Once I invite 45 members of my local rugby club back to the house. We consume a 50 gallon keg of beer, 32 bottles of scotch, 17 bottles of gin, 4 crates of wine and 15 dozen bottles of Newcastle Brown. Then we go for a cross-country run. Naked. Next day, when Jacquie sees the mess she says "It could have been worse. I suppose a lot of them were in training and off the drink."

Did I mention, Jacquie?

My marriage to Kate lasts ten years. We try to make it work but we were too young to get married. I told her that when she came in with the marriage licence. She puts up with my perpetual boozing but not my perpetual womanising. She ends it with considerable style. I was at our son's sports day and had just staggered drunkenly through the Dad's Race when Kate turned up, walloped me over the head with her handbag and packed young Mark off to live with her parents in a council house in Stockwell.

Jacquie was a dancer that I met while filming *Oliver!*. I would have made her the second Mrs Reed but she turns me down flat. She was much more realistic. As she says, "You're never going to get Oliver back at six o'clock every night for his 'cabbage'."

And so the famous piss-ups begin —

26

OLLIE *marks each session with a drink, by the end the bottle is empty*

Beverly Wiltshire Hotel, Los Angeles, my brother David's birthday, Keith Moon and Ringo Starr in tow, a stripper in the birthday cake and 10 thousand dollars worth of damage. 22 Brandy Alexanders — know how to make a Brandy Alexander, Paul?

Budapest, *Prince And The Pauper* wrap party, Mark Lester and Reg Prince and I decide to have the meal in reverse, 12 whiskeys to kick off, then 4 crates of red wine. The police were called before we finished the pudding.

Dublin, Alex Higgins, 15 Newcastle Brown Ales, 6 malt whiskeys and a pint of Chanel No. 5.

My stag do, White Swan, Surrey... 126 pints. How long have you got?

The Daily Mail reported that particular session as 140 pints, the Daily Telegraph 114. Brits delight in another's excess, revel in the fact that someone has the stomach (and the liver) to carry on as you wish you could —

Beats a tattoo on the surface of the bar

Peter the Great adored drummers! He'd interrupt the orchestra to take over on the drums. I had the same love for a mad drummer, Keith Moon of *The Who*. I'm lying in the bath, soaking out a few bruises, when I hear a tremendous roar. I run to the window... exposing my full frontal, and there's this strange, frail, punk-like creature sitting in a helicopter looking at me through binoculars and nudging a rather dishy girl. Causing havoc on my landscaped garden and frightening my horses. I think it must be some sort of a lunatic with a grudge against me, so I rush out brandishing an antique double-handed sword, which I keep for just such emergencies.

Sometimes when I tell this story it's a double-barrelled shotgun.

Keith ends up staying the weekend and adds considerably to the broken glass in my cellar.

Dear old Moon the Loon.

Cavaliers always die young.

OLLIE *pours himself a rum*

I knew the way to the bar but he showed me the way to the biz-arre.

One night while we were filming *Tommy*, he phones me up from his hotel room and says...

"Alright Oliver... get yourself round 'ere"

So I race round there and he says "'ere, give me a hand with this." So I get one end of the television set, he's at the other, and the ladies he was entertaining are over there. Anyway we heave it up and out of the window and it goes WHOOOMP. The porter comes running out and shouts "WHAT THE BLOODY 'ELL ARE YOU DOING?"

"ANSWER THE FUCKIN' PHONE!" Mooney replies, "OR THE WARDROBE'S COMIN' NEXT!"

Bah — it was fine. They were happy to pick up the pieces or mop up the vomit. Every broken window, broken nose or broken heart is a story to tell. "I drank with Keith Moon", "I wrestled with Oliver Reed," they'd say with pride.

I'm the biggest star this country's got, destroy me and you destroy the whole British film industry.

That's why I wouldn't go to Hollywood. I stayed put, even though, in the Seventies, the taxes in this country meant I could give myself a 40 per cent pay rise if I moved away.

And Hollywood came to me sometimes, I met Steve McQueen in Tramps nightclub, he came over to discuss a film for us to star in. I showed him some London hospitality - threw up all over him. The manager found him a clean pair of trousers but didn't have any shoes. McQueen spent the rest of the night walking around in Oliver Reed's sick.

Funny, it all went quiet after that...

Another rum

Just because I wouldn't play the game: Like Sean Connery. Or Michael Caine...

I turned down *Jaws* and *The Sting*, you know. I was even considered for James Bond.

OLLIE *sings the first few bars of the* James Bond *theme*

I wasn't going to tart myself about. Giving it the posh bit. I'd rather be in the pub. Drinking with REAL people:

Snotter, my driver, Norse, my minder, Dobbo, my head gardener, the most willing thrower down of a spade and picker up of a pint I have ever met.

So I bought myself a stately pile right here in England — 'Squire of Broome Hall' suited me rather well. Truth be told I was only looking for a field for a horse — ended up with 54 bedrooms. That nag became the most expensive beast that ever ate hay. I fixed Beerbohm-Tree's coat of arms above the door, sniffed the breeze, planted roses and worked the land.

I breed horses. I adore animals — my favourite co-star was Lucy, an Asian elephant — she had better manners than Raquel Welsh (and slimmer ankles). I breed heavyweight hunters — a horse that would carry a big man all day — a Bedford truck with a V8 engine under the bonnet!

Broome Hall is open house — every night a party, every day a piss-up, everyone's invited: builders, gardeners rock stars. Anything goes. I crash my green Rolls Royce in the drive. Bugger it. I never liked the colour anyway.

I decide we should hang one of the chandeliers from a tree — on an island — in the middle of the lake. So we row this great big chandelier out — it's the middle of winter and the water is Arctic, we're breaking the ice with the oars as we go. When we get back we wrap ourselves in towels, have a few brandies and admire our handiwork. It's a miracle nobody drowned.

And then I come back from another day on the lash at the Cricketers Arms, in Ockley, and Jacquie has gone...

Do you sometimes get the feeling that we're all just playing at being grown-ups? Do you ever get that feeling? I got it just now...

Another rum

So the Seventies roll into the Eighties and I'm still making movies. Hundreds of 'em. Not exactly packing them in at Leicester Square anymore. But there's alimony to pay, children to put through school, 30 workmen at Broome Hall, every day, for 8 years. So I'm trotted out to play the hard man.

As you know, I'm really quite good at being a bastard but now that I'm past 40 I'm too old to go around throwing punches at people. Acting hard is a good way to avoid a fight.

You know, the difference between the really dangerous man and the loud man is that the dangerous man has a great silence about him. I'm known in the business as 'the whispering giant', hated by the sound department. Because I never worked on stage and learned to shout like those RADA types.

You speak softly. AND YOU DON'T BLINK. Especially not in the cinema, where your eyes are six feet across — you don't want to be there, giving it like Bambi. Have you ever seen a cobra blink? Exactly.

I haven't really enjoyed making a movie since *Oliver!* — but I manage to entertain myself somehow. In Iraq, Libya, Minsk, fly-blown deserts and shit-hole towns, hotel bars and casinos.

31

I'm getting more and more bored, the older I get the fewer pretty girls I get to kiss. For years all I had to do was jump on Glenda Jackson and kiss her boobs but now the parts are for someone a little heavier and older. I had to lose two stone to fit into a tank for *Lion of the Desert* — it's boiled fish and boiled carrots and vodka not beer. But in most of the films I look like a fucking bank manger. It's fair to say that comparisons with *Citizen Kane* will not be forthcoming.

The occasional one gets some notice. Like *Castaway*. Though you could argue it was Amanda Donohoe's knockers that got all the notice in that one.

I suppose nobody wants to see an old Hellraiser's mighty mallet, eh, Alan? It's all about the peacocks now: bouffant hairstyles, perfumed bums, tight-arsed trousers and fancy underpants. ME... I'm never going to be a smoothie... like, like Richard Gere.

Another Beer

"I'm Oliver Reed from Wimbledon" I'd say to anyone I met. I outdrank, outspoke and outpunched everyone.

Listen, cocksucker, this is London not New York and that's the Thames out there, not the Hudson. And I'm the bucko boy and you're not — so fuck off!

Winner said: "If you look at Oliver's career as the career of an artist, the career of an actor. It went into the toilet: it basically vanished."

Quite honestly, I don't give a bugger what the critics say about my films. Taxi-drivers, the man on the street they're the people whose opinions I trust. Jack the lad.

Joe Bollocks. All that lot. "Fucking good luck to you, Ollie", they say. And that's good enough for me.

Then a second WIND. Pardon me? An old Act-OR coming back as a Rock-n-roll-OR.

I'm in Daytona in the early Nineties, walking past a shop that's selling rock 'n' roll jackets . There's one with Mickey Mouse on the back and it says 'WILD THING'... I say "WOW, look at that, boy. I'm going to make a rock 'n' roll record and I'm gonna make it with the Troggs." Not the TRONKS! And that's what happens as it turns out. Me and Alex Higgins record a single with 'em.

"Wild thing...you make my heart sing..."

DOES ANYONE WANT TO ARM WRESTLE? WHO'S FOR A BLACK RUM? ALAN, WILL YOU GET DOWN HERE AND FIGHT ME? ANOTHER DRINK? COME ON.

OLLIE *grabs a bottle from the bar and swigs from it*

I do NOT want to grow old gracefully. I do not want this body, which is my temple, to decay around me! When the time comes, my son, Mark, will be expected to perform his sacred duty and put a shotgun in my mouth and pull the trigger.

Performs this violently

And when I'm dead I want all my friends to have a glorious wake. That's why I've put aside 10,000 crispies, from my estate to be spent at my local pub. But only those crying will be allowed in. And I do not mean crocodile tears. The solicitor who drew up The Last Will and Testament of Oliver Reed AKA Mr England was a

33

trifle worried about that clause. But that's his problem, not mine. My problem is how long I have left before that final piss up that I won't be attending.

When it finally happens, when I'm caught, out, heaving it towards the boundary one final time — I don't want to be laid out for days in my best Dougie Hayward silk pyjamas, my favourite rugger jersey or whatever, and have people come to gawp at me to see what a certified dead hell-raiser looks like.

And I do not want to be a BURNT OFFERING, either.

To buck and twist in the heat of the inferno, frying in my own fat until finally the skull disintegrates. And my skull is a good deal thicker than most.
And burial at sea is also definitely out. Being gobbled up by a shark and becoming excrement that is munched by a sprat whose doings are swallowed by a prawn? I don't want to be lying on a lettuce leaf being nibbled by a beautiful girl and then when I have passed through her, being flushed into a sewer and then out to sea again. I do not want, ladies and gentlemen, to be a PERMANENT SHIT.

I would rather end up as a fertiliser under a sunflower which is then made into a sunflower seed oil so that instead of nibbling me in her prawn cocktail, the beautiful girl can rub me into her BRISTOLS as she suns herself on the beach.
CORRR! The British public love it when I talk dirty. Don't they?

My mind is like my prick. Sometimes it goes up, sometimes it goes down, sometimes it explodes all over the place —

A large jug of gin and orange if you please!

THE DES O'CONNOR SHOW? What time's it on? 7 o'clock? I'LL DO IT.

"Hello Oliver, I understand that you have a tattoo in a ... a rather unusual place?"

Yes, it's on my cock.

THE LATE LATE SHOW? Go on with Susan George? I'LL DO IT.

"I understand you've spent the day at the races?"
Are you saying I'm pisht sir?

ASPEL AND COMPANY. Promote the single? I'LL DO IT.

OLLIE *re-enacts the incoherent song and dance from Aspel & Company*

I give people WHAT THEY WANT.

Are you not entertained?

ARE YOU NOT ENTERTAINED? Is this not why you are here?

And I'm in control. I'm not really drunk. On those shows. I'm a prankster.

AFTER DARK... What's that? Late-night discussion programme: 'Do Men Have To Be Violent?' Brilliant. I'LL DO IT.

Is somebody who knows no ill... goes to the palais de dance... and steals his heels in the air... because he's a... Celt. Why should he go down... why should he forgive himself?

Because he's a better dancer?

Why are we PONTIFICATING here? We're not talking about a BOX OF CHOCOLATES... we're talking about COMBAT.

Let's not piss about.

Look... I'll put my plonker on the table if you don't give me a plate of mushy peas...

THE WORD... the series every bugger's talking about? I'LL DO IT.

"Oliver, did you know we were filming you getting drunk in your dressing room?"

Would I know anything, madam?

OLLIE *sings* Wild thing

I said it's on my cock. Are you saying I'm pissed? Give us a kiss, big tits...
Sorry... sorry... Do you want me to go?

Have I upset you? Is it time for me to go?

You've missed the... point... Why do you have to take life so... so fucking seriously.

With this scarred face and these baker's hands, everyone thinks I'm a dustbin. They keep the cameras rolling. They want to kick me over and watch the garbage come out. And it does. But among all the garbage are, I hope, some flowers and bells.

I can be very content, in Ireland, where the people are kind and live close to nature. In bed by six thirty with a cheese sandwich, Radio 4 on, my dogs all around me. Walks on the beach, gardening, golf, the occasional game of cricket. And Josephine. I'm deeply, deeply fond of my current wife. The second and last.

We met when she was just 16 and I was, well, in my forties. People said it would never last. But it has lasted. Just last week I gave her the most beautiful gold bracelet for her 35th birthday.

There is a wonderful quietness about her: she's very good at keeping me on the straight and narrow.

But something always drags me away from this peaceful existence: "the ancient Romans built their greatest masterpieces of architecture for wild beasts to fight in." Voltaire said that.

What did he know? He was a frog.

They never did beat us blighty boys.

"Tend your own garden," that clever froggy also said. And I did. Or I tried to — my Broome Hall, my Toad Hall, my England, surrounded by faithful retainers — Ollie the Great.

But the taxman comes knocking, the man in grey, the little man. The roundheads win in the end, of course.

A bell rings last orders

Paul, one more drink. One more Sailor Jerry. One more. For the road.

A final drink

I regret not making love to every woman on earth, not kissing the wet nose of every dog on earth, not going into every bar on earth, but that doesn't make me a hell-raiser. If somebody punches me on the nose, I will punch them back; if somebody buys me a drink, I will buy them one back.

Final session: The Pub, Valletta, Malta, May 2nd 1999 — 8 lagers, 12 double rums and half a bottle of scotch.

Ha! still got it.

A bell rings. It is time at the bar.

Paul? Paul? Are you there? Calling time? At two thirty in the afternoon?

But I haven't finished the film.

(As PROXIMO *once more)* "WE MORTALS ARE BUT SHADOWS AND DUST.

Shadows and dust..."

NEWS READER: *(Recording)*
"Film star and legendary hell-raiser Oliver Reed has
died today in Malta where he was filming *Gladiator.* The
sixty-one-year old actor collapsed while drinking with
friends in a bar. He died shortly afterwards in hospital."

And what is left of this pub of mine when the floor's
been swept and the tables wiped down?

My work? Ghosts flickering in the darkness. My son
Mark and my daughter Sarah, I live on through them.
And you. I live on in you as you have lived through me.
And that is why I shall never grow old, carried back to
the pavilion on the shoulders of my peers.

It's all blue heaven.

Pause

I have something to say: bring a smile to their face. Or
bed 'em. Cheers.

Exit

'CONSIDER YOURSELF' from OLIVER! plays us out.

THE DAILY TELEGRAPH

"It's all great fun — as, one imagines, Reed was himself (when not recovering from what must have been appalling hangovers). Crouch's... Reed is uncanny... But there's also a poignant seam of self-awareness running throughout. Reed believes that he became the hard-living caricature of himself because that's what the public expected him to be. In today's bullying, Heat-magazine celebrity culture, that's never rung more true." LAURA BARNETT

THE GUARDIAN

"[There's] one hell of a performance from Rob Crouch, who enters wearing a gorilla suit and then manages to take things up a notch. The show celebrates Reed's lust for life (sometimes in all its rampant ugliness), but it also suggests the tragedy of the man. In playing the role of hell-raiser so consummately, Reed knew he had made a spectacle of himself from which there was no escape." LYN GARDNER

THE SPECTATOR

"A good title works wonders... 'Oliver Reed: Wild Thing' has a simple and succinct name that promises excitement, drama and celebrity gossip. And it delivers. Mike Davis and Rob Crouch's exhilarating monologue races through the chief highlights of Oliver Reed's career... Rob Crouch, a charismatic performer, shows us Ollie as a schoolboy, a movie idol and a grizzled, elderly drunk. He reveals his warmth, his volatility, and something else as well: the sheer village-idiot strangeness of the man. Reed had a marvellous knack as a phrase-maker and the script honours this talent to the full." LLOYD EVANS

BRITISH THEATRE GUIDE

"Beginning with a swagger and a clout, there is barely a moment in 'Oliver Reed: Wild Thing' when the charged presence of Reed isn't practically beaming out from within Rob Crouch and his boisterously eloquent portrayal of the man... When Crouch asked the audience if we are not entertained, there really was only one answer; the rapturous applause that met him as he took his bows. A fine and fitting tribute to a larger than life figure, brilliantly realised, skilfully written and touchingly performed" GRAEME STRACHAN

41

EDINBURGH EVENING NEWS

"This gregarious tribute to Oliver Reed's life is everything a biopic should be... Rob Crouch not only resembles, sounds, scares and excites as Oliver Reed. He's so convincing you feel like sharing a whisky with him afterwards in a bid to get even closer to the man who treated the pub as his theatre... Awe and respect are two different things," Reed once said. At this pub, you'll find both."
BARRY GORDON

THE QUOTIDIAN TIMES

"An amazingly well scripted show – by Mike Davis with assistance from Crouch... Crouch's performance is a tour de force. He somehow appears to be getting drunker and drunker – to great dramatic and comedic effect – as the production unfolds... Hellraising until the end, this show captures the pathos of a great man who lived his life exactly as he wanted to."

THE LIST

"In this excellent one-man show, the renowned hell-raiser recounts his wayward life from beyond the grave and, appropriately, during the course of a mammoth boozing session. Rob Crouch does a superb job of playing the British film star of the 1960 and 70s, nailing Reed's mannered English accent and idiosyncratic intonation, his insolent attitude, mischievous stare and macho swagger. It's an enormously entertaining, frequently hilarious performance that switches to sombre and serious as Crouch's Reed becomes fully inebriated and the recollections of the man who swore he'd drink himself to death reach the end of his life." MILES FIELDER

FEST

"Oliver Reed sits in a pub and, in a manner which manages to bridge the gap between thespian raconteur and the Ancient Mariner, fixes the audience with a glittering eye and proceeds to recount his life story. With extraordinary frequency he pauses to down a bottle of beer, a glass of wine, a large whisky, another beer... Not least admirable about Rob Crouch's performance as Reed is his bladder capacity. He is also superb at capturing Reed in all his fallibility, vulnerability and rabble-rousing

42

monumentalism... It is the type of theatre that catches you out. Reed enters in a Gorilla suit – you laugh, it is a reference to his Wild Thing. He regales you with anecdotes and you laugh. In the grandiloquent tones of a great actor he says things of such staggering egotism – you laugh again. But gradually you realise that all this grandeur, all this solipsistic insistence on being the "last of the shit-kickers" is a terrible defiant bravado; an attempt to prove to himself and anyone else that might be listening that although it became a tragic spectator sport, his life – like that of an ancient Roman gladiator – was still glorious." MIRANDA KIEK

BROADWAY BABY

"In this show from beyond the grave Reed seems to be saying, rightly, that we wanted the shocking stories and the punch ups and appalling behaviour. That's what we want from all our celebrities deep down, from Reed to George Best to Alex Higgins to Amy Winehouse. As Crouch asks, arms outstretched and looking threateningly into the audience, Maximus Decimus Meridius-like: 'Are you not entertained?' We were." ROBIN T. BARTON

THREE WEEKS

"A very charismatic performance, and whilst it's hard to relate to someone so completely off the rails, it's impossible not to be fascinated by tales of his excess. That fascination is what the play explores, and Reed tells stories of his early ambitions, his break into the big time, his debauched lifestyle and his later notoriety as a sort of proto-Charlie Sheen. He's mad, bad and dangerous to watch, and Crouch is utterly convincing." ROZ TUPLIN

TV BOMB

"Crouch, apart from a striking likeness to Reed, has charisma on tap – and Reed was nothing if not charismatic. He also has the remarkable ability to interact with the audience without losing any characterisation. But it is the grace of the delicate moments that makes the play great viewing, never just an impersonation of a drunken brawler, which it easily could have been." RORY EDGINTON

43